STREET

STREET LOGIC

BY

STEVE SUNDBERG

www.bookstandpublishing.com

Published by
Bookstand Publishing
Morgan Hill, CA 95037
3074_6

ISBN 978-1-58909-680-6

Printed in the United States of America

Street Logic is a work of fiction. It is based on reality, experience and actual miles logged.

This book is dedicated to the people who have lived on the street at one time or another, to those who are still out there, and to the extraordinary people who work in shelters and street outreach programs everywhere.

Special thanks to Hank Putnam, Pasquale Tato and Helen Coyle for their time and talents in helping put this together. And thanks to my family for all their support.

Please visit www.streetlogic.org to learn more

Chapter 1

September 2, 2003

The odor of rotten fish and feces hovered around the body of the old man. He was listing badly to port side, but had managed to stay perched on top of an upside-down milk crate. His head lay anchored firmly on his left shoulder at a ninety-degree angle and his mouth hung partially open. Dangling toward the ground, his left arm fell in a straight line, curled fingers an inch short from reaching an overturned bottle of vodka. An open bag of potato chips stuck out from the red-stained blanket across his lap. His other hand rested on top of the blanket. His eyes were closed.

On the ground next to him was a copy of the *Globe* sports section, and the remains of a crudely filleted fish. An empty jar of salsa rested next to it. I stepped away and looked at my partner.

"What do you think?"

Tina Rodriguez didn't answer. She crouched down and repeated his name several times, raising her voice with each attempt. While she continued to call his name, I used a plastic bag lying on the sidewalk, scooped up the fish, and dumped it in the trash can outside the bank.

It was a sunny Tuesday in Boston after a long Labor Day weekend of rain. The temperature was already in the high seventies, with no wind, and was predicted to reach the mid-eighties by afternoon. Tony Ruffo was covered up in an assortment of blankets as if he'd been expecting a cold nor'easter to blow through. Evidence from a meal of chips and salsa ran from his beard on down the blankets, leaving a spotty trail of red stains.

"Hey, Tony!" Tina said. "Can you hear me?" She looked closely at his head and shoulder. "I don't see any movement here, Axel, or any signs of breathing. Do you?"

I took a deep breath, squatted down next to her, and brought my face to within a foot of Ruffo's. The stench made me hold my breath. If he were dead, I figured he would have been on the sidewalk by now.

But who knows. People croak sitting upright on their couches, a bag of chips on their lap, watching television. I zeroed in on the long, straggly mustache hairs below his reddish nose, to see if they moved. They didn't. The only sign of life was a line of drool that hung from the corner of his mouth and pooled on the sidewalk next to the bottle.

I shook him gently by the shoulder.

"Tony," I said. "Open your eyes. Make a noise. Show me you're alive."

His head lolled slightly from my shaking him, then remained fixed in place.

"He's gonzo." Tina let out a deep sigh. She stood and walked a few feet away, muttering something in Spanish. I peered into Ruffo's deeply lined face and focused again on his open mouth. The line of drool was hard to look at, and hard not to look at. I was searching for a bubble or something to tell me he was breathing. After a minute, I let my eyes wander. Ashes from a cigarette stuck in his beard along with some crumbs and salsa. His creased forehead was encrusted with dirt, a few flies picking at things. I waved them away with my hand.

"This isn't good," Tina said, crouching down next to me again. I turned my head and saw her dark attractive features clouded with worry. Her pursed lips and narrowed eyes studied Ruffo as if she wanted to will him into consciousness.

"Has he been incontinent like this for very long?" I asked.

"Only recently. But even when he's passed out, he always wakes up and talks to me." She suddenly pulled the blanket off his upper body, scattering potato chips on the ground. "Before we call it in, I want to see if he's responsive at all." Through his Red-Sox t-shirt, she grabbed a chunk of skin high on his chest, and pinched it. Ruffo didn't budge. She did it again. His eyes were tight as clamshells. "Hmm. That usually does the trick." She took his hand and began searching for a pulse.

I grabbed an inch of skin near a nipple and squeezed. Gently at first, then a little harder.

"There's a very faint pulse here," Tina said. She stood back up abruptly, yanked her cell phone out from a back pocket, and started punching in numbers.

"One more blast, pal." I found a bigger piece of flesh this time and clamped down hard. His eyes fluttered for a split second and a low moan escaped his lips. "We have contact," I said over my shoulder. "Tony, can you hear me? Open your eyes, man. Let me see those baby blues of yours." He moaned again faintly. "We're getting you some help. Hang in there, Tony."

I stood up. Way more than just drunk, I thought. Incontinence is always a bad sign. Reminded me of an old family dog, an Irish Wolfhound we had named Maggie. When she couldn't get up on her long legs anymore, my brother and I had to clean her twice a day. She didn't get better after that. I started walking toward Atlantic Ave where the Big Dig highway project was in full swing, sending dust and dirt and noise into the air. Cops were usually stationed wherever the work was most active, but all I saw was construction workers and bulldozers. I went half-way up the block to the Dunkin' Donuts and stared through the window. A fifty-fifty chance. But there were no police in the crowded shop either.

Turning back to the street, I watched the last of the rush hour traffic roll along the expressway. Car windshields shone bright from the morning sun. Heat rose off the asphalt in little waves. From high on top of the gothic Harper Tower, the clock bells began ringing. I glanced up at the golden hands as I counted the ten chimes that cut through the city noise.

Tina was still talking to a police operator and gesturing with her hands. I lit a cigarette and walked toward the end of the block to stretch my legs, sore from yesterday's hike. It was day two of this job and I already had doubts. I was wondering what the odds were that we could even help someone like Tony Ruffo, or any of the other poor bastards. The day before, I had met about fifty men and women who were living on the street. Walking around the city with Adrian Dantley, the project director and a friend from my past, all the people we talked to were in various states of disrepair, with a host of different diagnoses. We must have walked five miles and all we achieved was to take one guy to the Massachusetts General Hospital to have his arm examined. Most of the time we stood around in the rain, on street corners, or down in alleys and under bridges, speaking to people who didn't want anything we had to offer. Except for clean underwear and socks. The guy with the injured arm, Brad Swaggert, had lost his patience after an hour of waiting in the ER with us. He walked out. He said he could kill the pain faster himself and that he'd survived worse. "It'll heal on its own anyway," he said. Street logic.

At the end of the block, I saw Jimmie Irons sitting on the sidewalk, legs stuck out in a v-shape, counting a pile of loose change. I'd met him yesterday in the same place. A tall, bone-thin man with a caved-in face that was permanently smeared with grime. Scraggly black whiskers sprouted unevenly from his pointed jaw. He looked up and held his hat out, smiled at two guys in business suits walking past him. One of them acknowledged Irons with a nod. They didn't stop.

"Have a good day anyway!" Irons sang out. He returned to counting his money and didn't see me. His long, blackened fingers turned each coin over slowly before stacking it on one of the piles between his legs. "Fucking suits," I heard him mutter.

Ruffo hadn't moved. Tina rolled her eyes at me, the phone pressed to her ear. She wasn't saying anything. I glanced at Ruffo's bent head and considered raising it upright, so he could breathe easier, but decided moving him might not be a good idea.

"Yes, he probably has toxic levels of alcohol," Tina finally said, frustration in her voice. "We're on Atlantic Avenue, a block from the Aquarium. In front of the Citizen's Bank." She listened for a moment and then said, "We'll wait here until the ambulance arrives." She gave her name and flipped her phone shut.

"Jesus, I should know better by now," she said, shaking her head.

"Know what?"

"That telling them I'm an outreach worker doesn't necessarily raise their interest level. The paramedics arrive, the person wakes up, and half the time refuses to go with them. It's a waste of their time." She shrugged her shoulders and managed a weak smile.

"I see."

A man came out of the dry-cleaners store just down from Ruffo, carrying a garment bag. He stopped in front of us, his face screwed up. "This guy is disgusting," he said, "sitting in his own shit like that." His voice was angry, almost shaking.

"He's waiting for a ride to detox," I said. "Going to give up the drinking."

Tina started to say something, and then laughed. Her laughter sounded unnaturally fresh against the harsh noise of the bulldozers and traffic and this furious little man with the red face.

"I hope to god that's true." He stared at us before turning quickly and walking off.

"Another Good Samaritan gone wrong," I said.

Tina was still smiling. "Believe it or not, when I first started, I actually did talk to Tony about detox. Once. He told me the vodka is the only thing keeping him alive."

"I suppose it is. Is he always in this spot?"

"Usually here or around back of the bank. I guess he's been on the waterfront for years."

Just then, a trim, dapper looking guy came out of the dry-cleaners and spotted us. He walked over and gave Tina a bright smile before it turned into a frown. "Outreach to the rescue, I hope?" he said. "How are you, Tina?"

"Hey Tim. I'm alright. How's things with you?"

"I'm good. But Tony looks awful," he said. "Was that the police you were talking to? Looked like you wanted to kill somebody."

"Just hung up with them. Tim, this is Axel Hazzard," she said, turning to me.

He shook my hand with a good strong grip. He was in his forties, with cropped blond hair, wearing pressed white pants and a yellow shirt. He trained his eyes on mine. "Welcome to the street, Axel." He looked toward Tony Ruffo. "The man needs to go somewhere else."

"I think he needs a little more than that," Tina said.

Tim shook his head. "I knew him in his better days, if you could call it that. If he was a relative of mine, I think I'd try to have him forced into treatment. But I guess that's hard to do."

He glanced away and his face showed something that told me he had a relative in mind.

"Sounds like you know him well," I said.

He let out a short, compressed breath. "It's like this – seven years ago, the man could walk and talk and get around like any of us. I've heard every story he's got. Football heroics at Ohio State, fishing and restaurant businesses on the north shore, the vacations in the Bahamas. Oh, and the great rides he's had. Caddies and Lincolns and Jags." He paused, and a smile passed briefly across his face. "Last year he was still doing alright. Not great, obviously, but good enough to get around. Now, well, you can see for yourself. I hope you've got a strong stomach there, Axel."

"A hundred and fifty sit-ups a day. But I don't think it's going to help me with this job."

He finally laughed. "Fast learner, huh. That's good. You'll save yourself a lot of headaches."

Tina's phone rang and she answered it before the second ring. I turned back to Tim. "No hope, then?"

He snorted. "I've known him ever since I moved the business here. Sits along Atlantic and stems for money to buy his vodka. Sleeps behind the bank, under that pine tree back there. Year round, rain or snow, he doesn't care. He's been stuck on the sidewalk here lately. Says he was a fisherman, but then again, he's told me all kinds of bullshit. And he loves to talk about freedom! Still does, when he's conscious." Tim stopped, his eyes straying toward Ruffo. "He actually used to get cleaned up now and then." He stepped closer to me and lowered his voice. "Between you and me, if he was my own father – and my father is a royal bastard – I'd have his ass hauled in for treatment somewhere. But he's not."

I just nodded my head.

"Don't get me wrong," he went on. "I believe in people being free to live however they want, right, according to their own needs, follow their own path, all that. But this?" He paused with his mouth open, grasping for the right words. "This isn't freedom. This is a goddamn travesty, is what it is."

I nodded again.

"Well, Axel, it was good meeting you," he said. "Hope you can get him out of here."

"Will do," I said.

He waved to Tina and went back inside. Tina leaned against the wall, flipped her phone shut, and let out a deep breath. I could see how tired she was.

"That was Adrian," she said. "Wondering if the ambulance had arrived yet."

"How about some coffee while we wait?"

She gave me a grateful smile. "Good idea."

We waited for the ambulance in the Dunkin Donuts next to Tim's laundry. The little shop was crowded, so I stepped in line while Tina took one of the round swivel chairs in front of the window, with a view of the street.

"What do you want?"

"One of everything," she said, eyeing the donuts and muffins. "But I'll settle for a small coffee, cream and sugar."

"No donuts?"

She made a face at me. Tina probably weighed all of a hundred and ten pounds - her tight jeans revealed the legs of a runner. She wore a short-sleeve, modest T-shirt, a little loose and un-tucked, but it couldn't hide everything. From Mexico originally, she'd told me that she'd lived in Boston for the last ten years. Her English was perfect, only slightly accented, and a lot easier on the ear than the hard, R-less accent of Bostonians. It would be hard to know that she was almost thirty years old. She looked closer in age to the kids graduating from Boston University.

"If you insist, make it a Boston Kreme."

"You got it."

I stood in line, occasionally looking out the window for the ambulance. The line moved fast, and in a few minutes I was standing in front of a grey-haired, fifty-something woman. Her name tag was pinned to her striped shirt.

"Hi, Mary. Two small regular coffees, please, and a Boston Kreme."

"Sure."

I glanced back at Tina. She shook her head at me, and waved to Mary.

"You're with the donut queen, I see," Mary said. She took two small cups and pumped cream into them. "Good kid. Always coming in here to get a cup of water for that poor Tony Ruffo."

"Yeah. Name's Axel, by the way. Nice to meet you, Mary."

"Nice to meet you too, Axel," she said. Her eyes were warm. "Are you working with Tina?"

"Started yesterday."

She spooned sugar into both cups and filled them with coffee from one of the pots on the warm burners behind her. "If you want my opinion," she said over her shoulder, "that man is going to need a miracle."

"Looks like it," I said. "We called an ambulance, and now we're just waiting. Hopefully they'll take him in." Mary muttered something I couldn't hear, then turned back with the two coffees and set them in front of me.

"If they leave him sitting there, I think I'm going to call the mayor myself."

She pulled a bag out from under the counter and went to the donut racks, using wax paper to grab two Boston Kremes and stuff them in the bag.

"Here ya go, Axel. Looks like you could use a donut yourself. On the house. You want a cup of water for Tony?"

"I don't think he can drink anything."

Tina came over to the counter and looked in the bag of donuts. "Another donut lover, I see." She pulled one out of the bag. "Mary, how are you?"

"Fine, sweetheart. Just hope they take him in somewhere. Hate to see him in such awful shape."

"The only good thing," Tina said, taking a small bite of the donut, "is that the worse he looks, the better the chances that they'll take him. And maybe keep him a while. You should have left that fish there, Axel, now that I think about it. Would have added to the scene."

"Oh, wasn't that disgusting!" Mary said. "Looked like he butchered it with a spoon or something."

I took my coffee over to the window. People were passing Tony on the sidewalk, some looking at him longer than others. I ate the donut and glanced at Tina standing at the counter and talking with Mary. I hadn't known Tina for more than two hours, but I knew she was committed to doing this work. I also knew that she liked Boston Kreme donuts, and that she jogged two miles every night around Jamaica Pond, with her dog, Sappo. She had a roommate. I thought she mentioned the dog a few too many times. After she graduated from Northeastern, she'd worked for a variety of social programs, the last one Rosie's Place, a shelter for women and children. Six months ago she began working for the street team. She said it already felt like a year and a half.

"Axel." She sat down on the stool next to me with half the donut in her hand. "Remind me to make sure to find out which hospital they take him to. So Medical Care for the Homeless can follow up with him." She licked the creme from the donut.

"Think he'll stay in the hospital for a few days, assuming we get him in? Or be ready to consider a treatment program?"

"I think? This kind of thing, with an older guy like Tony?" She glanced out the window and sighed. "It's been a long time in the making, and the fix won't be quick. A few days in the hospital can't hurt, though. A ten-day detox would be better. But as long as he can still manage, even as he is, what can anybody say?" She looked brightly at me and smiled. "In answer to your question – no."

I nodded, and found myself wondering which side of the fence she was on. Whether she was a realist, or a save-the-world idealist.

"What about legal maneuvers? You know, have him forced in for an assessment?"

"It's a long-shot," she said. "I've been doing this for six months now, which isn't that long in some jobs, but long enough in this one. What I've seen so far, with some of the nearly legless people like Tony who can barely get around anymore, is that this thing is bigger than we are, bigger than they are, and bigger than the health care system can handle. So I work on one principle, basically. Get them in. I can't control the outcome and I've accepted that." She used the back of her hand to wipe the last remnants of chocolate and creme from her mouth. "That's how I can do this job and not feel useless." She nodded toward the street. "Now you know what you're dealing with. And on top of that, it can be a pretty dirty business as well. Still up for it?"

I looked into her soft, brown eyes, and did my best John Wayne.

"Well, getting dirty never stopped me before, little lady. Shall we saddle up?"

Tina laughed, and her cheeks colored slightly. "I don't think anybody's ever made me an offer quite like that before. At least not on this job." She spun around, said goodbye to Mary, and headed for the door. Not the born-again-savior type, I decided.

A half-hour passed and the ambulance still hadn't arrived. Tina called the police dispatcher back twice to see when we could expect them. The second time, she snapped her phone shut and almost threw it. "Don't ever let me say I'm an outreach worker to the police again." She flipped her phone open again and punched in another number. I bent down to take Ruffo's pulse. Slow, but still pumping.

"No, still not here," Tina said. "Adrian, if I call them back again they're going to think I'm harassing them." She paused, listening. "OK. Thanks." She stuffed the phone in her back pocket and turned toward

Atlantic Avenue, searching the traffic. "Adrian's going to see if there's a van driver in the shelter who can come pick us up, and we'll take Tony to the ER ourselves. First, I'm going to call the police back, and pretend I'm some businesswoman or something, and see if that gets a response."

"I'll call if you want. Or we both can. I'll tell them I'm the bank president, and there's a dead guy on the sidewalk preventing people from getting into the ATM."

"That might be a little too much," she said, but the humor was back in her voice. "But it would probably get them here. Go ahead, do it. Maybe you should just tell them someone's unconscious on the ground in front of your bank's ATM. Let them think it's a regular citizen."

The traffic on the expressway was still heavy, but Atlantic Avenue looked relatively clear. Still no police across the street. The clock on the Harper Building rang out eleven times as a taxi rolled slowly past us. I looked at Tina. "Forget about it," she said. "Once they see Tony, they're gone. It's our last option. Let's give this thing another ten minutes and see if an ambulance gets here. If you want, go ahead and call the police."

The stench around Tony Ruffo was getting worse in the heat. I leaned down to look at his face. The drool seemed a little longer. "This is crazy, Tina. I'm going into the bank to see if the manager will make a call. Give it a little more clout."

I entered the bank and looked for the biggest office. There was one near the back with glass windows where a woman was sitting behind a large desk and talking on the phone. I knocked on her door. She looked up and I waved at her, and she pointed toward the row of tellers. I pointed outside to the sidewalk. She hesitated, and finally put the phone down and came to the door.

"Hi," I said. "I'm sorry to bother you. My name's Axel Hazzard. I work with the street outreach team from Evergreen Street." Something dawned in her eyes. "I need to ask you something about the man passed out on the sidewalk in front of your bank. Tony Ruffo."

As soon as she heard Ruffo's name, the look of annoyance immediately doubled, then vanished. "Oh my god," she said as she came out of her office. "I meant to call 911 first thing when I walked in! Then I had an emergency to deal with and got completely distracted."

"He's in pretty bad shape. We called an ambulance over an hour ago, and I was kind of hoping that you would..."

She started toward the entrance. "You work out of Evergreen Street, did you say?" She walked quickly across the floor and pushed the door open.

"Yes," I hustled to keep up with her. She stopped in front of Ruffo and examined him for about five seconds, and then she turned and headed back to the bank. "I'm calling the police right now," she said.

Tina's exasperation eased up a bit. "Well, that was a good idea. I hope they listen to her and get here soon." She looked at her watch. "It's past eleven now." Her cell phone rang. It was Adrian. "No, they're not here yet," Tina said. "But now the bank manager is calling the police. After Axel seduced her." She winked at me. "Maybe we'll get some action soon. Any luck with the van?"

At the edge of the street, a taxi slowed and the driver looked at me. I pointed toward Tony Ruffo. He pulled over and I stepped up to his window.

"For him?"

"I work for the shelter. Just to get him to the hospital. I have a voucher. I can put a big tip on it."

He looked over at Ruffo and shook his head. "What, we gonna carry him? Sorry, buddy. Call the police. I can't take that kind of responsibility. Jesus, I can smell him from here."

There seemed to be nothing to do now but wait. Tina was still on the phone. Up the block near Jimmie Irons I saw a construction worker in dusty overalls come out of the 7-Eleven store. He was a big guy, six-four or more, solid as a rock. He took in Tina as he walked over and stood in front of Ruffo. After a minute, he squatted and stuffed a bill into his hand.

"Poor son of a bitch," he said as I walked up.

"An ambulance is coming. Know him?"

"Talked to him a few times. Looks like my uncle Jack. I guess he ate the fish."

"You gave him the fish?"

"Ten pound cod. Caught it last week. Told me he was a fisherman. So I thought what the hell, and packed it in ice and brought it down here Friday."

"I'm sure he enjoyed it."

He gave me an odd look, and then nodded toward Tina. "You working with her?"

"Yeah."

"Some kind of church, shelter?"

"Ever heard of Evergreen Shelter?"

"Oh yeah. Who the hell hasn't?" His eyes soaked up Tina one more time as he turned to go, and then he stopped. "Mack," he stuck his hand out. "They call me Mack. You guys have a card or something? I see Tony every day, he needs something, maybe I could call you."

I reached into my back pocket and pulled out one of the cards Adrian gave me. "Here you go. Thanks." I shook his hand.

"No problem." He crossed the street and I turned back to Tina.

"No van," she said. "It's being used, and the other one is in the shop. Adrian's trying to track down another one from somewhere, in case we still need it."

"I tried a taxi. You're right, nothing doing. But at least you've got an admirer." I nodded toward the construction worker.

"Him? That's all I need." She watched him as he crossed the street. "My ex was a pipe-fitter. Real asshole. I already know most of the jokes about the profession – unless you have one I haven't heard."

I shook my head. "Can't help you there."

From her expression, I didn't think I'd tell her even if I knew one.

We heard the siren and both turned to look for the ambulance, spotting it as it emerged from behind a row of traffic stopped at the intersection. They pulled up in front of the bank and a young guy jumped out of the side door and came toward us. Tina told him what was going on, not letting him interrupt her. The driver of the ambulance, an older, heavy-set guy with a tired expression, opened his door and stepped out slowly.

"Tony, Tony, Tony," he said in a friendly way. "I knew it was him when I heard the address."

They took his pulse and blood pressure, and then the driver said something to the young guy, who hustled back to the ambulance and opened the rear doors. He pulled out a rolling stretcher, unhooked the legs, then pushed it over to Ruffo and lowered it to the ground. After they removed all the blankets, they repositioned him so he was lying flat on the sidewalk. Then they eased him carefully on to the stretcher. Once he was strapped down, they spread a white sheet over him.

The driver looked at us as they began wheeling Tony toward the rear of the ambulance. "I know, I know: he's not dead. The sheet is just standard health precautions, when someone is in this, uh, kind of shape." They opened the doors and slid him into the back. The younger paramedic jumped in and pulled the doors closed. "We'll get him in, checked out, and cleaned up. Probably be seeing you all again, I'm sure," the driver said. "You're from the outreach team, right?"

"That's right," Tina said. "Which hospital are you taking him to?"

"Boston City. You know what I think?" He lowered his voice. "I'm glad he's out like a light right now. If he was conscious, he'd tell me with his last breath to leave him alone, that he doesn't want to go to the hospital. And to be honest, I can't take him against his will. But, between you and me," he winked, "I've done it a few times. When he was too tired to keep protesting. If it was up to me, he wouldn't even be out here on the streets anymore."

Tina and I watched him get into the ambulance. The bank manager came out and stood next to us. "I see they finally made it." She held her arms tight across her chest. "I hate to say it, but I hope I don't see him back here." There was a small note of compassion in her voice, mixed with relief that he wasn't in front of her bank anymore.

The ambulance driver turned on the sirens and flashing lights and pulled out on to Atlantic Avenue, made a u-turn at the light and raced off toward the expressway.

"Thanks for your help," I said to the woman.

"Oh, not at all." She shook our hands and said goodbye.

Tim came out. He shaded his eyes with his hand as he watched the ambulance take the southbound ramp. "I don't even want to know how much that costs the city," he said. "Probably not the ride he wanted, either."

"Not like one of his old Caddies, Lincolns or Mercedes, right?" I said.

Tim laughed and shook his head. "Jag," he said. "Always said he wanted a Mercedes, though."

Tina grabbed my arm and began steering me toward the 7-Eleven up the block. "He got just the ride he needed," she said. "See you later, Tim.

Tina called Adrian to fill her in. "They're taking him to BCH," she said into the phone. "We'll probably get some lunch soon."

We stood outside the entrance to the 7-Eleven, listening to Jimmie Irons barking at people for spare change. Tina let out a long sigh. "Axel, let's stop for a minute. I can't handle any more just yet." Against the storefront, she raised her leg slightly and did ankle rolls with one foot, then shifted her legs and worked the other ankle.

"Sore?"

"A little," she said. "Ran a ten-k this weekend."

"This street walking doesn't help."

"No, it doesn't." She was quiet for a moment, then gave me a small grin.

"You know what, Axel? You may last a while at this job."

"What gives you so much confidence?"

"The way you went to the bank manager," she said. "Using the resources at hand."

"You telling me we don't have enough resources?"

"We have some," she said. "But not a lot of direct power. We have to focus it. There's an entire community of professionals we can access

– doctors, nurses, social workers. But what we just did, getting an ambulance, is sometimes about the most anyone can accomplish." She reached into her pocket and came out with some bills and loose change. "What you were asking earlier, about legal maneuvers, as you put it? Adrian and I are looking into the possibility of having Tony sectioned, committed for treatment. We have to establish that he can't care for himself adequately. Not many doctors are willing to put their signature on the line, or spend their time on pushing that kind of case in front of a judge. It's a hard case to win, I've heard. And a nasty ordeal for the homeless person, usually."

"Why?"

"Because it rarely works out. Judges tend to rule in favor of the homeless person's freedom. They're wary of committing a person to long-term treatment, for whatever reason, lack of programs, the right to make your own decisions, I don't know. Money, probably."

We heard the sound of a bottle breaking around the corner, followed by the loud, hoarse shout of Jimmie Irons. "Aw, shit! Son of a bitch!"

I ducked around the edge of the building and saw a young guy in a suit and tie standing in front of Irons, apologizing. A bottle lay cracked on the sidewalk, the spilled contents running toward the street.

"I'm going to get something to drink," Tina said, "before I can talk to him. You want a juice or something?"

"No thanks. I'll be out here."

"Be right back," she said.

I stood off to the side and watched the action. Irons attempted to stand, balancing briefly on one leg. He wobbled a moment and fell back on the sidewalk. "Fucking shit!" he cried out, banging against the wall. "That was a full mother-fucking bottle!"

"I'm sorry," the guy in the suit said. "I didn't see you there. Here, let me give you a hand up." He leaned down to help Irons stand, but Irons took a swing at his outstretched hand and cursed him.

"Fuck you, asshole! Go home to your nice little wifey and kiss her ass for me."

"Hey, man, no need to be hostile," the guy said.

A few people slowed down to watch. People in business clothes, a few tourists in hats and t-shirts. All of us kept a safe distance. Irons glared at the man as if he might swing again. After a minute, Irons' expression changed. A dark, toothless cave of a smile crept slowly on to his narrow face. "Sorry, pal, didn't mean it," he said. "Listen, could ya spare a few bucks? That was all I had." He looked sadly down at the broken glass next to him. The man hesitated. He cast a quick eye at the gathering crowd and then reached for his wallet. Irons followed his movements closely.

"Tell you what," the guy said. "I knocked it over, it's my responsibility. Here, take this."

Irons' arm shot out and he snatched the bill out of the man's hand. He examined it quickly and closed his fist around it. "God bless you!" Irons said. "Sorry for calling you an asshole, and that thing about your wife. I fly off the handle sometimes."

"That's alright," the man said. "Understandable," he added, turning to go.

"Hey, you're alright, brother!" Irons said. "God bless."

The small group of watchers dispersed. Tina was still in the store. Irons took a pack of matches from his shirt pocket and attempted to light the tiny butt of a cigarette.

"Here you go, Jimmie," I said, standing in front of him. I shook loose a fresh one from my pack and offered it. "Too bad about the bottle, but that guy was pretty cool."

He stared at me suspiciously as he reached for the cigarette. "And who the fuck are you?" he said. "How'd you know my name?"

"We met yesterday."

Jimmie looked confused. The tips of his fingers were dark brown from nicotine, and his hands shook so much that it took three tries to get it lighted. Finally, he inhaled gratefully, and then dropped the lighted cigarette on to his lap. "Goddammit!" he cried, fumbling to pluck it off his pants. He stuck it angrily back in his mouth and puffed. He blew the smoke out and coughed, then took another deep drag and blew a perfect smoke-ring that hung in the air above his head for a few seconds. He looked down the sidewalk to where Ruffo had been.

"I see they took Tony. Did you see that fish he had? Jesus fucking Christ almighty, they ought to lock him up. He can't handle himself out here anymore." There was a note of sympathy in his voice. He blew another smoke ring, opened his palm, and re-examined the twenty-dollar bill before stuffing it in his pocket. He cleared his throat and spit, and pulled an unopened pint bottle from his inside pocket. After he unscrewed the cap carefully, he put his free hand on the sidewalk to steady himself. Then he tilted the bottle up and drank. Finished, he capped it and slid it back inside his coat. "Ah, that's more like it," he said. "Good to have an extra, just in case."

"Always good to have back-up."

"Damn right," he grinned. "Say, you couldn't spare some change, could you?" He was still trying to place me.

"You don't remember me from yesterday? I was with Adrian. Evergreen Shelter?"

"Oh shit! Now I remember you. Another one of the outreach posse, huh?"

"I guess so."

"You'll see. Ain't nobody out here wants that kind of help. Not the kind you people are dishing out. No offense, pal." He smoked the cigarette down to the end and stuffed the butt in a pocket. "You ever fly?" he said, working his legs underneath him as he put a hand on the wall.

"I fell out of a tree once."

Jimmie sputtered with laughter and fell back. "Shit, that's funny, man," he said, struggling again to get up on one knee and get a hand on the wall. "It's this goddamn gravity that's busting my ass."

I put a hand on his arm and helped him to his feet. He leaned against the wall to catch his breath.

"Thanks."

"That's alright. Why'd you ask if I ever flew?"

He rocked forward, then sideways, nearly losing his balance again. I steadied him until he was able to hold himself up, but he kept his hand clamped to my arm. Once he was set, he used his other hand to reach into his coat pocket for the bottle. He held it under his arm as he unscrewed the cap with his free hand, took another short drink, then recapped it and put it away, careful not to drop it. "Because you must be flying with angels to do this kind of work," he said.

Tina came up to us, drinking lemonade with a straw. Irons greeted her with a big smile. "There's my girl!" He took a step toward her and lost his balance immediately, his hand squeezing my bicep as he tilted, but he stayed on his feet. "For fucksake!" he hissed. "Excuse my language, sweetheart, but this fucking foot sucks."

Tina shook her head and frowned at him. "I heard you fell off the wall around back and sprained your ankle a few nights ago. Is that right?"

"I did," he said. "I'm going to sit."

He slid down to the sidewalk with his legs spread in front of him. "Shit, I wish *I* could fly. Make things a hell of a lot easier." He laughed at his words and took the bottle out again.

"You want to go into the ER and have that ankle looked at?" Tina asked.

He considered her seriously for a moment before taking another drink. "Nah," he said, wiping his mouth with the back of his hand. "I'm not feeling any pain now." His smile showed the diseased gums, a few pieces of teeth still hanging on.

"Well, you know they'll give you something for that pain if you go into the Wilder and rest. Give your ankle some time to recover, watch some ball games in the lobby. What do you think?" Tina smiled at Irons as if she was certain he would take the offer.

"I hate that place," his smile was gone. "You know I hate that place."

"Well, it's a good place to heal up," she said. "You don't have to go now, you can go tomorrow. But if you keep trying to stand on that foot and walk, it's going to take forever to heal. You know that, right?"

"Yeah," he said quietly. "I know."

"So…" She changed her tone to cheerful. "Besides that, what else is new?"

Jimmie looked at her and shook his head. "Nothing's new," he said. "Same old shit. What's up with Tony? Are they going to lock him up?"

"I don't know."

"You know what's going to happen?" he said. "He's going to wake up in the hospital and walk out. That's what." He asked me for another cigarette, and I gave him one, lighting it for him this time.

"Know what's good about having no teeth?" he said, inhaling.

"Uh-oh," Tina said, "I think it's time for us to go."

"No, it's not what you think," he laughed with a harsh, raspy sound that came from his chest. "It's this." He blew several more perfect smoke rings, and Tina turned toward me and indicated with her eyes that she was ready to move on.

"Well, Jimmie, we'll see you around," she said. "And think about going in for that ankle."

He pulled the bottle out and shook it at her. "I'm gonna go real easy on it, sweetheart, don't you worry."

"Take care, Jimmie," I said. "I'll be seeing you around, I'm sure. You know, Tina might have the right idea. With the Yankees series coming up this weekend, could be a good time to go in."

"Fuck the Yankees!" he spat. "And fuck the Red Sox too, those fucking losers. Fuck all of them!" He dug through his pockets and spilled coins on the sidewalk. Tina moved toward the crosswalk on Atlantic Ave.

"Let's get that lunch before we run into somebody else."

"He's skin and bones, that guy," I said. "What's his story?"

"Jimmie kind of grew up out here. His father stays at Evergreen. Sometimes they're both there at the same time. Usually one of them gets into it with the other and they have to keep them in different lobbies. Jack Irons, hangs out mostly in Back Bay and the Commons."

"Father and son. Damn."

"Yeah. Jimmie's young, too. Early thirties, believe it or not."

"What a face," I said. "Looks fifty."

"That's why they call him the Bone Man."

Chapter 2

September 2, 2003 - 6:00p.m.

At the end of the day, I took the orange line train to Jamaica Plain and got off at the Green Street Station. Tina lived in a different part of JP and had ridden home on her bicycle. She said it helped her leave the day's work behind. Might be a good method, I thought, as I walked up Green Street, my mind still working over the details of the day. I was up to the part where Tina had told me about Jimmie Irons, the Bone Man, who was fifteen years old when he began staying at the shelter. With his father, Irons the elder. Jack Irons had been staying at the original Evergreen Shelter on and off for years, when it had been housed in a church basement near Chinatown. Tina had learned from one of the shelter counselors that Jimmie had received a lot of attention from the counselors at first, offering him something better before the habit of shelter living took hold. Job training programs, GED classes to finish high school, even a position on the maintenance staff. Jimmie had tried, apparently, for a few years. Until the street became his permanent address.

At the package store on Seaverns Avenue, I picked up a six-pack of beer and a pint of Jimmie Beam. I asked the pot-bellied guy behind the counter for some cigarettes, and while he searched for them I watched the small television set on the counter – the Red Sox had just won an afternoon game in Cleveland.

"They're teasing us again," the guy said. He slid a brown paper bag and my change across the counter. "September, and they're still alive. Everybody starts believing again, and then they break your heart. Nobody learns."

I looked back at the television. They were re-playing the three-run homer Ortiz had belted out of Jacobs Field in the top of the ninth. I held back my own groan of disappointment at the Sox rally. Having grown up in Ohio, I was an Indians fan. But I didn't think it was worth mentioning.

"Ortiz is hitting the hell out of the ball," I said. The pot-bellied guy agreed, rubbing the tattoos running up both his arms.

"Manny is Manny, and he's great, but Big Papi is the man."

"He's the man, for sure." I picked up the bag and asked him how late he stayed open.

"Until ten," he said.

As I turned to go, the news switched to a story about a missing kid. A photo flashed on the screen of a young man wearing a white shirt, tie, and jacket, in a graduation picture from high school. He was a good-looking kid with a shaved head, Michael Jordan style, and a big smile on his face that said no worries, the future is bright. The newscaster said he was a college student at the University of Massachusetts in Amherst, last seen two weeks ago. His family was offering a reward for any information. Something was mentioned about a possible psychiatric illness.

"Kid's probably dead," the tattooed guy said. "Lying in a ditch somewhere, offed by some asshole for no good reason." On the TV, the boy's parents were speaking from the front steps of a large two-story house, pleading for public assistance. "Crazy world," tattoo guy muttered, shaking his head and cracking his knuckles. "Last week a gang of fifteen-year-old punks shot at a car driving up Seaverns. I saw it from the door right there. Number one in violence, baby, that's us. And with this jackass running the show, the numbers keep going up. This country has lost touch with reality, if you ask me."

"I'm with you on that, man. Take it easy."

This was a fairly peaceful area of Jamaica Plain, but I kept an eye out for teenagers as I walked toward Underwood's house. All I saw were a few people walking their dogs and some elementary school kids trying to ride skateboards.

I had rented a basement studio apartment from a friend of mine, Paul Underwood. Back in the mid-eighties, the apartment had been an actual recording studio. When Underwood bought the house, he renovated the soundproof room into a livable apartment with a kitchenette, and added a jacuzzi bathtub in what had been the sound technician's booth. Underwood lived on the first floor, and rented out rooms on the second and third floors to a couple of graduate students and a friend of his, a fellow musician. It was a good deal for me all around. Especially the soundproof feature, which ranked higher for me than the jacuzzi. I couldn't hear a thing from the rest of the house, and heard very little from the street when the double-pane windows were closed.

I've always been a light sleeper.

When I was a kid and the battle between my parents was over for the night, I'd fall asleep to the sound of eighteen-wheelers rolling along the expressway on the edge of town. I still liked that sound, because it had lulled me to sleep many times. But silence worked best. The basement studio was perfect. Just a short ten block walk from the station, but far enough that the Amtrak commuter trains were only a distant hum when the windows were open.

The house sat back from Alveston Street at the end of a long gravel driveway, surrounded by enough trees to give you the impression that you were in nature. I stopped to wipe a few fallen leaves off the front window of my eighty-five Lincoln Town Car. It had been sitting unused in a barn in Maine, and had been practically given to me by my friend Dave, who wanted it gone. So I ended up with a gas-guzzling beast for the price of the transmission repair. It wasn't my style, but I needed a ride. After a while it grew on me.

I pushed the steel-framed basement security door open and entered the narrow hallway. Since the studio used to house some expensive equipment, the door had an electronic lock. I punched in the numeric code, heard the click, and turned the door handle. Inside, it felt like a cave. Dark, cool, and far from downtown.

I opened a beer, put the rest in the refrigerator, and poured a shot of bourbon into a glass. At the far end of the studio, I sank into the worn black leather couch. The furniture remained from the recording studio days. I unlaced my boots, kicked them off, and rubbed my feet. Somewhere, in one of the boxes or duffel bags piled in the corner, were my sneakers. Since I'd moved down from Maine four days ago to start this job, I'd only unpacked one bag, the one with jeans and t-shirts.

The studio doorbell jarred me. I picked up the remote control from the glass table to open the door, something Underwood had installed when a paraplegic graduate student had rented the place. The door clicked open and swung quietly into the room.

"Bravo, dude!" Underwood boomed. "I see you're getting the hang of things! Damn convenient, that little clicker, isn't it? Care for a drink?"

"I'm ahead of you."

Underwood came in the room, ducking his tall frame under the door. He took a seat on the couch, put a bottle of Glenlivet Scotch on the coffee table, and picked a glass from the shelf underneath it. After he poured a shot, he pulled a joint out of his shirt pocket. "You know, I gotta tell you something, man. I admire you for taking that job. To work with those kind of people on a full-time basis. I mean, it sounds like some kind of secret mission, but, at the same time it's, uh…"

"Madness?"

Underwood laughed. He was a Vermonter, a philosopher and a musician. He played drums with a local blues band and had regular gigs around the city. We had met almost twenty years ago, working in the same group home for young mentally ill adults. He'd been studying to become a psychologist then, but after a year at the group home, he dropped out of the university and went into music full time. Our bond had always been deeper than our mutual interests in philosophical bullshit, lifting weights, and drinking.

"I wouldn't say that. Anyway." He lit the joint. "Tell me something that will shake my belief system."

"Ah, it's pretty much what you would expect. Lot of sick people out there. Feel like I walked ten miles today, but it was probably more like six." Paul passed me the joint. I declined. "No, thanks, it'll knock me out. I want to write some notes later, while they're still fresh in my head."

"Street journal? Cool." He stood up and paced the room, waving the joint in the air. "Write that stuff down! Great idea, man." At the other end of the room, he disappeared into the sound tech's booth. A minute later, John Lee Hooker blasted from speakers in every corner, and a few in the ceiling. "Awesome system, hey!" Underwood shouted. He grinned and ducked back inside to lower the volume, then came back and sat on the couch.

Underwood had maintained most of the original studio design. Black padding lined the walls, silver carpeting wall to wall, an oval-shaped table that I could use for a desk. The stereo system was still in place, with turntables even, set up in the jacuzzi/sound booth bathroom. The track lighting was adjustable by another remote control.

"Hey, Axel. It's good to have you back in Bean Town," he said.

I raised my beer. "Good to be back. Two years in Maine was great, but it gets a little quiet up there."

"Start having conversations with yourself?"

"Gotta watch out for that. At least the street's entertaining."

"Lay it on me."

I picked up my notebook from the glass table and opened it. "OK, these are short-takes. I'll tell you about Tony later. Now, on Newbury Street, right outside of a travel agency and a jewelry shop, there's a woman who sits there cross-legged on neatly folded blankets…"

"Like Buddha?"

"Yeah, just like Buddha. Sits there and stares straight ahead, meditating, or whatever. She has a little sign asking for spare change. And when someone tosses a coin into her bucket, she slowly turns her head to them and smiles. Opens her eyes, gives them this huge, beatific smile, doesn't say a word. Then she resumes her meditation and closes her eyes."

"Sounds like a mime I saw in Key West once."

"Everyone knows her, but no one knows her real name. Calls herself Star. We sat at an outdoor coffee shop and watched her for a half-hour. She made a few bucks." I reached for my beer and took a drink. "Tina, my partner, offered her some coffee and something to eat. But Star wanted a double-caramel latte and a slice of chocolate cake. When Tina said that she could only get her a coffee or a juice, and a bagel, real food, you know, Star screamed at her, 'Suck my dick, Outreach!' We finally had to leave."

Underwood laughed. "Maybe she was a He?"

"No, she was a She. And she knew what to say to get people away from her, I'll give her that." I turned the page and came to Antonio Sorelli. "Eighty-one year-old Italian manic non-drinker, reportedly. Overly friendly, wanders downtown area talking to anyone who'll listen. Wears a long overcoat in the heat, tells confusing jokes, and has a thirty year-old girlfriend who is a schizophrenic-obsessive-compulsive gambler. She uses Antonio's social security money to buy lottery tickets. He insists on buying Tina and me coffee. No medical concerns, he says. Sleeps in various shelters. Tina said he goes around all day meeting with other homeless people, buys them coffee if he has any money, happy as hell."

"And he's really not a drinker?"

"Doesn't appear to be. Maybe he has a couple of pops every night before he goes into the shelter, who knows. Lot of guys do that – stay relatively sober until dinner hour, then knock back a few shots to deal with the crowds in the shelter."

"I'd do the same. So why is a happy old guy like that out there?"

I took a drink of the Beam and followed it with some beer. I began to relax and forget how much my feet were killing me. "That's the million dollar question, my friend. I don't know yet."

"Another cold one?" He got up and went to the fridge.

"Sure."

"Do you have direct access to housing for a guy like this Sorelli, if he wanted it?" He handed me a fresh beer and sat down.

"Well, seems there are some hoops to jump through. But the shelter has a special housing program for the elderly. If the guy wanted it, he could probably have a regular bed in the older men's program tomorrow, while someone helps him do the paperwork."

"And if he doesn't want to do that?"

"Then I talk sports with him, listen to his jokes, and drink coffee."

"Wow," he said quietly. Turning the glass of Scotch around in his hand, he stared into it. "Something keeps the guy on the street."

"Something must."

"Maybe it's not easy for some people to live indoors," Underwood said. "Remember how some of them were, in that group home? They start ransacking the place. Burning things and freaking out. I even had one here. This chick must have been Bipolar or something. Took all her clothes off one night and ran all over the house, screaming that someone stole her cherries."

"Get out of here."

"It's true," he said. "Had to call the police."

"What happened to her?"

"They came and got her. Took her to a hospital, and kept her for a couple weeks. Then one day she shows up, all zombied out on medication. Packed up a few days later and caught a bus to the west coast."

"Bipolar. That's a tough one."

"Yeah, wouldn't want that." He sat back in the couch, nodding his head. "To tell you the truth, Axe, I can't get my mind around it, that a job like yours even exists. Seriously, what do they expect you to accomplish?"

"Get them in, I guess. We're supposed to focus on the 'vulnerable' ones. They have a list of people who need help the most."

"The Most Unwanted?"

"Sounds like a great idea for a TV series, huh?"

"I'll tell you what it sounds like to me." He sat up. "It sounds like a great opportunity to study the underbelly of this fine, righteous nation of ours." Underwood poured a little more Scotch into his glass and then looked at me the way he does when his philosophical curiosity kicks in.

"Want to try some of this single-malt?" he asked.

STREET LOGIC

Chapter 3

September 3, 2003

The clock on the dashboard of the Lincoln showed seven-fifty. Starting day three with a slight hangover didn't seem like a good idea, but there it was, so I dealt with it. I swallowed some aspirin with orange juice and drove into work, reminding myself to be careful about bullshitting late into the night with Underwood when a bottle of Glenlivet was on the table. The morning rush-hour traffic gave me some extra minutes to recover. By the time I wedged the old beast into the employee parking lot, narrowly missing the bumper of an ancient Volvo, my recovery was still lacking somewhat. I fumbled in my backpack and found the matchbox, opened it and fingered the half joint Underwood left me last night. What the hell. It couldn't hurt. The last working cassette I owned of the Doors was playing "Light My Fire". A sign, no doubt. I did a quick surveillance of the tiny lot, saw no one in sight, and rolled down the only working window on the rear passenger side. Took another look around, and sparked it.

The Lincoln was falling apart but the seats were still luxurious. I leaned back in the worn leather and slowly exhaled, watching the bluish smoke roll toward the rear window and drift out in a small cloud. I took another hit as Morrison screamed out the final lyrics, and I already felt better. In a corner of the rear-view mirror, I saw a tall man stagger out from between two cars. He windmilled across the lot, arms waving, trying to maintain his balance. At the last second, he lunged against the Volvo and grabbed the trunk. Carefully, he righted himself, took a few unsteady steps, and wandered into the alley. I stubbed the joint out in the ashtray and rolled up the window. As I searched for some gum in the glovebox, I caught the movement of a shadow outside my window.

Pretending not to notice, I kept searching for the gum until my fingers felt the pack. I stuffed a couple of pieces in my mouth and slowly swiveled my head to see Adrian Dantley, standing there and smiling through the window, cup of coffee in her hand.

"Hey there." I grinned at her through the glass. "Be right out."

I chewed the gum. The smell of reefer filled the interior of the car. If I opened my door, the unmistakable scent of Al Green would follow me out. Adrian and I had gotten high a few times together, but this was work. I took a few deep breaths of spearmint to clear my lungs and began to fool around with the seat belt, as if it was stuck. Finally, I slid across the front seat to the passenger side, opened the door just enough to slip out, and closed it quickly behind me.

"What's up, AD?" I've called Adrian AD ever since we met. "Patrolling the parking lot? You just missed this big, dangerous-looking homeless guy who almost attacked my car."

"Lucky for you I scared him off." She seemed amused. "You always use the passenger door?"

"Since last week. Door jammed on me."

"That's inconvenient." She walked around the car toward me. "I thought we'd work together today. Tina's going out with Ripley." She looked at me closely. "Smells like ganja around here."

"Sure does."

"Listen." She stepped closer. "There's something I need to tell you." She came to about a foot from my face. I breathed slowly through my nose and hoped the gum was doing its job. "Since our, um, last little session," she paused, staring directly into my eyes, "I've learned something about myself." She shifted from one foot to the other and looked away for a second. "I've discovered something kind of big."

I remembered the last time. About five months ago at her place. My eyes automatically moved down to her belly.

"No, not that, you idiot," she said, laughing. "It's actually more like the opposite."

"The opposite?"

She let out a deep breath. "I have a steady partner now."

"Partner?"

"That's right. And we're living together."

"You mean?"

"Yeah, that's what I mean. You'll meet her someday."

"Jesus, AD," I said, relieved. She wasn't going to read me the riot act about smoking weed on the job. "Congratulations! That's great. Except for guys like me, of course." She punched me on the shoulder, in a friendly way.

We had met a year ago. I'd come down to Boston to visit Underwood, and we were listening to some blues at Johnnie D's in Davis Square. Adrian was sitting at the next table. One thing led to another, but it was short-lived. She told me that she was going through some changes. When she graduated from Boston College last spring, with her master's degree in social work, she took a job directing the outreach team at Evergreen Shelter. In the middle of the summer, she called and offered me a position. I'm a social worker by trade. By experience, without the degree. We set a start date and I spent the rest of the summer fishing and wandering the backwoods. The outreach job sounded pretty cool. And I knew the boss.

I gave her a hug. "Well, you go, girl! What's the lucky lady's name?"

She laughed, and a little red came into her cheeks. "Janice. And you have to put a little more emphasis on the 'go', Axel, if you want to say that right. But thanks."

"Hope it works out AD. You deserve someone great."

"Hey," she looked around and sniffed the air. "That was some strong shit, huh?"

I chewed the gum slowly, poker-faced. "Yeah. Potent."

She punched me again on the shoulder. "So now we have work to do. Need to go into the office for anything?"

"Naw, I'm ready for action, AD. Just put the old harness on me and head me straight to the field."

We walked to Copley Square through the South End. Adrian gave me the lowdown on what happened with Tony Ruffo yesterday. The hospital had wanted to admit him. His nutrition level had been at zero and they needed to run some more tests before starting him on detox.

After a shower and some clean clothes, he slept for a while. When the nurse went looking for him later, he was gone.

"Jimmie Irons was right."

"What do you mean?"

"The Bone Man predicted it. Said Ruffo would split as soon as he was able."

"Well," she said, "we know he can still get around, when he has to."

Adrian wanted to check on Frank Murphy and a few others who usually hung out behind the Boston Public Library. "This guy Murphy can be a nasty character," she said. "And he's beating up his girlfriend, Rose. She always has bruises on her face and arms. Plus, he's got Hepatitis for sure, and possibly HIV, to go with his sparkling personality and substance abuse issues. He's been tested for HIV, but refuses to go back for the results."

"Other than that, he's a wonderful guy."

"Be careful," she said. "He likes to instigate people."

"My favorite kind of person."

Adrian gave me a look. "Here's my research. When we interact with people who are prone to violence, like Frank, where it's bubbling under the surface at all times, we really have to tread lightly. Something about our efforts to help frustrates the hell out of them. I think it's because they know we're right. A guy like Murphy is flawed, of course, but he's not stupid."

"What's your theory, exactly?"

"Talking with them about their health issues and whatever's keeping them on the street, their addictions, for example, brings up their incapacity to deal with it. When we walk away, and they stay, especially when they need help, the failure on their part to act in their own best interest provokes them, unconsciously. I've seen some who take their frustration out on whoever's nearby. Their drinking buddies, a stranger, a girlfriend."

"Like kicking the dog? Or Rose, in this case."

"I'm sure you know how it works," she said. "Good thing to remember when you're talking to someone who can be as abusive as

Frank. Anyway, I want to get her away from him long enough to convince her to go in and see a doctor. Murphy has her under his thumb. Won't let her pee unless he gives the OK."

"A real gentleman."

We crossed Dartmouth Street and went down the street behind the library. A small group was gathered about halfway down the block, sitting on top of the iron grating that ran alongside the building. A man in an orange coat was bent over a shopping cart. Four others leaned against the concrete wall. The one in a jeans jacket with the bottle was my guess. His eyes followed us all the way as we approached them.

Frank Murphy was smaller than I'd expected. Along with the jeans jacket, he had on a clean pair of blue jeans and what looked like a brand new pair of Red Wing boots. I recognized them because I had the same kind. Insulated and waterproof, they're perfect in the winter or on a hiking trail. Not so good on the city streets, I'd discovered. Today I'd dug out my hi-top basketball shoes, with padded inserts.

Sitting next to Murphy was a woman with dirty blond hair, skinnier than Jimmie Irons. The bruises Adrian had mentioned looked to be fresh. There was one on her cheek and another nasty one on her arm. She sat against the wall with a blanket across her lap and her boney, bare legs sticking straight out. Her feet looked like a couple of dirty baked potatoes. When she saw us, she quietly put the aluminum foil pipe she'd been using under the blanket.

Murphy glared at us. His face was flushed and he was sweating. "Well, look who's here. Outreach. Who you got there, Adrian? A doctor?"

"Hey, Frank," Adrian said. "This is Axel, and no, he's not a doctor. He's working with us now." She turned toward Rose and nodded at her.

Murphy's bloodshot eyes inspected me. "Well, Axel," he said, drawing it out. "What special talents do you bring out here for us lost souls?" There were a few quiet laughs.

Ignoring Adrian's advice, I took a step closer and gave him a big smile. "Well for starters, I'm able to leap tall buildings and stop runaway trains." His tough-guy stare didn't waver. Maybe I'd played it wrong. The two younger guys sitting on Murphy's left did their best to look intimidating. Rose seemed to be shrinking away from him.

Murphy burst into laughter. "That's fucking great, man! You're gonna need superpowers to stop this train!" The two guys also laughed loudly. Murphy raised the bottle to his mouth and Rose made a sound like a hiccup. The guy in the orange coat didn't look up. He was sorting cans from bottles. He was about medium height, stocky, and was probably in his forties. Murphy finished his drink and passed the bottle to the guy next to him. He muttered something and they laughed again.

Dismissing me, he pushed his hair back with his hands and turned his attention to Adrian. "Can you get me in?" His rough voice had turned almost childlike.

Adrian stuffed her hands in her back pockets. "Where do you want to go, Frank?"

"Anywhere. Just get me in."

"How about New England Medical Center," she said carefully. "And while we're there, you can talk to that nurse who's been working with you."

Murphy gave her a hard stare. He shifted back to me. "What's your name again, buddy?"

"Axel."

He snorted. "Does a name like that come with car parts?" He laughed again and this time Rose joined in with a high-pitched cackle. Her remaining upper teeth hung precariously in front of her small mouth. Her thin lips were badly chapped and had open sores in the corners. Murphy's two sidekicks laughed with him. They were in their early twenties. Both had cans of beer and wore their baseball caps turned backwards. One offered the bottle to the guy standing by the cart.

Orange Coat refused the drink. "Don't be such a horse's ass, Frank," he said.

The young guys' laughter trailed off as Murphy grabbed the bottle angrily. He inspected the level of vodka and spit on the sidewalk. "Fuck you, Bernie! I offer to share my booze with you, and then you go and insult me?"

The man in the orange coat kept working. I heard a low chuckle.

Murphy shook his head as if he were waking up, and suddenly his face changed. "Shit, man. Sorry, Bern. I'm just fucked up." He checked the level of vodka in the bottle again and let out a deep breath. "Damn, I'm gonna have to send Rose to the fucking store again. Here, Axel." He leaned forward. "You want a little taste before it's all gone?"

"No thanks. I'm working."

"Never stopped me," he said, lifting the bottle to his lips.

Orange Coat had a square jaw and some miles on him. His nose looked slightly off center. He straightened up and put out his hand. "Bernie." His hand was rough, and strong. "Don't pay no attention to this clown. He's just pissed off at himself, that's all."

The two against the wall watched, quiet. Rose attempted to light her aluminum pipe. Murphy stared back at Bernie. "You always got to cut me down, don't you Bernie? Saint, my ass."

"Relax, Frankie, he's only trying to help," said Rose.

Murphy raised his hand, then dropped it. His look silenced her.

Bernie slowly shook his head. "Murph, sometimes we all need to take some advice." There was a quiet authority in what he said. He was taller than me, maybe five-ten, with a solid build under the bright orange jacket. It was the kind that highway workers wear, usually in winter. His jeans were stained and his boots were old and worn. One flapped loose at the toe.

"Yeah, right," Murphy growled.

"Well, I got business to take care of," Bernie said. He stepped closer to Murphy and leaned down, getting eye level. "Think about what these people are offering you, Murph." His voice was calm and carried no anger. He turned to us. "His bite isn't as bad as his bark."

Adrian smiled. "Everything all right with you these days?"

"I'm always all right. Sylvia, though. She's not getting out much from under that bridge."

"I know," Adrian said. "Tina and Ripley are going to check in with her today."

"That's good." He turned to go.

Murphy opened his mouth to say something, but seemed to think better of it. Bernie took the front edge of his cart and pulled it down the street. Murphy grunted and put his hand on the grate and tried to raise himself, but slipped and fell hard against Rose, who cried out in pain.

"Aw shut up, will ya goddammit!" he growled at her.

Adrian gave me a look. "Listen, Frank," she said. "You are a bit yellow in the face. Have you seen any of the street nurses lately?"

"Yeah, I saw them last night in the van. They wanted me to go in, but I was too tired to go anywhere."

"And now?"

He leaned back against the wall and looked at the bottle in his hands. "I just want to stay here for now," he said. "Maybe later." He turned his attention back to me. "Hey, listen, Axel? When you're not leaping tall buildings and refusing drinks, can you get me a winter coat and some sneakers? And maybe some of those new socks and sweatshirts I know they have at the shelter?"

I looked at his Red Wings boots, thinking they seemed better than my own. There was a dirty, heavy coat next to him. "Those Red Wings are pretty good boots. I wear a pair myself in the winter. And that coat seems solid. Sounds to me like what you really need is a little time to chill out somewhere, like Adrian was suggesting. Maybe the Wilder..."

"We could call them," Adrian said.

"Fuck you, Axel," he said, uncapping the bottle.

"Well, alright then," Adrian said. Her gaze shifted to Rose for a moment. "We're going to move on. But give it some thought, Frank."

Rose searched her pockets, talking to herself. She pulled out a small tin box. As we walked away, Murphy began to call her a string of names and insults. I stopped and looked back to see Murphy suddenly grab Rose by the hair. He jerked her head back and shook it hard, then pushed her away. She dropped with her hands around her head and made a low howling sound, and cowered against the wall. Murphy raised the bottle of vodka above her and swore he'd kill her. Adrian squeezed my arm.

"Hey, Murph!" I shouted.

He froze. "What the fuck do you want?"

"What's your shoe size?"

His rage turned to confusion. Then, seeing his advantage, his expression changed into the smile a child bully uses to charm.

"Ten," he said.

"Nike or Reebok?"

"Adidas, fool."

"I'll see what I can do." I stepped a few feet toward him, dragging Adrian with me. "You know, Frank," I tried to keep my voice neutral, "I feel like it's my job to let you know something, whether you care to hear it or not." Murphy's eyes narrowed. The smile disappeared. "I'd be glad to bring the van out here and get you into the hospital tomorrow, if you want. A little time off the street could do you a lot of good. Think about it. In the meantime, I'll try to score some Adidas, size ten, when a pair comes through at the shelter. Those boots are tough on the feet."

Murphy slowly brought the bottle down, muttered something, and drank the last few drops until it was empty. "Alright," he said. "I'll think about it. I feel like shit anyway." He grinned. "Better make those ten and a half's."

"I'll stop by here tomorrow morning, and we'll take it from there." I nodded at Rose.

"Bye." Adrian directed it at Rose. "See you soon, I hope."

Adrian let go of my arm as we walked away. "You know, that was a little risky."

"I reacted, AD. He was going to bust her head open."

"I know. And it worked. Now you know what I mean by being careful around this guy. What did you think of Rose?"

"If she stays around Frank," I shrugged, "bottles are going to be broken."

Adrian sighed. "More than just that, I'm afraid. I've been talking to her for the last three months about going into the Betty Jones house. For a rest, and some detox time. She came close to agreeing a few times, but Frank always intervenes. He won't let her go. I figure if we can get him off the streets for a while, to take care of his medical issues, maybe she'll agree to go somewhere."

"Good idea. Before he kills her."

"He's a pretty sick guy." We headed up Dartmouth to Boylston. "And angry and scared about it. I have actually had a few serious conversations with him, about the HIV test, and about different strains of Hepatitis. He's been out here all summer, since his last hospitalization."

"Hospitalization?"

"It was more like an accidental hospitalization," she said. "But at least he got some rest. He harassed a woman in the library, and the library called the police. Hard to imagine him fleeing from anybody, the way he looks now, but I guess he gave library security a run for their money. Just so happened that your old buddy Ken Easttree was in the library at the same time, seeing some of his clients. He convinced the police to take him to the Wilder instead of jail."

"Which of course, Frank had to agree to. With Easttree there."

"Beats jail, too," she said. "By the way, your friend gave you a great reference. Ken said this job should be right up your alley." She paused. "That was pretty good back there. The Nike or Reebok thing. They didn't teach me that one in graduate school."

"No, probably not. Just good old redirection. I learned it at home. You distract them with something they want."

"OK, professor," AD said. "Let's go try those tricks out on Lamar Cleveland and company."

We got coffee and walked up Newbury Street with it, passing Star on her folded blankets, her eyes closed. "Keep going," Adrian lowered her voice, "she always screams obscenities at me." At the corner of Mass and Newbury, we stopped in front of the Tower Records store. "Over there," she nodded toward the other side of the street. "That's his headquarters."

I could just make out two figures sitting in the shade at one end of a sheltered bus stop. Lamar and company turned out to be just Lamar and Bernie, of the orange coat. Bernie's shopping cart sat parked against the chain-link fence barrier to the Mass Turnpike that whizzed by below them. Lamar was known on the street as Tarheel, Adrian told me. A North Carolina tag. She guessed that he was about the same age as Tony Ruffo.

"He's usually got a gang around him," she said.

"Who, Lamar or Bernie?"

"Lamar. Bernie doesn't run with a gang. And he doesn't like Lamar's crack buddies, either. I've noticed they all split when he's around."

"Lamar's into crack?"

"No, just some of the people he usually hangs out with are. Lamar's a drinker."

"What's the story with this Bernie guy?"

"He's kind of a mystery. Usually by himself, although he seems to know everybody on the street. All he's told me is that he got in some trouble, years ago, and did his time." She tossed her coffee cup in the trash can and shaded her eyes, looking at the bus stop. "Assault with a deadly weapon."

"He told you that?"

"Yeah." She took out her phone.

"Gun or knife?"

"His hands. He used to be a semi-pro boxer, I guess. He steers clear of the law now, but he's still out here on the street. Told me he prefers to live outside the system. He has a place under the Storrow Drive bridge, built up under the highway rafters. I see him all over, but usually he hangs out around Horseshoe Park and the bridges. Collects cans and bottles and cleans up a bar near Kenmore Square. Seems like a decent guy."

"You mean he's not an asshole?"

"No, he doesn't bother anybody. And nobody seems to bother him."

"Murphy called him 'Saint.'"

"You caught that. They call him Saint Bernie. Or sometimes just the Saint. We guess that it's because he's rescued a few people from the river. Which reminds me," she flipped her phone open, "I want to see if Tina and Ripley saw Sylvia Tompkins yet."

"Bernie's an undercover outreach worker."

"I think it's his way of redeeming himself," she said.

I watched the scene across the street as she called Tina. Lamar was wearing dark clothing and in the shadows, he was hard to see. Bernie's orange coat was impossible to miss. They seemed to be engaged in a deep conversation, Lamar gesturing with his hands, head bobbing, occasionally shouting, with Bernie leaning forward and facing him.

Adrian hung up. "This Sylvia isn't a drinker, but she's as stubborn as Tony Ruffo and Lamar. Flat out refuses health care. Let's go talk to Lamar," she said. "If you can chat it up with him, I can see if Bernie has any pull with Sylvia."

We crossed the street. Adrian introduced me to Lamar, and asked Bernie if she could have a few words with him. Bernie acknowledged me for the second time today, with a slight nod of his head. "It's your hide, not mine," he said to Lamar. The small dark-skinned man muttered something in return as Bernie and Adrian went over to another bench and sat down.

I stood in front of Lamar. He had a short mustache and beard, and his low-cut Afro was peppered with grey. He eyed me for a minute and then his face relaxed. "Well, if you know Adrian, you can't be all that bad. You going to stand there blocking my view or sit down?"

"I guess I'll take a load off." I took Bernie's spot.

"Good. Hurts my own feet to see you standing there." His tone softened. "Adrian's a good woman."

"Yeah, she is. And she tells me you're a good guy."

"I don't know about that." He gave me a sly, loopy kind of grin. "I don't hurt nobody, if that's what you're talking about. Less I have to." When he shifted his leg, his face grimaced. "So tell me, young man, what can I do for you?"

"I was going to ask you the same thing. Since you asked first, I'll tell you. I just want five minutes here in this shade. Adrian's been walking me all over the city today. My dogs are killing me."

Lamar chuckled. "Well, then you just sit there and rest yourself. Mine are killing me, too." He took a brown paper bag out from his jacket. "Don't suppose you want a taste?"

I shook my head. "No thanks." Seemed like everyone wanted to drink with me. I looked toward the ground. One of his feet did appear to be killing him. Sockless, I could see the skin was broken and bleeding around one ankle

Once Bernie had left with his cart, and after ten minutes of Adrian's coaxing, Lamar agreed to let her call the nurse from Medical Care. "But you tell her I ain't going in," he said.

The nurse, Marion Shea, worked on the streets two days a week. She met us a half-hour later. Lamar didn't want her to examine his feet at the bus stop. After some complicated negotiations, we eventually agreed to use the foyer of a small office building a block away. There was no security or doorman.

"This here's my private office," Lamar said, and sat on the floor. Marion helped him remove his shoes. The rash covered his right foot, but it also ran up the back of his lower leg, as well as under his armpit and the back of his head. It bled and oozed an ugly yellow pus where he'd been scratching it, especially on the foot and leg.

"You want to go to the Wilder?" Marion asked him.

"Hell no! I already told them that."

"How about Saint Elizabeth's? You know I can't treat it properly out here. It's infected, Lamar, and just going to get worse out here."

He put his shoe back on. "Not today," he said quietly.

Marion tried a few more times. Finally, she said she had to get downtown. Adrian and I walked with Lamar back to the bus stop, and I sat with him while she went to get him a cold drink and some chicken nuggets. We talked about old movies and sports while we waited. Lamar liked *The Towering Inferno* and *The Getaway*.

"That Steve McQueen, now he was an actor," he said. "Liked to race them cars too. Killed him in the end." He didn't care much for the Red Sox or the Patriots. He preferred to talk about the old Cleveland Browns. "That big ol' buck nigger used to carry four, five of 'em into the end-zone, right on his back. Had himself that white woman, that singer. Remember the one I'm talking about?"

"The singer, or the big ol'…?"

He shook his head sharply and cut me off. "Listen here! I'm only talking about the greatest running back of all time! Don't tell me you never heard of... "

"You mean Jim Brown?"

"That's the one! And that white woman, what was her name? The skinny one, sang all them show songs, cabaret songs, I think. Her mama was that girl on *Wizard of Oz*."

"Liza Minelli?"

"That's her! Lord, those white women loved his big black ass!" he chuckled. "And his big fat bank account, too. Although that one was a rich woman herself. Probably had more money than him." He switched back to movies. "Now, remember the one where Steve McQueen is the firefighter, and that other guy, the good-looking one, Newman whatshisname, see, he's the boss-man. And he don't like this McQueen, who wants to put out the fire no matter what it takes, and finally orders the water tanks on top of the tower to be busted. You remember that?"

"Sure."

"You know something?" He leaned toward me. "You look kind of like him, that firefighter. You better watch yourself," he grinned. "Anyway, he didn't care what the boss-man said, he just went ahead and ordered them tanks to be broken! And he was right, too! It put out that fire, sure enough." He set the brown paper bag on to the bench between us, and pulled out his smokes.

"He made the tough decision."

"That's right, that's right! Now you're talking. Ended up the hero." He lit his cigarette and leaned back. "Had all kinds of money, too, that McQueen. Not as much as Jim Brown, but he had enough to go around. And women were crazy for him! Now if I had that kind of money, you think I'd be out here?"

"No, I imagine not."

"Damn right. I'd be drinking some of that Russian stuff and riding in one of those big old cars, like that one going by right now, see, across the street? Like that." A white stretch limo cruised across the bridge. "That's what I'd be riding around in if I had some of that Jim

Brown's money. Here, you sure you don't want a taste?" He held out the paper bag again.

"No thanks."

He took another pull on it and set it down again on the bench. A bus rolled along the bridge followed by a dump truck, and their weight caused the bridge to tremble. Lamar put a hand on the bottle.

"So tell me, how long you been a drinker, Lamar?"

He nearly spit out his drink. "Now why the hell you going to ask me something like that!"

"Didn't mean anything by it, Lamar. Just curious. I guess it's kind of a dumb-ass question, come to think of it."

Lamar muttered something I couldn't hear, but I could read his face. I thought about Adrian's theory. Don't poke the bear in his own den. I leaned forward and got ready to move. His lips started to curl into a snarl, and I was about to stand when he suddenly broke out in laughter. "My wife," he said, "my second wife, that is – she asked me that same goddamn question when I met her. Course, I lied. Told her I only touched it now and then, on special occasions."

Adrian returned with a bottle of orange juice and the chicken nuggets. "Here you go, Lamar," she said.

He took the juice and bag from her and put them down on the bench.

"Thank you," he said. "I'll save these for later."

"Make sure you eat them," Adrian said. "Gotta keep your nutrition up."

He gave her a big smile. "I will. I like them chicken nuggets. Not as good as chitlins, but they'll do. Sit down for a minute before you rush off, unless you got somewhere to go."

"We have some time," Adrian said, and sat on the other side of me. Lamar lit another cigarette and offered me one.

"No thanks," I said.

"Good. Don't start."

He stretched his bad leg out in front of him, the one with the rash. The effort caused him to wince. "I been drinking longer than I can remember," he said quietly. The traffic on Mass Ave forced me to lean closer to hear him. "But I was sober for a time. Once. Yes sir, when I joined up with those Christian folks in Springfield. They didn't go for no drinking. After a while, well, I had to leave. Had to leave a lot of places. 'Course, I got my boys out here, watching my back. And this is where I'm staying. I ain't going back there."

I didn't ask why.

"Where would you like to go back to?" I said.

"There ain't no anywhere to go to. And I sure as hell ain't going to that Wilder Center, or that Evergreen, or any one of those goddamn places! So don't even say those names to me."

"I won't. But how about that one you said you liked. Out in Brookline. What was it, Saint Elizabeth's?"

"That's right."

"They treat you well there, do they?"

"Yes sir, they do. But I ain't going there today. You gonna be out here tomorrow?"

"I'll be out here tomorrow," I said.

"Good. What time?"

"How about ten o'clock?"

"Ten o'clock. Good. I'll be here. If I'm not here, then I'll be across the street in the subway."

The next day I arrived with the van and parked around the corner from the bus stop. Tina came with me. When we found him, he only wanted some new clothes.

"Wait a minute now, Lamar," I said. "Yesterday, you told me that you wanted to go to Saint Elizabeth's, and have your rash treated. To meet you here at ten." A couple buses roared past and drowned out his response. The look he gave me said he wasn't going anywhere.

"Well, alright," I said, sitting down next to him. "You have to do what you have to do." He grunted something, and looked down at his leg. "But if you're dead set on not going to the hospital today, how about this. If you want, we can go get some clothes at the shelter, and kill two birds with one trip. You're going to want a shower probably, especially to put on some new threads, right? And the clinic has a good shower. It's private. While you're there, a doctor can examine those rashes and tell you what you can do about them. You don't have to stay there."

He closed his eyes and sat back against the corrugated siding of the bus stop. I thought he'd dozed off. Tina said she was going to check on the van and make some phone calls from there, so we wouldn't get a parking ticket, and to call her when I was ready.

I waited, watching the foot traffic pass along Mass Ave. Mostly college students. Young people carrying their instruments to class at Berkeley College of Music. Future rock stars. I tried to pick the ones that looked like they might make it. After maybe ten minutes and spotting only one contender, a Janis Joplin look-alike, I heard Lamar begin to shift around. He pulled out the paper bag from inside his jacket and took a short drink, then capped the bottle and stuffed it away again.

He cleared his throat. "I'm taking my bottle. Or forget about it. You gonna bring me back?"

I knew we weren't supposed to transport anyone with an open container. Adrian had warned me about that. And the general practice was to take people in, not out. They came in because they wanted to sleep a few hours on the lobby floor, or see a doctor or nurse in the clinic, or eat. They either stayed or wandered out to the street again, on their own. Taking a person back to the street didn't make sense. But I'd seen how difficult it had been for him to even walk a block.

"I'll tell you what. Bring it with you. Just promise me that you won't drink it on the way in. When you're done at the clinic, and they've had a look at your rashes, I'll bring you back here. Clinic, shower, clean clothes. How's that?"

"You gonna do that for me?" He stared at me, his eyes wide. "Gonna bring me straight back here?"

"That's right. So what do you say? Let's do it?"

"You know," he gave me that loopy grin again, "You a pretty nice fella, Axel. You married?"

I stood up and grinned at him. "You're not going to ask me to marry you, are you, Lamar?"

"Lord have mercy!" he said, laughing. "You got a better sense of humor than I thought. What I was gonna tell you, is that you need to find yourself a good woman and settle down." He took a drink and then wrapped the bottle tightly in the bag, and buried it in his pocket. "Yes sir, that's my advice."

Chapter 4

January 5, 2004

The bell began to toll as the sun descended over the top of a long row of maple trees. It was one of those iron bells that weigh a ton and hang from a steel rod, with a rope to pull on and make it swing. A young boy was pulling on the rope. He leaped and yelled with joy at the sound of each gong. The deep notes carried half a mile and called the workers in from the field. The workers, in faded, dirty clothes, straggled up the dusty street. Their faces looked tired, but they seemed happy as they traded jokes. Then the deep tones of the bell changed. It rang at a higher pitch. And the boy was gone. I searched for him and saw him running across the field. Then the field and the green trees and the workers faded away. The bell turned into smoke. Ashes fell as the smoke rose up in a great black cloud.

But the ringing continued.

I opened my eyes. The ringing was coming from the cell phone in my backpack, on the couch. The clock radio read 6:15a.m. I rolled out of bed. The carpet was cold under my feet. Slowly, I shuffled across the room in the dark to the couch. The ringing stopped. I turned on a lamp, sat down, and dug through my pack until I felt the phone. It began to ring again as soon as I pulled it out.

"It's me." Her voice was so soft I could barely hear her. "Sorry to call you so early. It's about Tony Ruffo."

"Hang on, AD, let me adjust the volume." I thought I heard her say someone was dead. "OK, now I should be able to hear you. Did you say he's dead?"

"No," she said, speaking louder. "I said that I dread seeing what kind of condition he's in, with this weather. The cold front came in last night, just like they were saying it would. It's close to zero already. The van offered him a ride last night, but he refused to come in. So," she paused, "can you do us all a big favor?"

I pulled the window curtains aside to see outside. Pre-dawn darkness. I rubbed my eyes and looked over at the clock again. "You're already in the office?"

"Came in early."

"Alright, give me forty-five minutes or so to get down there, and then I'll call you."

"Thanks, I really appreciate it. I'll call the taxi company for you. What's your address again?"

I gave it to her as I made my way over to the kitchenette in the corner of the studio.

"Use a voucher. And call me as soon as you know anything, will you?"

"OK." I lit the burner on the stove and put some water on to boil.

"Because I want to know if we need to call Emergency Services and have him sectioned. It's better if he'll come in on his own. You can even bluff him and say that the mayor's called a state of emergency or something like that, and that everyone has to take shelter."

"Did the Mayor actually do that?"

"No, not yet. And maybe you can leave Ken Easttree a message, just in case we need his help in pushing for an evaluation. He can mobilize the Emergency Services Team faster than I can."

"OK." I found a filter and stuck it inside a large mug, and tossed in some ground coffee. "I'll call you as soon as I get down there."

"Oh, and one more thing. There was a message on our phone about a woman on Washington Street, which is on your way. Can you keep an eye out for her? She's a black woman, in her forties, camped out by a fence next to Vinnie's Pizza. A few blocks before you hit Mass Ave. The guy who left the message said she showed up two days ago and has been sitting on her suitcase next to his shop. He also said she's babbling and singing to herself, and that she refused his offer of free pizza."

"Wow. Vinnie's has good pizza."

"Right. If she wants transportation, call me and I'll find someone to get her. Or bring her in the taxi if you can."

"Got it. Black woman, Vinnie's Pizza, fence, Washington Street, babbling and singing."

"I owe you one." She hung up.

I poured hot water over the coffee grounds and took a glass of water over to the window. Outside, the street lamp at the end of the driveway lit up the waving branches of bare trees. I traced my finger along the frosted edges of the window. First week of January. Zero degrees already. The birds weren't even awake yet. I got into my work clothes: a union suit of long johns, thick socks, a thermal shirt over the union suit, and fleece-lined, winter pants. When the coffee was ready, I sat down on the couch with it and had a cigarette. I was worried about Tony Ruffo. The New England fall had been beautiful, but winter had arrived early, and now it was blasting the coast with sub-freezing temperatures and nasty winds. Tony had weathered worse, and apparently, he was trying to add another winter to his belt. The few times he came into the shelter were only for a shower and some new clothes. Especially after the street nurses stopped giving him sponge baths in the back of the outreach van. During Thanksgiving, the banker lady had even invited him to her house. They picked him up at the shelter, she and her husband and two children. Just trying to do something good. Ruffo had showered and dressed for them in an old three-piece suit and a heavy long overcoat from the tons of donated clothing. Crazy as I thought it was, it was a nice gesture by the banker's family. Only problem was that Tony couldn't hold his bowels, and they had to put him in the shower in the middle of the dinner and then dress him again in one of the husband's sweat suits. When they brought him back to the shelter for the night, he never went in. Later, one of the counselors was doing rounds and found him laid out in a doorway of the building next to Evergreen. Alive, but unable to walk.

I heard the taxi beep twice from the end of the driveway. As I closed the back door, Paul came out on to the deck above me.

"It's a cold one out there today, buddy!" He looked wide-awake. "Got your thermal jock on?"

"Fleece-lined. What the hell are you doing up so early?"

"I like to see the sunrise from the pond, now and then," he said. "Had a late gig last night. That your taxi?"

"Yeah. I gotta go. Enjoy that sunrise."

"Sure thing," he said, saluting. "Hey, how's that Tony Ruffo guy doing?"

"I'll let you know, I'm going down there now. He's still camped out on the waterfront."

"One tough bastard."

"I guess so."

"Bring him in before he's an ice sculpture."

The taxi driver told me it was seven degrees below zero with the wind-chill factor. He drove fast along the dark, empty streets and we were on Washington Street in under ten minutes. Near Mass Ave I told him to slow down. There was no one on the sidewalk. Then I saw her, or someone, huddled against a fence, not far from Vinnie's.

"Pull over in front of that pizza shop, could you," I said. "I'll just be a few minutes. You can keep the meter running."

He turned around and looked at me. "I don't think Vinnie is doing business this early, pal."

I opened the door. "Listen, any chance we can give that woman a ride? The one sitting over there?"

He glanced through the windshield and whistled. "You serious?"

"Yeah. I don't know if she'll go. But it's too cold out there."

"A ride to where?"

"The Evergreen Shelter."

He thought about it. "Long as she doesn't mess up the back seat, I'll take her. It's too cold out there for anyone."

"Alright, thanks. I'll be right back."

The wind hit me in the face as I hurried over to where she sat against the chain-link fence, tucked back in an alcove that was slightly out of the wind. She was rocking back and forth and singing to herself, softly, eyeing my approach.

"I need a little coffee for my sugar, baby," she sang. Her voice was clear and sweet. She repeated the phrase, over and over. I stepped closer.

"Coffee sounds good right about now. You want some?"

She stopped rocking and lowered her voice, until I couldn't hear her. Her big brown eyes peered up at me from under a purple wool hat that was pulled low over her ears and forehead. Her white parka was un-zipped and she had an overcoat on underneath.

"So, how about it? Hot coffee, and I can also offer you a ride to…"

She clapped her gloved hands together. "You want to pay my rent?"

"Were you evicted?"

"Oh, honey, worse than that. But I had time to grab my clothes before that bastard threw me out."

"That doesn't sound too good." I moved my feet to keep warm.

"Hell no it wasn't! You want to pay my rent?"

"Sorry, I can't do that. But I can offer you some coffee, and a ride over to the Women's Inn at Evergreen. It's warm there and they have plenty of sugar to go with the coffee."

She clapped her hands again and whooped as if it were all a joke. Maybe it was to her. Then she scowled. "That ain't gonna help me pay the rent. They a bunch of crazy women down there anyway."

"Well, it can get crowded. But it's a lot warmer than here. Even for a little while."

"I know what happened to me." She suddenly glared at me. "You don't know shit. He shouldn't have thrown me out. It's my place, you know!"

"I'm sure the counselors there would be glad to help you sort that out."

"How they gonna do that?"

"They can make some phone calls for you, find out what's going on, talk to your landlord." I knew I was reaching. "They can see if there's something they can do. And you can warm up at the same time and get something to eat."

"I don't want nothing to eat," she said. "Some motherfucker tried to give me a whole pizza, but I know what he really wanted."

"Listen, my name is Axel. I work for the shelter. Can I ask what your name is, ma'am?"

"You can ask, but that don't mean I got to tell you."

"You don't need to tell me your name if you don't want to, but I can go with you and introduce you to the counselors."

"Nope," she said. "I'm just fine right here."

The end of my nose was icing up. The wind was howling up the sidewalk. Even a desperate prostitute wouldn't be out here in this cold. But this one wasn't going to come with me, I could tell. No matter how long I stood there.

"How about if I come back in a little while and see if you want to go in then?"

"If you gonna come back with my rent money, I'll be here."

I smiled at her. "I'll be back. I hope you'll think about it. It's below zero out here, you know."

"It don't bother me none," she said.

"See you in a while, then."

When I got in the taxi, the driver looked at me. His eyebrows went up. "Well? She coming?"

"No. Let's go," I said. "Atlantic Ave at the Aquarium."

"They're not going to be open either at this hour," he said, as we drove along the street. "But I don't suppose that's why you're going."

I called Adrian to let her know about the woman on the suitcase, telling her it was a no-go. After he parked in front of the Citizen's Bank, the driver inspected the voucher I gave him, and turned toward me. "You work for the shelter, huh?"

"Their street outreach team."

"Must be tough work."

"If you like results, yeah."

"Know what you mean," he said, smiling. "Don't freeze to death out there, pal."

"It's OK. I was a Boy Scout." I stepped out of the warm cab and into the cold wind.

"Hey!" the driver shouted, before I shut the door. "Don't forget your backpack!"

"Thanks."

"Always be prepared." He laughed and drove away.

Across the street, the Big Dig site was silent. Only a few workers were beginning to gather. According to the clock on the Harper Tower, it was 7:05. I stuffed my hands deep into the pockets of my goosedown parka, and hurried up Seaward Street toward the waterfront. Passing the entrance to a parking garage, I saw Stella Simpson sitting cross-legged on a pile of cardboard and blankets, almost hidden. She seemed to be asleep. I went over and stamped my feet in front of her. Her eyes opened to narrow slits on her bony, crack-addled face.

"Hey, Axel. You come out here to see me?" Her smile was hideous. A Halloween skeleton mask. She seemed to be oblivious to the temperature.

"You're a mind-reader, Stella. You know what else I'm thinking?"

"You're wondering why a beautiful woman like myself is sitting out here in the cold." She had on several wool caps. The outer one was a blue Patriots hat. "You know the answer, Axel, you know the answer already. Whenever you want to take me to your place, I'll go. I already told you that a thousand times. All you have to do is say the word." She laughed like a hyena.

"How about some coffee, Stella?"

"I only want you, Axel, only you. But if I can't have that, I'll take a hot chocolate. Now, what's on your mind?"

"It's too cold for anyone to be out here. You really should consider going into the Women's Inn for the day, have some hot food, a hot shower."

"You already know the answer, Axel."

"You're a tough one, Stella. But I had to try."

"Appreciate the effort, sweetheart."

"I'll be right back."

"I hope so," she said. The wind carried the rest of her words away.

I hustled back up to Atlantic and into the Dunkin' Donuts, anxious to get to Tony Ruffo and evacuate him from his spot. When I entered the warm shop, I nearly slipped on the wet floor.

"Be careful, I just mopped there!" Mary cried out.

"Now you tell me," I said as I managed to straighten up. "Beautiful morning out there today, huh?"

"I wouldn't call it that." She looked worried. "You're here early."

"Unfortunately. I'm kind of in a hurry…"

"I walked by there this morning, Axel. The man was buried under all those blankets and I didn't want to move them. I was afraid he might be, well…" She paused.

"What?"

She leaned across the counter. "Dead."

The door opened and cold air rushed in. A guy in a long overcoat, hat and scarf almost slipped in the same spot as I had.

"Mary, can I just get a …"

"I would hate to see him freeze to death," she said, grabbing a medium sized cup. "Knowing he's there, just out back, and it's so cold."

"Yes. Just a quick hot chocolate, please," I said.

Behind me, the man walked carefully up to the counter. His briefcase bumped me in the leg. I glanced back at him. Impatience and aggravation were already set on his face and it wasn't even 8:00a.m.

"You know what, Mary? I wouldn't be surprised if he was already frozen solid like a fish. The Mayor should call a state of emergency and force these people in. Or we're going to have of lot of frozen Tonys around the city." The man behind me cleared his throat and bumped me again with the suitcase. I turned back to stare at him. I kept talking. I didn't like the look the guy was giving me. "That stubborn old fisherman has been flaunting death for years. Today really could be his last." I turned back to Mary as she poured a coffee. "Just the hot chocolate." I pulled out some cash.

"The coffee's for you." She pushed my money away. "On the house."

"You're too good, Mary." I grabbed both cups and turned to go.

"Damn cold out there today, isn't it?" I said to the guy.

"Yes. Terrible."

"Be worse to be living out there. Makes you appreciate what you have." I glanced at his long coat and wool scarf. "Boggles the mind sometimes."

He looked closely at me. "What do you mean?"

"You walk by here every day?"

"No. I'm from out of town." His accent sounded familiar.

"Oh. Well, there's a homeless guy who camps along the waterfront in back of this building. Thought you might know him. I was hoping to outrage you enough to call the mayor's office and see if they're going to do anything for this guy. You know, just a concerned citizen's call. Where you from?"

"Cleveland."

"Cold out there, too." I headed for the door.

"What about shelters?" he said.

"He refuses to go. Thanks, Mary. I'll let you know what happens."

"I'll call," the man said.

I turned around at the door. "Good. You can make up anything you want. Tell them you voted for the mayor. Tell them it's about a guy named Tony Ruffo."

Stella took the hot chocolate with both her gloved hands. Her Halloween smile made me want to hurry. "Thanks, sweetheart." She pried the lid off the cup and smelled the sweet drink.

I turned to go. "Stay warm, Stella. Think about going in."

"Don't worry about me, Axel. I'm always taking care of Stella."

He was covered in a white blanket of snow, under a pine tree. His eyelids were lightly dusted with snowflakes. "Tony!" I shouted. The wind was stronger here along the harbor. Slowly, he opened his eyes.

"Axel," he croaked.

"Jesus. I thought you were a goner."

"Still here," he said.

"It's below zero, Tony. With no sign of stopping. I think you've got to come in."

He stared at me solemnly. "Promise me something, will ya, Axel?"

I leaned down to hear him better. "What?"

"Can you apologize to Tina for me?"

"For what?"

"She knows." The wind blew snow off the branches of the tree, sending more flakes on to Ruffo's face. He lifted a gloved hand and wiped them away.

"You mean about her wanting you to come in? About going to the Wilder Center for a few days?"

He made an effort to lift his head, but it was too much. His face contorted. He tried again, and fell back. He lay still, his breath coming out in short vaporous puffs.

"Axel," he gasped. "Promise me another thing."

"I haven't promised anything yet, Tony. But I can promise you one thing. You won't make it out here in this cold. Not for long. I think you need to let me get you out of here."

"I want…" He started to say something and began to cough. As I waited for the hacking to stop, I stood to the side and looked out to the harbor. It had frozen in some places along the wharf and next to the breakwater. Farther out, the waves pitched furiously. The sun was still hidden in the dark grey sky. I may have been a Boy Scout, but I wasn't prepared for this. I couldn't imagine spending the night here, even with a tent.

He was up on his elbow now and his hands were out from under the blankets. On one hand he wore a blue ski mitten and on the other he had a black glove. My phone rang inside my jacket. By the time I located it, I'd missed the call.

I hit re-dial. "Hey," I said, when Adrian answered. "He's alive. I'm just about to read him the riot act. I'll call you back in five."

"Tell him we have the van on the road already."

I bent toward him. "The van is on its way. Mayor's orders. Until the weather clears, everybody has to get off the street."

He grunted something and reached behind him into the snow bank, dug around, and pulled out a quart-sized bottle that he held up for me to inspect. "See this?"

"I see it."

"I know you mean well, Axel." He had no fight in his voice. "But I'm not going in."

"You can bring it with you."

He shook his head and took a long pull from the icy booze. When he was done, he stuck the bottle back in the snow.

"You know what Woody Hayes would say right about now?" I said.

His hand was still tightly wrapped around the neck of the bottle. A smile started to form and he cleared his throat. "He'd say, Ruffo, get me five yards or I'll skin your ass!"

"That's right. And he'd probably say 'Ruffo, you got to get up now and win one for the Gipper!'"

He fell back on to the snow. His laughter was short and raspy. "That was Rockne, Knute Rockne. Notre Dame, for chrissakes." He raised the bottle and took another long drink. "I can't do it, Axel."

I threw my last card on the table. "OK, Tony, I can understand that. But here's the deal, no bullshit. The Mayor himself called us this morning and said he's authorized the use of the police to get people into shelters. You can come with me, and bring your stuff, or wait for the cops to hogtie you and stick you in the paddy wagon. Think of it that way."

His blue eyes were weak. He glanced at the water. The wind was coming in sharp gusts, sending spray into the air. The coffee I'd set down in the snow had already blown away. The wind flapped the pine branches with a fury, sprinkling more snow down on us. I pulled out my phone and stuck it to my ear, and then leaned down closer to him.

"It's the Mayor calling again! You want to talk to him?" I held out the phone.

Ruffo looked surprised, his blue eyes wide. "Really?"

"Really." I nodded.

He glanced up at the sky, and shook his head slowly. "No. Just tell him I'll go."

"That's the spirit, Tony." I placed the phone to my ear and said loudly, "Yes, Mayor, he's going in." Then I punched in Adrian's number and turned away. "OK, Coach, he's ready. Have them pull the van around to the back."

"Did you have to twist his arm?" Adrian asked, after we had dropped Ruffo off at the shelter's clinic.

"I resorted to football heroics. And lying. You know that Tony won the Heisman at OSU, didn't you?"

"Of course. What was the lie?"

"I told him the Mayor was on the phone."

"And he fell for that? Well, that's a new weapon to add to your arsenal. Threaten them with the Mayor."

"Desperate times..."

"Totally. Speaking of which, are you going back to see that woman on the suitcase?"

I had forgotten about her.

"I'll go with you," she said.

We drank gas station coffee and listened to the van's radio on the way. On Washington Street, I pulled up in front of Vinnie's Pizza. "I don't see her," I said, as I opened the door and stepped out. Adrian followed me to the alcove. Where the woman had been sitting on a suitcase this morning, there was just some loose trash swirling in the wind and a rusty old padlock rattling against the chain-link fence.

Chapter 5

January 23, 2004

A trail zigzagged through the snow. Mounds of two and three feet had formed overnight. "Ready?" I started down the slope, through knee-deep drifts. "Follow me," I said. But she moved past me, veered off the path and pushed her legs like a cross-country skier. Her long brown hair was swinging loose. It didn't matter what the weather was like, she wouldn't wear a hat. Unless it was a Red Sox cap, and that was only during September. "Watch yourself, AD," I said. "There's a manhole cover and a pothole ahead." The alley behind Station 33 slanted downward and split off with a ramp to a parking lot. The rest of the alley ran for another hundred feet. At the end, against a brick wall and under a narrow roof of concrete, was Frank Murphy's spot. I didn't think Adrian and I would be able to get him out of there on our own.

It was seven-thirty on a Tuesday morning, a few weeks after Tony Ruffo had gone in to the shelter. Because we had threatened to tell the Mayor about him, Ruffo stayed for a couple of days. Then, one morning he was gone. The overnight team found him hunkered down in Chinatown, and he accepted a ride back to Evergreen. As weak as he was, he left again a few days later wearing a new outfit, and returned to resume his post by the waterfront under the pine tree. At least he was well dressed.

Today, we had gotten a phone call from one of the firefighters at the station. He'd spotted Frank in this alley a few days ago. He'd tried to talk him into going to a shelter, but Murphy had refused. I'd seen Murphy every day for the last two weeks and he'd turned down my offers as well. As the weather grew colder, he just got more blankets from the overnight team when they checked on him. The temperatures had been in the teens for the entire week and now Adrian wanted to see Frank Murphy's situation for herself.

She stayed even with me until we reached the bottom of the slope. Murphy was about a hundred feet away. Adrian's foot suddenly caught on something and she lost her balance. As she tried to keep from going down, her feet kept sliding and she began waving her arms frantically. She was still laughing when she slipped again and went down, reaching for me. I was only a couple feet away and grabbed her hand, but it caused me to slip, and we spun around as her momentum brought us both down. I went into the snow on my back. With a bounce, she landed right on top of me with a small scream. All that hair fell on my face. Startled, she lifted her head, her nose covered with snow.

"Nice move, AD. What kind of conditioner do you use?"

"Whoops," she said softly. She had incredible blue-green eyes. "Sorry."

"No problem."

Her face was only inches from mine. She grinned, and planted both hands on my chest, straddled me, and pushed up until she was standing. Then she reached for my hands to help me up.

"Told you to be careful there." I dusted the snow from my coat.

She grabbed my arm and started pulling me down the alley. "Let's go do this thing."

"Right. But follow me, this time, OK? I think I know where the, uh, hazards are in this territory."

When she saw the pile of blankets, she got down and began brushing the snow off the top one. "Hey, Frank!" she said, in a loud voice. "It's Adrian and Axel." Adrian wrinkled her nose.

"Yeah. Smells a little like the waterfront," I said.

"Frank," she repeated. "I need to talk to you."

A muffled sound came from somewhere under the layers of tangled blankets. "Wait a minute," we heard him mutter. The pile began to move. A wool cap emerged, and Murphy looked up at us. It took him a minute to adjust his eyes to the brightness. An arm snaked out and he tried to rise, but immediately he fell back, howling in pain. He began to make choking sounds and as he turned to face us, his mouth opened and he gushed a torrent of dark vomit. I grabbed Adrian's coat and yanked her back. We tumbled into the snow and again she landed on top of me. This time Adrian quickly got to her feet.

"Missed us," I said. "You OK?" Steam was rising from the bile.

She helped me up. "Yeah. Close call. You alright?"

"Yeah." Murphy lay on his side, heaving. "Want me to call?" I said.

"Yes, please." Adrian started to pull off the outermost blankets. Frank was flat on his back now, groaning and protesting.

I speed-dialed the Boston Police emergency operator. If you dial 911 like everyone else, the call is answered out in Framingham, where it can sometimes take an extra minute of answering questions. The operator then transfers you to the appropriate station in the city, where you get to explain it again. But a cop working in the shelter gave us the direct number, and told us to use it in an emergency.

"This is 911, do you have an emergency?"

"Yes I do. I'm with a man who's buried in the snow, in a back alley in Back Bay. He's vomiting blood and has a broken arm. He can't get up. He's also wet and freezing."

"What's your exact location?"

"He's in the alley behind the firehouse on Boylston Street. Station 33. It's the alley off Hereford Street."

"Is he conscious?"

"He's vomiting blood. Yes, he's conscious. But he's in terrible shape, and in danger of frostbite as well."

I heard some clicking noises on the phone. "Do you know his name?" the operator said.

"No," I said. I'd learned that one from Tina. Never give names. "He appears to have been assaulted." That was rule number two, my own particular favorite. Lie.

"Your name?" I gave her the first name that popped in my head. Henry Miller. She recited my cell phone number from her caller ID and asked if the ambulance driver could use it if they couldn't find the man. I said sure, and that I'd be waiting with him. That also did the trick. Knowing somebody was going to be there to witness their arrival helped. The police operator said an ambulance would be there soon.

Adrian had all the blankets off except for a sleeping bag. I bent down and looked for the zipper. "Here," I said. "We have to unzip this thing, Frank. You hanging in there?"

He tried to focus on me, but his eyes were circling around in their sockets. He lurched to the side and heaved again. Nothing came out this time. After a series of dry heaves, he fell back and gasped for air. "I think I'm dying."

"No you're not, Frank," Adrian said. "You're sick and you're going to the hospital." She found the zipper and worked it down until she could pull it partially away from him. There were more blankets underneath, and they were soaked. The odor of urine, feces, and vomit hit me and I stepped back.

"What are you people doing to me?" he cried.

"We're getting you out of here," Adrian said. "An ambulance is coming soon."

"I'm not going anywhere." He closed his eyes.

"Frank," I said. "Is your arm broken?"

He opened one eye. "Axel," he grunted. "You son of a bitch! How the hell are ya?"

"I'm alright, buddy. It's you we're worried about."

He tried to laugh and had another spasm of dry heaves. When he finished, he lay still. Spittle was running down his chin. "Everything's broken," he said, finally, his words faint. "Every fucking goddamn thing."

He closed his eyes again.

The firemen shoveled out a path for the two paramedics who carried the stretcher into the alley. When the paramedics saw who it was, they gave each other a look. One of them made a comment I couldn't hear. The lead guy grunted a response, and they went to work on Frank. They cut the sleeping bag away from his body and attached a brace to his arm. Next, they lifted him on to the stretcher and covered his entire body with a clean white sheet, all the way up to his head, and strapped him down. Through the whole process, Murphy cradled his face with his good arm. Now and then he groaned in pain. Rather than try to wheel him through the snow, the two firemen helped the paramedics pick up the stretcher. Each of them took a corner and they carried him out. Adrian and I followed. As they slid Murphy into the ambulance, Adrian waved to him.

"What time is it?"

Adrian looked at her watch. "It's only eight o'clock. Jesus, these rescue operations completely disorient me."

"Let's get some coffee."

We trudged along snowy sidewalks for a while and then walked in the street. Snowplows had already cleared Boylston. We took our time. At the Copley Mall entrance, we ducked inside and stood next to the heaters. She gave me a curious look.

"Who'd you say you were this time?"

"Henry Miller."

"Who's he?"

"Just some writer."

We wandered through the mall and headed for the food court. On the way, we passed several homeless people we knew. Adrian slowed and we looked at each other. They were warm, and all doing a lot better than Frank Murphy. "Coffee," she said. We kept walking.

STREET LOGIC

Chapter 6

February 20, 2004

By the third week of February, the severe cold had emptied the streets. Temperatures hovered around zero, and a state of emergency declared by the Mayor had chased many of the most persistent holdouts indoors. After Frank Murphy's hospitalization even Tony Ruffo was forced to come inside again. People who had never stayed in shelters before suddenly found themselves at the Evergreen.

Ripley Novak, Bette Malloy, and I were lingering a little longer than usual around the shelter, too. None of us wanted to set foot outdoors but Adrian was pushing us out of the office and into the streets almost as soon as we arrived and got a brief on the overnight report.

Tina had already left with a nurse to visit a few diehards who were living in the subways. Adrian was taking a phone call in her office, so I leaned back in one of the broken armchairs in the conference room. Five more minutes, that's all I wanted. I put my hands behind my head and closed my eyes. I wished I could close my ears.

Bette Malloy was telling horror stories. As the new psychiatric clinician, maybe she felt the need to impress us. She was describing in all too vivid detail the time she found a three-month-old baby in a lit oven. I cracked one eye to see if she was serious. The bright colors of Bette's snowsuit made my head hurt. The purple bib overalls and yellow fleece underneath made her look like a painted Easter egg. Her round cheeks flushed as she told us how the mother reacted when the police knocked the door down with a battering ram. Fortunately, the oven hadn't gotten hot yet, she said. I glanced at Ripley, who frowned at me. Ripley had been working at Evergreen for ten years, and he didn't impress easily, or scare easily, for that matter. Adrian's door squeaked open and Bette stopped in mid-sentence.

"Yes, that is strange," Adrian was saying, striding purposefully toward us, cell phone pressed to her ear. "Especially the part about running away." She came to a halt in front of me. The shiny silver belt buckle on her low-rider jeans was right at eye level. I blinked, and decided to focus on her belly button ring instead. Our offices were warm, so Adrian had a habit of taking off all of her outer layers of clothing as soon she arrived. Her short t-shirt didn't completely cover her navel. "Yes, at the very least, we can offer this person a bed in the shelter," she said.

I couldn't help admiring the top of her serpent tattoo. The fangs of the cobra were visible today. "I'm going to hand you over to Axel Hazzard," she told the person on the other end of the line. "He's my most experienced man." Ripley winked and saluted me from the other end of the table.

I recalled that the tail of the snake went below her waist and circled her thighs in a masterpiece of tattoo art. The night we met, I asked her why she chose the image. She told me it symbolized her liberation. From what exactly, she never explained. Now I understood.

"Hold on," she interrupted. "He's right here. You can tell him yourself. Let me know if you need any more help." She pressed the phone against her chest and smiled. "Good morning, Axel. How are you? I have a park ranger on the phone, and he wants to know if we can send a team out there to assist him."

"The Commons?"

"No. The Blue Hills."

"Ooh, that sounds exciting!" Bette said.

"Someone's camping out in the park there," Adrian went on. "The ranger is worried about the guy's safety, and he hasn't been able to get to him. He'll explain it all to you."

"Now that I have my snow suit, I'm ready for anything," Bette said.

Adrian lowered the phone and held it against her thigh. "Good. The ranger thinks it might be a psychiatric case. The camper is a couple hundred yards in from the road. Would be good if you could go, in case we need to arrange for a hospitalization."

"Absolutely," Bette said. "We're prepared, right guys?"

"Ever-ready," Ripley said. I knew he hated the cold. He and Bette began to debate the depth of the snow in the hills. They were wondering if we would need a team of sled dogs as Adrian held out the phone to me.

I looked up from the cobra. Her blue-green eyes were watching me as I spoke into the phone. "This is Axel Hazzard. How can I help you, sir?"

Sometimes, the scope of our operation stretched into uncharted territory, beyond our grant's mandated jurisdiction. I guess we felt that the federal grant reviewers didn't really need to know if we had to work outside the city limits occasionally to help people. We were supposed to focus on the main areas of the city – Downtown, Back Bay, the waterfront. Not the Blue Hills.

On our way out of the building, we stopped at the bottom of the stairs to put coats, hats, and gloves on. I opened the side door that led to the parking lot.

"Wow, it's freezing out there!" Bette shrieked. She was struggling with a zipper on one pant leg and trying to light a cigarette at the same time.

"Hold on Bette. You've got it stuck here. " I took the zipper and pulled it down to her hiking boots, a shiny pair of rubber things that looked like duck's feet.

"God, I'm not even out of the building yet and I'm having a crisis," she giggled.

We could hear the loud rumble of voices in the lobby through the metal security door. It sounded like a hundred drunken Irishmen in there. "Look at that, will you." Ripley peered through the unbreakable glass window in the door. "There must be two hundred people today."

Evergreen had two ground floor lobbies that were used for the meals and cots. Men congregated at tables, sat on benches, and on the floor when it was crowded. I looked through the window. Bodies were stretched out in long rows and covered most of the floor space. Some were lying face down with their cheeks right against the hard tile floor.

I spotted Jasmine, a hooker we'd met a few weeks ago, sitting in a corner with a man on either side of her. She gave me a naughty smile and blew me a kiss. The men beside her were grinning as they spoke to her. Jasmine's long blond hair was tied back and her face seemed to glow from all the attention. Tina and I had found her under a blanket in the Public Gardens. There had been some discussion about whether to take her to the women's side of Evergreen, or the men's. The policy at the time was that males, even if they'd had a few operations and considered themselves to be women, still went to the men's section. Jasmine hadn't minded.

"She's going to love this place," I said.

"Or it's going to kill her," said Bette. She stood on her toes to peer through the window. "I still think she should be in the women's shelter."

"She looks like a woman to me," Ripley said.

"To me, too," said Bette.

"OK," I pushed the exit door open again. "I'm going to go start the van. You two can stay here for a few minutes and discuss her finer points. I'll honk when it's warmed up."

"I can't get over her butt," said Ripley.

"I'd kill for a body like that," Bette said.

We stopped first at the gas station next to the shelter. While Ripley went in to buy three coffees, I told Bette the story. "The ranger said he's been tracking this guy from one end of the Blue Hills to the other. In this kind of cold. Can't catch up to him. Have you ever hiked around there?"

"Are you kidding? The longest hike I take is to the grocery store." She lowered the window and lit another cigarette. "Until this job, that is. I smoke too much as it is. I need to quit."

"Well, maybe you'll quit after today's hike."

"The job or the cigarettes?"

"Both, maybe." I had to laugh. "The weird thing is that the ranger has only been able to spot Long Hair from a distance. He's never been able to actually talk to him."

"Long Hair?"

"That's what he called him."

"Who's Long Hair?" Ripley asked when he returned with the coffee.

"The mystery camper," Bette snorted. "This ranger sounds like a rookie. He can't sneak up on somebody in his own woods?"

I pulled out into traffic and took the entrance ramp for I-93 south. "And another thing: he thinks Long Hair can somehow sense his presence, always in time to escape."

"Damn!" Bette spilled a little coffee on her ski suit as I hit a pothole. "This is brand new!" She held the cup more carefully, out in front of her. "So, the only thing we know for sure is that Long Hair is camping in ass-freezing weather, and running away from the ranger like the roadrunner from the coyote?"

"Which cartoon characters does that make us?" Ripley said.

Bette laughed and nearly spilled her coffee again. "Well," she said confidently, "sounds perfectly clear to me that this person is trying to escape from something, and I don't just mean the ranger."

We drove along the interstate in silence for a while. To the east, the sunlight sparkled on the rippling waves of the ocean, like glitter. The air was so cold it made everything look clearer, sharper. The sky appeared a deeper blue, the grays of the ocean beyond Dorchester Harbor seemed darker. The Blue Hills would be beautiful in the snow.

"You've got a point there, Bette," I said, as we neared the town of Quincy. "I've done some winter camping myself. If all you're doing is camping, and a park ranger approaches you, why the hell would you run?"

"Exactly. Must be a reason," she said. "The ranger probably thinks Long Hair is nuts, which is why he called us. But if he thought he was dealing with a criminal type, you know, a killer, maybe, on the run, then he'd be going in with cops. Right?"

My cell phone rang and rather than answer it, I tossed it to Ripley. "Outreach," he said. "No, this is Ripley Novak." He listened for a few minutes, and said we were coming up to the exit. "We should be there in about ten minutes, Jim. See you then." He hung up. "He wanted to know how close we were. Said he's got a feeling that Long Hair is about to make a run for it."

Bette lit another cigarette and adjusted her purple wool cap. "I feel like we're a team on a rescue show."

I parked behind the ranger's pick-up truck across from the water reservoir. He waved through his window as we stepped into the harsh, frigid air. Leafless trees dotted the silent white landscape, along with a few stands of green fir. Huge piles of snow lined the curved road that led up to the overlook, where the skyline of the city can be seen from ten miles away. I started toward the ranger's truck as he stepped out.

"I'm glad you made it," he said. "Roads are a little slippery still. Jim Hudson, with the park service." Bettes's guess was right. I put him at no more than twenty-three years old. A pair of heavy binoculars hung on a cord around his neck. Ripley and Bette came around to the front of the van, and Jim shook hands with everybody as we introduced ourselves.

He pointed toward the hill that rose up alongside the reservoir. "As you can see, the subject is camped there, just over that small rise and behind that grove of trees. You can almost see the tarp, but it blends in well with the pines. I spotted him moving around up there about fifteen minutes ago. Haven't seen him since. He's elusive, I'll tell you that."

I looked to where he'd pointed and only saw the trees.

"You need these," he said, passing me the binoculars.

As I scanned the area, a figure walked into view over the hilltop. Whoever it was had an armful of sticks, and appeared to be dressed in heavy winter clothing. Both the head and the face were covered by a scarf, and long, brown hair flowed out from under it. Long Hair dropped the wood in the camp, turned, and stared directly at me.

"I think we've been spotted."

"Can you see him?" Jim asked.

"Somebody wearing a blue scarf." I passed the binoculars to Bette. "With long hair."

"That's him. Been watching me, too, it seems," Jim said. "He's been set up there since yesterday morning. I came across his camp while I was checking the ice on the reservoir, but he wasn't there. The fire was ready to light, though, and the tent was up. Funny thing is, he's never around when I show up. And he moves his campsite from time to time. I came back later yesterday afternoon and saw him with the binoculars from the road here. Still haven't been able to get a facial profile. When I reached the tent, he was gone again. This time, I figured it would be better to go in with a few more bodies, and with something solid to offer."

"How did you know to call us?" Ripley asked.

"I called the shelter, thought it might be an option. They connected me to Adrian."

"I think he's got a dog," Bette said. "I see a large bowl at the edge of the camp." She passed the glasses to Ripley. "Have you seen signs of a dog, Jim?"

"Good eyes," Ripley said. "I never would've spotted that."

"I've seen tracks, but I thought they belonged to some other hikers. Who knows." He pulled the ear-flaps down on his hat, and kicked his boots together to get the snow off. "I don't imagine you people get out to the woods much in your line of work."

"Not since the time they called us out for the Blair Witch investigation," Ripley said. "Speaking of which, if we don't know what or who we're dealing with out here, especially with this deep snow, maybe we shouldn't all hike in. I mean, something's a little weird, huh? Maybe we should leave one person down here just in case."

"Yeah, no kidding," Bette said. "I was kind of thinking the same thing. Now that I'm seeing the layout here, there's no backup for us if this person turns out to be a madman of some kind. What if things get ugly?"

"I'm not getting a sense of danger. Just someone who probably needs shelter. Anyway," Jim opened his jacket, "just in case, I'm armed."

"Oh, shit," Bette said. "I don't know…"

"If I thought we needed firepower," he went on, "I'd be going in with the Staties."

"Staties?" Bette asked.

"State Police," I told her, looking back towards the camp. I didn't see Long Hair anywhere. "Listen, Ripley's right. Maybe we should leave one person here." I looked at Bette. "Anybody want to stay?"

She glanced in the direction of the camp and hitched up her snowsuit with a determined expression. "Well, we're here, aren't we? I don't want to miss out on any excitement. So we might as well all go. Safety in numbers, right?"

The air was crystal clear. Fresh snow from last night had added to an already deep snowfall, and in places, we sank up to our knees. Jim blazed the trail. Ripley, Bette, and I followed. We moved steadily. No one spoke.

About a hundred feet in, Bette stopped. She was breathing hard and her face was flushed. "I need to rest," she gasped. "You can go on if you want. I'll catch up with you."

Ripley stopped for her. "You all right?"

"I don't know," she said. "These legs aren't what they used to be. I just need to stop for a few minutes."

Jim handed Bette a water bottle from his backpack. He pulled out his binoculars and watched for activity at the camp. "Maybe he's already gone," he said.

Bette leaned against the trunk of a tree and drank some water, then passed it around. When it came back to her, she took a few more short gulps, handed the bottle back to Jim, and pulled out her cigarettes. "You guys keep going," she said. "If old Long Hair makes a run for it and comes my way, I'll offer him a smoke."

Ripley laughed. "Jim, maybe you can wait with Bette a couple minutes, until she's ready. Axel and I can keep going. You two can catch up with us."

"Sure, why not." Jim put his binoculars away.

Ripley and I forged ahead, moving slowly up the slope of the hill. We got another hundred feet up and he stopped. "You know, this just seems odder than hell to me. And way out of our jurisdiction."

"Ten miles out."

"They should have sent a cop with us."

"We've got Jim."

Ripley grinned. "And he's packing heat."

I glanced behind us. Bette made a thumbs-up sign and waved her cigarette at us. We started uphill again. I half expected to see Mr Long Hair up there watching us. Five minutes later, we reached a shallow dip, just below the camp. We caught our breath and listened. Silence. Then the wind kicked up and we heard the sound of a tarp, or tent flap, snapping in the breeze. Ripley's eyes met mine. As he opened his mouth to speak, we heard sticks breaking. I put my finger across my lips. He nodded back and mouthed "Blair Witch" at me. The wind rippled through the branches of the trees and dusted us with light snow. More sticks were breaking in the camp above us. I found my cell phone in my parka, switched it to walkie-talkie, and scrolled down to Bette's name. "Long Hair is in the camp," I whispered into the phone. "We're going to approach." I turned it off immediately so she couldn't respond, and gestured for Ripley to do the same. He shook his head no. He put his forefinger and thumb in the shape of a pistol and pointed at Ranger Jim. We looked back down the trail. Jim had stopped and was staring at something. Bette was clutching his arm and had an odd expression on her face.

"What do you want to do?" I asked Ripley. There was only silence now from above.

"Against my better judgment, I say, let's do it."

"OK." I climbed up the slippery embankment to the camp and hollered out a friendly hello. There was no one there.

"We got a regular Houdini here," said Ripley, when he reached the camp. "Big Jim was right. Whoever this is gets out of Dodge fast."

It was a level spot, still a hundred feet from the highest point. There was a good view of the reservoir and the road below, unless you were behind the pines. That's where the tent and the tarp were set up. A few short tree stumps ringed the edge of the campsite. One was covered in plastic, with a couple of stones holding it in place. There was a fire pit in the middle, lined with rocks.

"Looks like he went that way." Ripley pointed at some tracks. The trail led from the camp to a thick group of fir trees above us.

I did a slow three-sixty and saw no one. "He picked up on our approach alright, didn't he? Not that it would be too hard. Must have just been here, with those sticks snapping."

"Let's look around before Jim and Bette get here."

The silence was filled with the sounds of the wind, whistling through the trees. Ripley started inspecting the plastic poncho on the tree stump as I headed for the tent. I noticed that the campfire was piled with dry sticks and pieces of newspaper to light them. Always be prepared. The tent, one of those high-tech mountain designs, sat back against the trees where the tarp was strung. I stopped in front of the entrance flap. "Hello, anyone home?" I watched for movement inside, then spoke a little louder. "Hey, is anybody in there? Everything all right?" No answer from the tent. I surveyed the woods, looking at the trail where it disappeared over the hill. Ripley had found something under the poncho. I announced loudly that I was going to open the tent, and pulled the zipper down.

A heavy, goose down military sleeping bag took up most of the narrow space inside. Plastic bags lined the sides, containing clothes. There were piles of books. Some were open. On top of a small backpack in the corner was a music player with headphones. Four thick insulated socks hung from a makeshift stick hanger in the center of the tent, but it was a tiny pair of black thong panties, dangling in between them, that caught my eye. Black thong panties with white crystals of frost clinging to them.

I looked around and spotted an open notebook, half-covered by the sleeping bag. I read what I could see once, and then read it again. I was inspecting the black thong when I heard Bette scream. I dropped the book, scrambled out of the tent, and ran to the edge of the camp. Ripley was already there, staring down the hill.

"Uh-oh," he said. "Bette was right about a dog."

A short distance below us, Bette and Jim were standing together, stock-still, facing an enormous black dog. "It's just standing there," I said. "Where the hell did it come from?" Bette's eyes darted in panic from the dog to us.

"Big Jim is freaked," Ripley said. "What do you…?"

"We have to go down there and scare it off."

"Shit," he said, "I guess you're right. Maybe we can distract it, throw something at it."

"No, the best thing is to run like hell, screaming and yelling, straight down the hill toward them."

"We need weapons." Ripley ran back to the fireplace and picked up a large stick. He tossed it to me and grabbed some of the rocks in the pit. I saw the dog start moving slowly towards Jim and Bette, and its tail wasn't wagging. I jumped off the embankment and took off running, waving the stick in my hand and hollering. Jim looked up and raised his arm, pointing. Something dark moved on my right. It hit me from the side and sent me facedown into the snow.

"Don't move Axel!" Ripley yelled. "It's another dog! I'm going to throw a rock at it. Protect your head!"

It had me pinned to the ground. My face was buried deep in the snow. I felt the dog sniffing around my ears, and lay perfectly still. The snow burned my face. Then I heard a sharp whistle come from above the camp. Immediately, the dog scrambled off of me. I raised my face and looked sideways, but kept my head low.

"It's alright!" Ripley shouted. "It's moving away!"

I lifted my head slowly. The dog was the spitting image of the one near Bette and Jim. A big black mix of Labrador and German Shepherd. It stood just a few feet away and watched me closely, making a low growling sound. I saw Ripley staring somewhere above the camp. He let the rock fall from his hand. I followed his stare. A woman stood at the top of the hill. The blue scarf we'd seen earlier was wrapped around her neck. A wool hat now covered what was actually long golden hair. With a slightly amused expression, she watched us for a moment. Then, in a clear, pleasant voice, she shouted, "Kill!" I raised my arms instinctively, but the dog only whimpered, looked up toward the woman, and then sat.

She was wearing a pair of heavy, insulated overhauls, the kind that construction workers wear during winter months. Over that, a thick, dark green parka. From a distance, with the bulkiness of her winter gear and the hats and scarves that covered her face, it made sense that we'd mistaken her for a man. But not now. I just stared at her, struck by her beauty. Bette and Jim came into the camp followed by the other dog. Bette was still a little spooked, and held on tightly to Jim's arm. He seemed dumbstruck. He was staring at the young woman, too. Ripley seemed to have forgotten how to talk.

"Sorry about that." She turned to face me. She looked about twenty years old. "They're a little overprotective." Her big brown eyes were bright as she took in Jim, in his official ranger's hat, Bette in her multicolored snowsuit, and Ripley, rooted in his spot. She smiled. Her white teeth were perfect.

"Are you OK?"

"I'm fine," I said, shaking the snow off my coat and pants. "Beautiful animals. And well trained. I like your commands."

"Eat!" the young woman said. Both dogs trotted over to her, wagged their tails, and sat down. She put a gloved hand on each of their heads. "I learned that from a book I read. This guy trained his dog to respond to commands that an enemy wouldn't expect. Stay means kill, for example."

I noticed the dogs were wearing something on their paws. "Nice booties. You make those?"

"My own handmade creations." She lifted one of the dog's paws and readjusted its snow boot. "Otherwise they'd freeze their paws off out here, when I have them with me."

Bette opened her mouth to say something. She looked at me and waited.

"My name's Axel, and this is Bette, Ripley and Jim, who's with the park service. Sorry to have, uh, invaded your camp. The reason we're here is, basically, to see if everything's all right." I glanced at Jim. "We understand that you've been living out here in the Blue Hills for a while."

She laughed lightly. "I know it must appear a little strange to you, someone camping out in this kind of weather. But I'm here by choice, if that's what you mean. Am I doing anything illegal?"

When Jim didn't respond right away, Bette said, "Sure is cold out for camping."

"It's not that bad." She patted the dogs. "I have good gear, and sometimes I have good company." She bent down to light the fire and the paper caught immediately. "The thing is," she pushed the smaller sticks over the flames, "I lost my place. Actually, my parents lost their house. I was living there and going to school, working part-time. They had to move in with my grandparents in New York. I stayed with some friends at first, but that sure didn't work out. The guy was a…well, it doesn't matter. Anyway, since I practically grew up with these woods as my backyard, I thought, well, I'll just do what Henry David Thoreau did." She gestured to include the woods, the sky, and the water in the reservoir. She sounded honest. Confident.

"Just like Walden," I said.

She glanced up from the fire and gave me a tiny smile. Bette parked herself next to the growing flames, as close as she could. The girl put down a blanket for the dogs. They soon closed their eyes and forgot about us.

She made the whole thing sound almost plausible. Five days a week, she told us, she hiked through the woods to the Furnace Brook Parkway and caught a bus to UMass. On the weekends, she went into the city and studied in cafes, sometimes staying a night at different friends' places. "I like it," she said. "It works out well. My dogs are actually living with our old neighbors. My parents couldn't take them. So sometimes I bring them up here, so they can hike around. Right, boys?" She patted their heads again. "It's their old stomping ground, too. But most of the time, I'm at school."

"But isn't there some place you could stay?" Ripley asked.

"Well, it's kind of a money issue, too. I thought I'd try this for the rest of the semester." She stoked the fire and hung a kettle of water over it to boil. "Then I'll probably have to go to New York, unless I can get a job for the summer and find a cheap place."

Bette cleared her throat. "We normally work with homeless people, in the city," she explained. "When we heard about you out here, we thought maybe you needed shelter."

"Really?" the girl said, surprised. "That sounds like a pretty cool job. So, you guys are like what, Rescue Rangers, or something?"

Ripley laughed. I smiled, unable to take my eyes off of her.

"I think the homeless should have shelters out in nature," she said. "Someplace natural, you know? A big farm. The kind of environment you're in can make a huge difference to the psyche. I've walked past the Evergreen before. It's not in a very pretty area."

Finally, Jim spoke up. "Well, ma'am, I have to warn you that there's no camping in this park. And no fires are allowed." He cleared his throat. "I mean, after this one."

She nodded and took a plastic bag from under the poncho. She brought out coffee mugs, a jar of instant, and asked him if he took sugar in his coffee.

"Well, yes. One."

She went to the tent. The flap was still open from my attempt at trespassing. After a few minutes she came back with another small pack. Using another tree stump for a table, she pulled out more cups and some small bowls.

"I'm afraid these bowls will have to do," she said. "Anybody else take sugar?"

We all did. She opened sugar packets, dumped them in, and threw the paper into the fire. After she poured hot water into each mug or bowl and handed them out, she made one for herself. "Well, don't worry." She looked at Jim. "I can assure you that I'll move on from here today. And no more fires."

"That would be great, ma'am. I still have to issue you a warning, though."

"You have to do your job," the girl said.

"Your name, ma'am?" He set his coffee down on the stump and pulled out his notebook.

"Holiday Golightly."

He began to write it down and then stopped. "Say that again, please?"

"Holiday Golightly," she repeated. "Spelled G-O-L-I-G-H-T-L-Y."

"That's a pretty unusual name." Jim looked up from his notebook. "Your first name is Holly?"

"No, Holiday. Like Holiday Inn."

"That's your real name?" Jim said.

"It is now."

Jim accepted that, and scribbled a few things on his warning ticket.

"So you're alright, then?" Bette said.

Holiday Golightly gave Bette a gentle smile. "Oh yes. And I really appreciate you guys coming all the way out here! But I'm fine." She did look to be in excellent health. She had a great tan on her face from living outdoors.

"I know of a place where you might be able to stay," I said. "A friend of mine likes to help people when he thinks they're doing something worthwhile." She seemed to consider that, but didn't say anything.

We finished our coffee and Jim handed her the ticket. Bette gave her a warm hug, and Ripley shook hands with her, wishing her luck. Everybody started for the trail and the dogs jumped up to accompany us, wagging their tails and racing down the hill.

"I have one question." I stopped at the embankment and turned back. Ripley and Jim started down. "And you don't have to answer it, if you don't want to." Bette halted her descent. "Does your father know where to find you?"

Holiday's upbeat expression turned neutral. She stared back. "No," she said.

"Does he know you're camping out?"

"No. My parents have enough problems without having to worry about me."

I gave her one of my cards. "If you need anything at all, you can call our office number."

"How about some extra blankets?" Bette offered. "We have plenty in the van."

"No, thanks. I have an awesome sleeping bag." She looked at my card and then back at me. I thought I saw something vulnerable there, for just a moment. "It's OK," she said. "Everything's OK. You shouldn't have gone in my tent, but I guess I can kind of understand that." She hesitated, and then looked me directly in the eyes. "I appreciate the fact that you cared enough to ask." She turned and called her dogs back to the camp.

I took the back roads through Lower Mills and Dorchester so we could stop at The Harp and Bard for a late lunch. Bette sat quietly in the front seat as I drove. Ripley was stretched out on a pile of blankets in the back of the van.

"Hey," he said. "That was pretty interesting back there. Bette, what was your take on Miss Holiday Golightly?"

"She seemed mentally stable as far as I could see." Bette cracked her window and lit a cigarette. "Still, that's a lot more than I would have ever done to stay in college. I would have found a place to crash somewhere, even if it was just on a friend's kitchen floor."

"Same here," Ripley said. "That's some serious dedication. Her story sounded genuine, though. She didn't seem to be too worried about anything."

Bette turned to me. "I'm curious, Axel. Why did you ask her that, when we were leaving? You know, that thing about her father?"

I kept my eyes on the road. "Well, while you and Big Jim were being treed by that dog, Ripley and I had a chance to look around a little. She wasn't there when we first showed up. I was worried somebody might be hurt, injured, or whatever, in the tent. When nobody responded, I took a look inside. There was an open notebook on her sleeping bag."

Bette waited for me to finish.

"It was right there," I said. "I thought it would give us a clue as to what was going on there. Anyway, I only read a few lines before I heard you scream."

She didn't say anything for a few minutes. She threw her cigarette out the window and said quietly, "It was about her father?"

I nodded.

"You going to tell me what it said?"

"It wasn't much, just something about how she was feeling a lot better since she moved out of the house, and got away from her parents. Especially her father. I figured that if she was bullshitting us, and was actually on the run or in trouble of some kind, or maybe hiding from someone, that if I mentioned her father, I might get a reaction from her. Something, you know. And it would show on her face. Remember that character, Golightly, in Capote's book?"

"Wasn't she running away from a bad situation?"

"As far as I can remember. And running toward something she thought was better."

Bette raised her eyebrows. "So, did you see a reaction?" she asked.

"No."

Ripley had moved up and leaned in between us. "What did you ask her?"

"If her father knew where to find her," I said.

"What did she say?"

"She said no, and that she didn't want to worry her parents."

Bette interrupted. "You know what it sounds like to me?"

"Yes," I said. "But who knows for sure. Like you said, she seemed to be on top of things. Aware of what she's doing, mentally stable, not at risk. She's safe. She may just be taking care of things her own way. She looked pretty capable."

"She looked pretty, all right." Bette winked at me. "She's cute! Really cute. God, I hope she's going to be OK."

We had burgers, fries, and coffee at the Harp. Bette entertained us with another horrific story. This one was about a girl and a stepfather. I managed to tune out most of it with the news on a television at the bar. I was thinking about Holiday Golightly, and what it must be like for her out there at night, in those cold woods, alone.

STREET LOGIC

Chapter 7

May 21, 2004

Tina and I had made the rounds from Fenway Park to the Public Gardens, where we met a pregnant and scared twenty-year-old abandoned by her boyfriend a couple days ago. From Georgia. Apparently they'd been traveling in a van, and he split. She readily accepted Tina's offer to take her to a women's shelter while she figured out what to do.

Nothing much was shaking in Copley Square, so I bought some coffee at Finagle a Bagel and took it toward the alley. I stood at the entrance and peered down the narrow, grease-stained strip of asphalt, at a woman stepping out of a back door and lighting a cigarette. She wore a white cook's apron, and after she took a few puffs, she untied her hair, shook it loose, and then leaned against the brick wall. Except for the cigarette, she looked like Holiday. I'd been wondering how the winter had turned out for Long Hair. Mostly I'd been thinking about how stunning she had appeared in the midst of that white wasteland of snow and cold, dressed in construction thermals and looking at us like we were in her living room.

The woman's hair was the same golden shade, between blond and light brown, and she had the same height, too. I took a few steps into the alley toward her when she suddenly cocked her head toward something. Even her profile reminded me of Holiday's. But now I could see that it wasn't her. Different cheekbones.

At the greasiest spot of the alley, we met. She flicked her cigarette away and looked at me, somewhat startled. "Morning," I said.

She must have decided I wasn't a menace. "Hey," she said and turned her head back to where she'd been staring. I followed her gaze and saw Frank Murphy, tucked into a corner and surrounded by cardboard boxes, with his legs raised up on a pile of blankets. One shoe was off. Something looked wrong.

"So, can you do it for me?" Frank said.

I slumped down in the chair and watched Ken Easttree let Murphy's question hang in the air between them, while he stared at Murphy's foot. We were in Easttree's basement office at the Wilder Respite Center. After I'd helped Murphy sit down, I'd nodded at Ken that it was all his. The two men sat on opposite sides of a steel-grey metal desk. The warm air felt heavy – apparently the air-conditioning was on the blink. Neither man spoke for a full minute. Murphy's foot was propped up on the corner of the desk like a hunting trophy.

Easttree closed his eyes and rubbed them wearily. I imagined that he was probably reminding himself of what he had told me many times, that our clients not only tended to let things hit bottom, they often managed to discover newer, deeper levels of bottom. That none of them had signed up for these kinds of futures. Children, as he liked to say, even in the midst of some god-awful desperate and impoverished life, with losses mounting up, couldn't anticipate the kind of horrors waiting for them. Or they would shut down completely. Permanent loss, of the kind now on display in his office, was as real as the loss of hope.

Easttree let Murphy's question about the pair of Levi's drift away. When he finally opened his eyes, he stared again at the foot, or half-foot, until he seemed to realize what the expression on his face must have looked like. Shifting in his chair, he cleared his throat and met Murphy's broad smile with a grim, slow shake of his head. "Well, this is something, all right."

Murphy leaned across the desk and offered Easttree a cigarette from a crumpled pack of Camels. Easttree responded with a thin smile, and took one of the last two smokes. "Sorry, Axel, no more," Murphy said out of the corner of his mouth. "Looks like Tree needs it more than you." Easttree pushed the pile of reports on his desk away from the leaking foot and reached into his top drawer. He set the souvenir Bruins ashtray in front of him, spinning it around with his finger before sliding it gently across the desk toward Murphy. It came to a stop a few inches from the foot, like a hockey puck stopping just short of the goal.

Murphy lit his own cigarette first and then reached across the desk with the lighter still lit. Easttree stood, and was forced to bend over Murphy's foot to accept the light. The smoke he exhaled didn't come close to covering the rotting smell that filled the room.

"A real prize-winner, huh?" Murphy's voice chirped. He must have been still under the influence of whatever painkillers he had on board when I found him in the alley. "Wouldn't you say, Tree?"

"I'm not sure I'd put it like that, Frank," Easttree responded.

Glad I wasn't in Ken's chair, I went over the facts in my head. Franklin Delaney Murphy. Born in 1970, he was only thirty-three years old, but looked closer to fifty. From Easttree's records, I was aware of the roller-coaster ride Murphy had lived with his cocaine-addicted mother in the Heath Street projects. Maybe as an escape, Murphy had joined the military. He'd survived the Gulf War by taking some shrapnel in his ass, which gained him an early exit. After Operation Desert Storm, he'd started his own assault on the streets of Boston, selling and using heroin, cocaine, and the wonder drug Oxycontin, for which he proudly claimed to have a military prescription. Occasionally he got some rest from this activity in the Area A police headquarters. Once, in the mid-nineties, he'd spent six months in a sober half-way house.

"How would you put it, then?" Murphy dropped the ashes on the floor, ignoring the ashtray. The top half of Murphy's right foot had been removed soon after Adrian and I sent him into the hospital from the alley. Frostbite took all his toes. After three months in recovery at the Wilder Respite Center, Murphy had checked himself out against medical advice and hit the streets again in a wheelchair, getting back to his business.

"Tell you what," Easttree said. "If it were me, I'd put it in the hands of Dr Huffman and the nurses here, and this time leave it there until it's fully healed."

The bandages were worn off. The place where his toes should have been was now a raw, dark piece of meat. There were maggots working on it. Easttree and I had seen this kind of thing before, on a Maliseet Indian from Maine who parked himself regularly in Downtown

Crossing. One time, he had an infected leg wound that he refused to treat. Maggots turn out to be a plus, in some cases, because they eat the infected areas.

Murphy seemed oblivious to the activity at the end of his leg. "I wouldn't mind putting it in the hands of that blond, Jane."

Easttree took a last hit off his cigarette, and stood up. He ground the butt out in the ashtray and walked around his desk to the bookshelf in the corner of his office. From the top shelf, he picked up one of the long sticks of incense I knew he used to conceal his smoking, and took his time lighting it. I looked at the items on his shelf – the collection of books he'd acquired on clinical practice, a photo of him standing in front of Fenway Park with his wife Rebecca and children, Kyle and Melissa, a tiny statue of a fat smiling Buddha, and a plastic model of a sailboat, complete with little sails. "Hope the smell of patchouli doesn't bother you, Frank."

"Nope," grunted Murphy. "Whatever the hell it is. So, listen, how about it? Can you get those Levi's for me?"

Easttree stared at the Buddha, quiet. Probably hoping to gain some of that peaceful serenity. I knew his technique from our numerous bull sessions of psychotherapeutic strategies, and I'd seen him at work with clients we shared. He held to the idea that the main thing was to get inside the person's world long enough to see the angle to approach them from, and then retreat to do the work. Keep your own emotions in check, but pay attention to them. And use your client's emotions. That's the rule. I watched to see how he'd handle Murphy's repeated request for a pair of Levi jeans.

"You know what, Frank?" Easttree turned around. "You might just be one of the best I've ever seen. I mean, you toughed it out in Iraq, not to mention Heath Street, and you've survived on the streets of Boston with the best of them. You're one hell of a survivor, there's no question about that." He paused, his face frowning as he held his hands together in front of him. "But this time, this thing..." His gaze moved to the maggots feasting on Murphy's foot. "Here's the deal, Frank. I don't want to talk about blue-jeans. I'm not in the clothing business, I'm in the social work business. I'm your case worker. I know my job can sometimes entail such things as finding someone a new pair of jeans, but we're going to have to talk about more important things first."

All of Murphy's smugness transformed instantly.

"Shit, Easttree!" he barked. "Your job is to help me! I don't want any of your psychology bullshit here, all I'm asking for is some goddamn Levi's!"

I sat up in my chair.

Easttree held Murphy's stare and kept his voice calm. "Alright, Frank, I hear you. But I'm going to put that issue on hold for now, and ask you to look at priorities, OK? Tell me, honestly – what are you going to do to prevent yourself from losing the rest of your foot?"

"That's my problem, not yours," Murphy growled.

Easttree turned away and picked up the model sailboat from the bookshelf. Kyle had made it for him, for his fortieth birthday in March. He turned it around in his hands. "My job," his voice calm, measured, almost sounding faraway, "is actually to help you work on yourself. Not your wardrobe, but you. Your self-understanding, your ability to make good choices, to prevent further..." he turned and faced his client. "Losses."

Murphy didn't give up. "I'm just asking for a fucking pair of blue-jeans, size thirty-two, uh..."

Easttree's cell phone rang, startling all of us. He silenced the ringer and said, "Thirty-four. You know what's wrong here, Frank? I know your pant's size better than you do. But I don't know how to help you, if you won't help yourself."

I went out to use the restroom down the hall. When I returned, Murphy was glaring at Easttree, who was back behind his desk.

"Alright, Murph," he was saying quietly. "Let's make a deal. I'm going to be honest with you. I'm willing to work with you, but what I'm mostly good for is positive change. Not just a change of jeans." He paused, looking at me. I nodded, and sat back down. Easttree continued. "I can't force you to address your issues, but I want to remind you that this is your chance to start making better decisions. You owe that to yourself. Then, maybe while you're here, having your foot taken care of, we'll see about those Levi's. After your foot is completely healed, and you're cleared by the doc to leave. And while you're here, you come and talk to me. OK?"

Murphy's face went through a series of contortions.

"Fuck you, Easttree! I lost half my goddamned foot and you're sitting there telling me I need to talk to you about it? Let me tell you something, Mister clinical fucking social worker! I don't need this kind of shit, I have enough to deal with on my own!" Murphy abruptly lifted his foot off the desk and swung it to the floor, reaching for his crutches. As he jumped up and hopped on one foot, the damaged foot banged against the side of the desk. Murphy howled, losing his balance. I stood quickly and reached for him, but it was too late. He hit the floor hard, landing on his side. "Son of a bitch! Goddamn this fucking thing!"

Easttree moved fast around the desk and helped me pull Murphy up, each of us taking an arm, until we had him positioned back in his chair.

"Jesus, Frank," Ken said. "You alright?"

"Shit." Murphy winced. His face was red, but the anger was gone now. "Yeah, I know, I know. I'm a fucking asshole. Always was, and probably always will be." The fight was gone from his voice. "OK, Tree. You win. I'll do it your way."

"It could be your way, Frank, if you want it. I can only help you if you're willing to work with me."

Murphy sighed. "I know. Can you do me one small, tiny favor? If it's not asking too much?"

"If I can," Easttree said.

"Will you call Jane to come and get me?"

Easttree smiled. "Now we're talking business. I'll see if she's available, but no promises. They're busy as hell up there today and she could be tied up with something else. You never know."

Despite the pain, Murphy grinned. "I wouldn't mind tying her up. She's one stone fox."

Easttree paused, and held the phone up in the air. "You have to treat her with respect, Frank. Got it? Or else I'll have to call Big D to come down here to get you."

Murphy laughed. "Alright, alright," he said. "Not Derrick. I'm only playing with you."

Easttree dialed the extension to the nursing desk. When he got Jane Winslow on the line, he made his request and put the receiver down.

"She's coming," he said. "Now, as far as our agreement goes, I'm going to visit you upstairs, every day for a while, and we're going to talk about more than Levi's and the Red Sox, OK?"

"Yes, boss."

I stepped out to the hallway to call Tina. She was still with the pregnant woman at the shelter. I filled her in on the episode with Murphy, half-listening to them talking about the Red Sox as they waited for Jane Winslow to arrive with a wheelchair. When the tall blond stepped off the elevator pushing a wheelchair, I hung up and waved at her. Her smile was stunning. Easttree rose from his chair as she stopped in the doorway. Murphy might be damaged goods, but his vision was in good working order. Jane Winslow was by far the most beautiful woman working at the Wilder.

"Nice to see you again, Mr Murphy," she said, her large blue eyes sincere and sympathetic. "I hope you'll stay with us for a while." She ignored the foot and joked with Murphy as Easttree helped her get him into the wheelchair.

"I'll call Dr Huffman and let him know Frank's here."

"Oh, that's OK, Ken," Jane said. "He's upstairs, I'll tell him."

"You're the best, Jane. And thanks for coming down to fetch him. He's promised to be a good patient, and stay until he's completely healed this time. Isn't that right, Frank?"

Murphy gave him his best smile. "You're the boss, Tree."

The statuesque nurse wheeled Murphy up the hallway to the elevator, making light conversation with him. Probably only twenty-five years old, I thought. Easttree and I waited until they were in the elevator, and then stepped back into his office.

"Good job riling up Murphy, by the way," I said. "Seems to have worked. And that must be the finest looking nurse I've ever seen."

He ground out the smoking stick of incense and picked up the tiny sailboat again. Turning it around in his hands, his expression was distant, as if he were picturing Jane Winslow on the deck of the boat, wearing little more than a smile and with nothing but blue skies and aquamarine water for miles and miles. And no homeless people anywhere. He put the model back in its place on the shelf and got himself together, grinning at me. "No doubt," he said, and picked up the phone. He called someone from maintenance to come and disinfect the desk and floor where Murphy's blood was smeared.

We walked out to his car. It was after five o'clock, and I'd talked him into coming down to Bukowski's for a quick burger. "I was hoping to go see this woman, Sylvia Thompson, this afternoon, before I got caught up with Murphy. Maybe we could take a little walk over there after we eat. She's in rough shape. And it's Friday, I won't get another chance until Monday."

"Duty calls," he said. "Then maybe we can get a beer."

Easttree backed his old Honda Civic into a metered parking spot across from Saint Cecilia's Park, on a small street behind the Back Bay Hilton. We sat in the car and stared at the park for a moment, listening to the engine tick as it cooled down.

"I've been wondering lately if I'm losing the touch," he said.

"What do you mean?"

"Ah, I'm getting a little crispy, that's all. Well, I guess that's all." He mustered a smile, and shook his head. "Vacation time, soon."

We stepped out of the car and lit cigarettes. The sun was low in the sky and clouds were changing colors. He mentioned something about heading for the Caribbean and a sailboat, or maybe taking a week off and driving north to Vermont to camp out.

"Good idea," I said. "Either way, south or north. Change of scenery is always good." We started walking. At the end of the park, he stopped and pointed at the statue of the Virgin. Only her face caught the last rays of the sunset.

"Look at that," he said. Before I could respond, we heard voices behind the statue.

"She's mine, you cocksucker!" a male voice shouted.

STREET LOGIC

We peered through an opening in the bushes. Three people were standing behind the statue, two men facing each other and a woman standing off to the side. We recognized the woman with the tangled bleached-blond hair, even though the hair covered most of her face. She was Rose Sullivan, Frank Murphy's long time street partner. She showed up now and then at the Wilder, and Easttree had almost convinced her to enter a sober house. The one who'd shouted was Dennis McFarley, who was jabbing a short, stocky man in the chest with his finger, within head-butting range. "If I have to kick your ass right now, buddy, then I will," McFarley was saying. "Just say the word."

Easttree turned toward me. I shook my head. This wasn't our battle. And I knew that if we didn't get under the bridge before it started to get dark, we could be risking some bad confrontations ourselves.

"Let's grab that quick burger," I said.

We entered the dark, narrow bar. The loud punk rock made me want to order a beer immediately. The happy hour crowd hadn't arrived yet and only a few of the padded stools were occupied. We wandered over to the bar and took a seat. The bartender was an attractive young woman who looked barely legal to be working in here. I'd met Sabrina a couple of weeks ago, on her first night in Bukowski's. She and her sister Wendy had just been hired and they were an added draw at my regular hangout. She flashed us a smile from the other end of the bar and yelled that she'd be right there. Above the liquor shelves were sketches of Bukowski, with some of his poems painted on the walls. I read one, having to do with waking up in a strange city. Sabrina squatted to pull a cardboard box out from a low shelf in front of us. Her red shirt slid up her back and revealed a tattoo at the base of her spine. The narrow white string of her underwear cut across the image of wings. Her jeans were cut so low we could see about half of her ass. Easttree allowed himself a good look before he turned to me and muttered something I couldn't hear. I took another look at her, still bent over and taking something out of the box. It was a beautiful tattoo.

Finally, she closed the box and straightened up, bouncing a little as she faced us.

"Hey, how's it going, Axel?" she said. "Sorry about that. What can I get you?"

"Nothing to be sorry about," I said. "Just the dollar burger, well-done, no cheese, fries. And a glass of ice water."

"Sure thing." She turned to Easttree. "My name's Sabrina. You know what you want?"

Easttree opened his mouth, hesitated, and then said, "Tree. Haven't seen you here before."

"Yeah, just started a couple of weeks back." She filled a pint glass with ice water and slid it across the bar to me.

"I'll have the special, medium, with the works. Mashed potatoes," he said.

"Mashed it is," she nearly shouted. "Hope you like loud music!"

"I like it loud," Easttree shouted back. She laughed and headed for the kitchen at the other end of the bar. We both watched her go the distance.

"Hey, is the tattoo plus g-string the new fashion standard these days?" Easttree smiled over his burger at me. He was nodding at the waitress who'd dropped our food off, another one with the same low-cut uniform of Sabrina. After she had leaned down and kissed me on the mouth, I'd introduced her to the surprised Easttree as Sabrina's sister. "This is Wendy, poetess of the dark truths. Meet Ken Easttree, prober of the deeper madnesses of the human psyche." Wendy, true to her California upbringing, gave Tree a warm hug and kissed him on the cheek before she left.

I grinned at Tree. "Where you been, man, holed up at the Wilder too much? But by god, you're right. And what a great trend it is, I have to say. I don't know which sister is hotter. I came in here last Friday after work, and Wendy and I hooked up that night. Guess L.A. got too crazy for them, and they hit the road."

"I feel like doing the same thing."

"So you're more than just crispy, huh?"

"Tell you the truth, lately it's a struggle just to remind myself how to do my job. Hard to tap the positive energy required," he said.

I gave him a look. "Things OK with Rebecca?"

"Yeah, I guess. It's me, really. I just need to do something, take a break. Do something completely out of the normal routine."

"Early prevention?"

He laughed. "Early burn-out prevention, more like."

"By the way," I stuffed some fries in my mouth, "I appreciate you coming out here to help with this woman, Sylvia. It's getting pretty serious."

"How bad?"

"She hasn't moved from her spot under the bridge in weeks, and I don't think she's eating much. Won't even think about coming in. During the winter, she was forced into the women's shelter a few times by the police, and the medical staff there had some concerns about her health. She wouldn't consent to being examined."

"Crazy?"

"No, not clinically speaking. Just street crazy, from years of living out there."

"That would make anyone crazy. I'm going to get some ketchup." Easttree stood. "Be right back."

He walked up to the bar. When Sabrina handed him the ketchup, she leaned forward and her torn punk-style t-shirt opened slightly. From where I was sitting I could see she wasn't wearing a bra.

Back at the table, he almost looked happy. "She asked me if I wanted anything else."

"What did you say?"

"Told her the truth."

"Which is?"

"A week sailing in the Bahamas."

"Smooth as always, Tree. Did she respond to that?"

"She shook her finger at me and said she'd been studying B.F. Skinner's Behaviorism theory, and believed that if you act happy, you'll feel happy."

"Wow," I smiled. "Did she see you looking down the front of her shirt?"

"Caught me red-handed."

"Did she look happy?"

"She was smiling," he said. "But then I really dazzled her. Said I don't believe in Skinner's theory. Only in what happens."

"Was she still smiling?"

"Mouth wide open, silver stud in her tongue flashing. Guess what she said then?"

I raised my eyebrows and waited for him to tell me.

Easttree kept his face straight. "She said, 'At first, I had a hard time swallowing it. But now I like it.'"

"Get the fuck outta here."

He poured ketchup on the burger and took a bite out of it. He took another bite, then another, and when he finally put it down he sat back and chewed slowly, looking over toward the bar.

"It's tempting, isn't it?" I said.

Easttree nodded and continued eating. We didn't talk until we were finished. Wendy came for our plates, and I gave her some money. "It's on me this time, Tree."

Wendy whispered something into my ear before she left.

"It seems you've charmed the sister."

Easttree looked to the bar again. "That's flattering."

"It sure is. How often does a guy your age have a young woman who looks like that flirt with him? Listen, I know you're a married man and all that. But it's always nice to have a fan." I slapped him on the back. "Come on, let's go do this thing. I want to get out there before the crack rats return to their camps."

As we left, Easttree gave Sabrina a small smile, and she waved back. Outside, the early evening light cast long shadows. The street lamps were already on. "So, tell me more about her," Easttree said as we started walking.

"Who?"

"Sylvia Thompson."

"Of course," I said. "Well, like I said, she's not moving much from her spot. Doesn't even sit up when I go by to talk to her. Her voice is weaker. Seems pretty sick. But she doesn't complain about anything."

"You think it's time to have her evaluated?"

"Close to it." We walked along Boylston Street to Mass Ave, moving through the after-work crowd. "It's incredible to me, still, how they can hang on to whatever freedom they believe they have," I said. "She's got to be in her sixties. And seems totally unconcerned about the danger of being under that bridge with all those crack-heads at night. Bernie says she's safer there than anywhere else on the street."

"That's a reassuring thought."

"I don't think we'll have any company down there just yet, it's still early."

At Mass Ave, we crossed Boylston and walked past the Tower Records store. I pointed out Lamar Cleveland across the street. "I love that guy. Stubborn as hell. Won't go anywhere unless he's in severe pain, and then only to Saint Elizabeth's. I'd like to get him over to the Wilder."

"Maybe I can meet him sometime," Easttree said. He sounded like he wished he were still back at Bukowski's. The wind was picking up as we crossed Newbury Street, coming in strong and warm from the river.

"Sylvia used to talk with me a lot," I said. "But in the last three, four months something changed. Maybe she had a minor stroke, lost some of her mental functions. She isn't making any sense now."

"Did she ever?"

"Well, no, but she could take care of herself. Now she's created a whole new fantasy, completely different from her old story of being a cook at Bunker Hill Community College. Claims there are creditors chasing her for money, that she actually owns an apartment, but can't live there because of electrical problems, that her son's getting married next week in California. And, she says she's planning on going."

"How?"

"American Airlines."

Easttree laughed. We crossed Commonwealth Avenue and I picked up our pace. "Come on, man, I don't want it to be pitch-black under there," I said. The evening traffic moving across the bridge had turned its headlights on and the buildings at MIT were lit up. Street lamps illuminated the sidewalks. I stepped over the short fence on to the steep, grassy embankment. Easttree's cell phone rang. I waited while he spoke quietly.

"All right," he said. "I really have to go. We're at the Mass Ave Bridge, about to go under." He put the phone away and stepped over the railing. "Rebecca."

"Everything alright?"

"Yeah, yeah," he said. "A little tense lately."

I could hear it in his voice. "Let's wrap this up and then you can tell me about it. You all set?"

We hiked down the embankment. Easttree nearly slipped once on the slick grass. When we reached the base of the bridge, the rush of the local traffic along Storrow Drive seemed to wake us both up. Easttree scoped out the area while I dug through my backpack for the small flashlight.

"We should've come an hour ago," I said. "My fault."

Both of us stared into the dark space under the bridge, which appeared to run on forever but actually extended about a hundred feet until it reached a low wall. Beyond that was a fifty-foot drop-off to the Storrow Drive express lanes.

I shone the narrow beam of light in an arc along both sides of the underpass. A few broken chairs on their sides were scattered around a fire pit, my light reflecting off the shards of bottles and cans that covered the ground. Fortunately there was nobody in sight. I swept the entire area again, and then aimed it toward the drop-off. "She's back there."

"Jesus," Easttree said.

I started moving carefully across the rocky floor. "Watch your head over here." I pointed the light at the series of crossing support beams. "I banged the hell out of mine on that one time. You don't want to do that."

"Ten-four."

We picked our way over the uneven ground. Traffic rumbled overhead along Mass Ave. The fire-pit looked recently used, smelled like burnt charcoal. As we neared the drop-off, the roar of the rush-hour traffic along Storrow intensified. I stopped as Easttree came even with me.

"You smell anything?" I said.

"I'm afraid so."

I continued toward the low wall where Sylvia had been set up for as long as I'd been working on the street. Easttree followed, bent over, keeping his head down. "There." I pointed with the flashlight, revealing a dark pile of blankets. We moved closer. "Sylvia? It's me, Axel. You awake?" The smell was stronger here. I reached into my pack and pulled out some rubber gloves.

"Here, put these on. Just in case." Easttree took the gloves and slid them over his hands. I crept up to the pile of blankets. Standing a foot away, I raised my voice. "Sylvia! You there?" There was no response. I panned the blankets with the weakening light. "Sylvia! Hey, Sylvia! It's me, Axel!"

Her face was covered by a scarf, with only her forehead exposed. I held the flashlight under my arm as I put on a pair of the rubber gloves, then handed the light to Easttree. I poked the blankets near her shoulder. Getting no reaction, I peeled the scarf back. Easttree put the light on the old black woman's face. Her eyes were wide open.

I dropped the scarf to the ground and took one of her hands, pushed the sleeve of her coat back and felt for a pulse. I kept my hand there for a few minutes, moving my fingers around her thin, bony wrist. "Shit," I muttered, and gently lowered Sylvia's arm. "Let's get out of here and call it in."

I started for the entrance, my cell phone already in hand. After a few feet, I turned and saw Easttree looking once more at Sylvia Thompson. He had the light on her face still, and I could see her profile. He noticed something and bent closer to her. I flipped open my phone and punched in 911.

We waited on top of the bridge, smoking cigarettes and looking out at the river. Neither one of us felt like talking. When we heard the siren coming up Mass Ave five minutes later, I waved it down. Two paramedics followed us back under the bridge to the body, carrying a stretcher. We stayed back and let them do their job. It didn't take them more than a few minutes to strap Sylvia's body on to the board and carry it out. The hike up the embankment was a little more difficult. It took all four of us. As the paramedics slid the stretcher into the back of the ambulance, Easttree's cell phone rang. He didn't answer it.

"Bukowski's?" he asked, as he turned toward me.

I walked in ahead of him while he called Rebecca to let her know that he would probably be a while. When he finally came in, the foam of the two Guinness pints had settled.

"And a couple of shots of Jim Beam," Easttree said, sitting next to me.

She reached up to the top shelf and pulled down a bottle of Jameson instead. She poured two shots and placed them on the bar. "This is better," she said. "What a terrible experience that must have been!"

"To Sylvia," I said, raising my shot glass.

Easttree picked his up and knocked it against mine.

"Yes," he said. "To Sylvia."

Easttree tipped his glass, drained it in one swallow, and set it back down on the bar with a loud bang.

"Two more?" Sabrina asked.

"Please." Easttree said.

I sipped mine. Wendy came out from the kitchen and stood between us. "You two look like you've seen a ghost." She put her arms around our shoulders. "What happened?"

"Well, we found that woman I was telling you about," I said. "But it was too late."

The music in the bar was loud and distracted us. We watched the Red Sox open up a six-run lead over the Tigers. The drinks appeared before us without our asking for them. Wendy came by and kept asking Easttree if he liked tattoos. At one point, she and I went outside when she had a break and walked down by St Cecilia's park to smoke a joint. The moonlight glanced off the stone face of the Virgin while she recited a poem she wrote. I couldn't follow it, lost in my own thoughts. When we returned, I saw Easttree standing at the bar, leaned over and in close conversation with Sabrina. Taking the seat next to him, I heard her tell him that her shift ended in a half-hour. "Stick around for a little while." She patted his arm and poured me a pint of beer before she left.

"Well, now you've gone and done it," I said. Easttree shook his head, and checked the messages on his cell phone.

"I have to go soon," he said.

Two drinks later, Sabrina was sitting next to him. Easttree remembered the piece of paper he'd taken from Sylvia. He straightened it out on the bar, and we stared at it, each reading it silently.

"Wow," Sabrina said. "That's her final message…" Her voice was swallowed by the music, cranked up louder by the manager as the signal that it was almost closing time.

I picked up the paper and read it again. 'Nothing solid to sit on but smoke' was scrawled on one side. I flipped it over, saw two words written in large block letters. 'DO SOMETHING.'

We stood outside for a while and looked at the moon, then wandered down the side street to Easttree's car. Wendy and Sabrina conferred quietly in front of us, while Easttree and I had a cigarette. He didn't seem too drunk, but then he never did.

"Well, that was one for the record books," he said.

"A first for me," I said. "And probably not the last, if I stick with this job. You ever found a dead body before?"

He stopped at his car, and we leaned against it, looking at the sky. The moon was nearly full, casting shadows of the trees on the grass of the park.

Wendy came over and took me by the hand.

"No, not until today," he said.

Wendy pulled me off a little way, then stopped and pressed herself against me. "The moment of truth," she said as she looked over my shoulder before kissing me. When I looked back, Sabrina was standing in front of Easttree, putting her arms around his neck. "Let's go to my place," Wendy whispered in my ear.

The ringing of my cell phone woke me. The clock on Wendy's nightstand said 6:10a.m. Her arm was thrown across my chest, and one leg lay in between mine. She moaned as I untangled myself and reached for the pocket of my jeans on the floor. It was Easttree's number.

"Hey," I answered.

"She just left." Easttree's voice was dry. "Axel, I'm fucked."

"Where are you?"

"In my car. Shit, man, I feel like someone took a brick to my head." He told me that when he first woke up, he thought they'd been in a car crash. He was stretched out on the back seat of his Honda with Sabrina laid across him, her head hanging toward the floorboards.

"Anybody hurt?" I moved Wendy's leg and she groaned louder, then turned over on her side and pulled the pillow over her head.

Easttree let out a deep sigh. "No. Not yet. Hungover," he said.

"Did you drive anywhere?"

I heard his cell phone fall to the floor and his voice muttering as he searched for it. The sound of phone connecting with bottle rang in my ear.

"Sorry, lost it," came Easttree's voice. "But I found the rest of the Jameson. No, I'm still parked in the same place."

"Tree, hold on," I said. "Let me relocate." I slid carefully out of the bed and picked up my jeans, then walked out into the living room.

"OK," I said. "Go ahead."

"This is a mess, Axel. Out all night, not answering my phone, another woman…" He told me to hang on while he looked for a cigarette. I looked for one myself. A pack was sitting on Sabrina's futon bed and I ducked into her room and took one. When Easttree got back on the phone, he said he'd found a red card tucked into the pack. "Get this," his voice was quiet. "It says 'Call me'. And on the other side, she wrote, 'We can DO SOMETHING again sometime, if you want.'"

I found a lighter in the kitchen. Easttree was babbling about tattoos and body piercings when I heard footsteps outside the front door and a key being inserted into the lock. "Tree, I think Sabrina's..."

"Jesus, now I remember," he said. "That's how it got started. Showing me her tattoo and some of the other..." The door handle turned.

"Tree, I'm in their apartment. She's walking in. Want to get some coffee?"

There was silence on the phone for a moment. Sabrina opened the door and stared at me in surprise, then made a sheepish grin.

"Sure," Easttree finally said. "Christ, I've even got a little Irish to add to it."

STREET LOGIC

Chapter 8

May 29, 2004 - 8:00p.m.

It was still early on a Saturday night. I'd just finished running along the Charles River and was sitting in my car outside a package store on Mass Ave. Starting the second part of my weekly ritual. Some beer, some smokes, and a pint of Jim Beam lay on the seat beside me. I said a short prayer, promised that whatever I didn't drink or smoke that night, I would donate to the sink or give away, and charge into the week burned clean. It was a bargain I made with myself a few years ago. Every Saturday, no matter where I was, rain or shine, I went for a run. Then I could break out the good stuff. From Sunday until mid-week, I usually stuck to my agreement. Lots of water, push-ups and sit-ups. Certain things should be within our control, I liked to think.

On the radio, I searched for something better than the slick, commercially-produced whine that passed for rock. I found an oldies station that was playing Tom Petty and turned up the volume. The windows were down and the night air was cool. It looked like the clear weather we had been enjoying earlier in the week had been a big tease. Rain clouds were rolling in. I opened the ashtray and pulled out a pre-rolled mix of some Jamaican blend and Danish tobacco. It was my own version of a Saturday Night Special.

I was parked a few blocks from where Easttree and I had found Sylvia Thompson's body last week. The rear-view mirror picked up the lights of the cars crossing the bridge as Petty wailed about running down a dream. I lit the Special and cracked open a beer. "Thank you," I said, as I exhaled into the night. "Thank you for getting me to another Saturday night." As I leaned back and relaxed into the seat, it occurred to me that after my little prayer to the only God I knew, maybe I still needed to talk to a saint. I watched the action on the street. A few couples were out for a stroll. Some college kids were hanging around outside the package store. My cell phone rang.

"Hey," I said.

"Did you grab some bourbon?"

"For me. Didn't think you were drinking the hard stuff these days." I could hear CJ, Easttree's golden retriever, barking in the background. "You want me to pick up some more?"

"Anything but Jameson."

"Alright. I don't want to get you into any trouble."

"I'm already in trouble," he said.

The college boys were negotiating a deal for booze with a man going into the store. He looked familiar. "I should be there in a little while," I said. "I just finished my run, and I'm on Mass Ave now."

"Got any…?"

"Yeah, I got some."

We hung up. The kids were waiting for their guy. A few minutes later, Lamar Cleveland came out carrying two paper bags. He handed one to the kids. They all shook hands and went their separate ways. Into their own Saturday nights. I sat there a few minutes longer and watched Lamar shuffle along the sidewalk to his bus stop shelter. He was moving in an awkward way tonight, favoring his bad right leg. His mysterious infection had never completely healed. At the corner of Commonwealth, he stopped for a drink. As he lifted the paper bag to his mouth, the bottle inside slipped out and fell on the sidewalk. He quickly picked it up and inspected it. Apparently, it wasn't broken. He took a short pull on it and then hid it in a coat pocket. I took another hit of the Special and silently toasted Lamar, then put it out in the ashtray.

I started the Lincoln, and eased it into the light traffic. At Commonwealth, I turned right, cruising slowly under the Storrow Drive bridge and past Horseshoe Park. Split by Comm Ave, with the bridge overhead serving as protection from the rain, it wasn't really a park so much as a discreet and dry place to hang out. Standing at each end of the space were fifty foot high concrete walls, supporting the bridge and providing secrecy to whoever needed it. One wall faced the Charles River and the other one fronted the Mass Turnpike. The place was known as Horseshoe Park because of the curved shape of the walls, and also because the turnpike side was convenient for shooting horse.

Horse, the old name for heroin, had enjoyed a revival when they made it easier to do. When the powdered form got popular back in the early nineties, I'd even tried it a few times myself. Just to see what I was missing. It was like taking a horse tranquilizer. Made me sick. There were still needle users on the streets, though, and the turnpike side of the shoe provided the privacy to tie off and shoot up. No apartment windows or sidewalk pedestrians, only traffic rushing by at sixty miles an hour.

If it wasn't for the orange coat, I wouldn't have seen him. The sun was down now, but Bernard Marseille practically glowed in the dark. He appeared to be alone, sitting on a concrete bench in front of the turnpike wall. I slowed and parked the Lincoln on the next block at a meter. Cigarettes in pocket, I stepped out of the car and walked toward the park.

I had a question only the Saint could answer.

The people on the street first started calling him 'Saint' Bernard after he'd saved all three Lewis brothers from drowning in the Charles River a few years ago. The Lewis brothers had been living behind the turnpike wall one year, drinking and shooting heroin with the money the youngest one collected from a construction job injury claim. About fifty feet from shore during a family swim challenge, Harry, the oldest, had started floundering. Bernie swam out with an inflatable rubber mattress and retrieved all of them. Over the years, he'd pulled a few other drunken swimmers from the swampy, muddy waters. Now, he always kept a few long tree branches next to the river to fish people out with. His most recent rescue was old Honey Crawfish, a year ago. There had been a fire-setter loose on the streets, for about two months, setting four homeless people on fire during his rampage. He doused his victims with alcohol while they were passed out, and lit them up. No one knew for sure who was doing it, but there was talk about a drifter from out west named Billy Northrup. He'd showed up shortly before the first incident. One night, Bernie saw Northrup running away from a small fire in the Horseshoe that nearly roasted Crawfish. Fortunately, Bernie had been able to put out the flames before too much damage could be done. Still, the skin on Honey's upper legs and stomach was singed pretty bad. If there was any advantage to incontinence, Honey Crawfish's private parts could testify.

Bernie usually spent his days collecting stuff in his carriage, and then drinking near Kenmore Square or under one of the ramps or bridges nearby. He'd shown me the small shelter that he'd built under the girders of the Storrow Drive overpass, next to the river. He'd built it with wood planks and sheet metal that he picked up from the leftovers at construction sites. By using the steel girders of the bridge as support beams, he'd created something like a tree house up under there. Inside, the ceiling gave off the constant thump thump thump of the highway overhead. He had pieces of good scrap carpet on the floor, and a twin-sized bed. High and dry, it was even protected from the wind.

Walking across Charles Gate West Street I left the sidewalk, and moved into the park. I went slowly so he could see me. Bernie and I got along well, but he wasn't used to seeing me at night and I didn't know if he would recognize me in the dark. As I crossed the rocky ground, I checked out the bushes along the edge of the stream. It wasn't really necessary. Anywhere around Bernie was safe. No one bothered him, not even the police.

"Hey Bernie," I said.

He raised a cigarette, took a long drag on it, and stood up. He had a beer in his other hand. He wasn't a huge guy but he looked powerful, still a little like the promising boxer he'd once been. Now, he drank beer and smoked marijuana, religiously, as he put it. Said it kept him on an even keel.

"What brings you out here on a Saturday night, Axel?" His deep gravelly voice sounded like it had rocks in it. He had a small radio propped up on a wood crate, with the Red Sox game playing.

"I was just driving by. Saw your coat from the street."

I walked up and put my hand out. He set his beer down on the crate and shook my hand, gripping it tightly as he always did.

"Beer?"

I thought about it for two seconds. "Sure, why not."

He handed me a can of ice cold Schlitz from the cooler next to him, and took another one out for himself.

"Cheers," he said.

"Cheers."

I put the beer on the ground and pulled out my cigarettes.

"Axel," Bernie said, "how long you been working these streets? Almost a year?"

"About that. Long enough to know better."

He laughed. I offered him one of my smokes and he took it.

"Feels like it, I bet," he said.

"Sometimes. Other times, it seems like a short time."

Bernie grunted. "Short time is more like three months. Although nothing is short when you're on the inside. I did six months once that felt like forever, and ten years that seemed to, well, that was a whole different thing." He opened a leather pouch that was hanging next to the radio and hunted for something. "I remember when you first came out here with Adrian. Indian Jack was just out of jail and raising hell all that summer and fall, before they arrested him."

"Yeah. I haven't seen him in a long time."

"He's down south somewhere now. Has family in Florida, I guess."

"Ever been there?"

"Never. Not planning on going, neither. Too hot."

The wind kicked up and sent a piece of newspaper whirling in the air in front of us. Across Commonwealth, in the other half of the park, someone had started a little fire near a wall.

"Assholes. They'll get busted," Bernie said. "Can't be out in plain view like that." He clicked his lighter. "To old Crawfish. The son of a bitch has his own place now, but he still likes to sleep out once in a while," he chuckled. "Won't find a better man out here. You won't be offended if I smoke a little Mother Nature, will ya?"

"No, go ahead."

He lit it and took a few tokes, and then passed it to me. I took a ceremonial hit and passed it back. We watched the shadows of the fire across the street dance on the wall. I had never drunk or smoked pot with anyone on the street before. But tonight, it seemed like the thing to do.

"Axel," Bernie said. "Did I tell you about the last week of Sylvia's life?"

I wouldn't even have to ask him about it now. I picked up my beer and listened.

"She hadn't moved from that spot under the bridge for at least a month," he said. "I knew something was wrong with her, but she just said she was tired. She used to go into Kenmore to McDonald's every morning." He glanced across the street at the growing fire and muttered under his breath. "Anyway, that month, the outreach van was bringing her food at night and during the day, I'd take something back there for her. But she wasn't eating."

He offered me another toke. I thought it would be rude to say no.

"I think she knew what was happening," he went on. "There was something she kept saying, every day that final week. It wasn't until afterwards that I gave it much thought." He took a drink and sat quietly for a minute as the wind whistled past us. I passed back the joint. "She said that for some people, there's nothing left for them to stand on but their own breath. That life was like trying to stand on words. Words, or smoke, she said. I guess it all made sense to her somehow."

I told him about the letter Easttree had found on her.

The gravel rattled in his deep voice. "'Nothing solid to stand on but smoke.' Perfect."

Bernie stood up, handed me the joint again, and walked over to the edge of the wall. The fire across the street was going full-tilt now, and lit up half the wall. I could hear Bernie singing softly to himself as he peed in the night air. My beer was empty. It seemed like a good time to go. When Bernie came back, I handed him what was left of the joint and gave him a few cigarettes. He took them without a word, just a grunt. He reached down into his cooler and pulled out another cold can of beer and handed it to me.

"Don't drink and drive," he said, and laughed at his mixed message.

"Thanks, Bernie. What do you think she meant by that note?"

He lit a cigarette, and stared into the darkness. "You know, I was thinking about that. All I can come up with is, there's a whole lot of people blowing smoke about helping the homeless, but not much action."

"Uh-huh." I didn't know what to say to that.

"Hey, I know you people are trying," he said. "Trying hard. It seems to me, though, that some people, when they're in a condition like she was, they just need to be taken in someplace. Whether they want that or not."

"I hear that, Bernie. I think the same thing myself at times."

"Well, go easy, Axel. And watch out for the police."

Still thinking about the note, I walked back to my car. When the engine cranked, the oldies station was playing "Light My Fire" by the Doors. Again. Back at Horseshoe, I saw figures racing away from the flames as a police cruiser pulled into the park, its lights flashing. I drove under the bridge, but when I searched the shooting gallery wall, Bernie's orange coat was no longer visible. I put the can of Schlitz in the bag with the rest of the beer and moved it to the back floorboard. Then I drove toward Roslindale, where Easttree lived.

STREET LOGIC

Chapter 9

May 29, 2004 - 10:00p.m.

I turned on to the dead end gravel road and drove under a dark canopy of trees to the last house. Easttree's old Honda was the only car parked in the driveway. I pulled in next to it, cut the engine, and heard the sound of crickets, and nothing else. I sat there for a minute, admiring the large oak trees that stood like sentinels on either side of his three-story house. Listening to the night sounds. The only light came from a second floor window, where Easttree had an office. I grabbed the bag from the package store, and walked up the brick path to the front door and rang the bell. Immediately, CJ started barking from somewhere deep in the house. After a minute, I heard some furious pounding on the stairs accompanied by more anxious barking and Easttree's voice. When he opened the door, Easttree had CJ by the collar.

"Sorry," he said. "I was on the phone."

"That's alright, Tree."

As I entered, I bent to scratch Carl Jung behind the ears and give him a moment to remember me. He licked my hand until Easttree turned toward the kitchen, and then he darted ahead of us.

"I would've been here sooner," I said, "except I ran into Bernie on my way through Kenmore."

"Saint Bernie?"

"Yeah. So how're you doing, man?"

"I'm all right, I guess," he said.

He didn't sound all right. When I could see his face better under the kitchen light, I knew he wasn't. His eyes looked tired and there were dark circles underneath them, but what really concerned me was the expression he wore.

"Well, actually, I feel like shit," he said. "Have a seat, I was just cooking some pasta. Gotta keep eating, right?"

"That's right. Like the Italians."

"Exactly," he said.

He handed me a beer from the refrigerator and put the sixer of Sam Adams I'd brought in the freezer to chill. He set the pint of Jim Beam on the counter. I hadn't bothered to buy another.

"First we eat," he said. He loaded piles of spaghetti on two plates and placed them on the round, glass kitchen table. After he ladled sauce on to each of them, he took some bread out of the oven, set it next to a bowl of salad, and sat down.

"Thanks for coming by," he said.

We ate and talked. He went to the fridge for fresh beers. He told me that Rebecca had discovered Sabrina's thong under the seat of his car. He'd somehow forgotten to get rid of it. Maybe it was a new twist on the Freudian slip, he tried to joke.

"Or just sheer exhaustion," I said.

"Within an hour, she packed up the kids and went to her sister's house in Brookline."

"Are you talking to her?"

"I was just on the phone with her sister. She says she isn't ready to talk to me yet. The whole thing was pretty sloppy on my part."

"Did you have a chance to explain?"

"What's to explain? That it's because I'm burned out at work? That I discovered a dead homeless woman under a bridge, and that I needed to get shit-faced and make out with some stranger in my car? No, Axel," he said, reaching down to pet CJ. "There are some things that you just can't explain."

He gave me a long look, and slid his plate over to the side.

"I should've seen it coming," he said. "It's the job, mostly. I knew I needed to take some time off, chill out, and relax for a while. She and I have both been working too much. The kids demand a lot of time, but that's often the best part of my day. I just fucked up."

I drank some beer.

He stood and went to the cabinet for two glasses, filled them with ice from the freezer, and grabbed the Sam Adams.

"Come on up to the den," he said. "Bring the Beam." He tried to smile, but it was weak.

As he led us up the wide staircase, I noticed that he didn't look at any of the family photos lining the wall. At the top of the landing, he came to a stop in front of the last one. It was a shot of all of them at the beach.

"That was last year," he said. "The sand dunes outside of P-Town." Easttree had his arm around his wife, everyone was smiling. "A lot can change in a year."

"For sure."

"Come on," he said. "Sorry."

I put a hand on his shoulder and swung him around to face me.

"It's all going to work out, Tree. I know you. You'll work it out. Something with a strong foundation can even survive a hurricane, right? I think you told me that one."

He grinned. "OK, captain. Follow me."

We went down the hallway to his study. It was a large room that spanned the front of the house, and had an outdoor balcony. Some blues were playing on his stereo. In the middle of the room was a round wooden table between two soft leather chairs, where we'd sat on numerous occasions. Up against one wall was his desk. It was loaded with papers and books. A long brown sofa lined another wall. A worn plaid blanket was spread across it. He put the two glasses on the table, took the bottle of bourbon-whiskey from me and poured until the glasses were full. I pulled out two beers and opened them. Easttree opened the porch doors and we sat down in the two armchairs.

"Airs out the place a little," he explained. "CJ has been laying some horrendous stink-bombs lately. The vet says it's natural for a golden retriever at his age. Smells highly unnatural to me, though." Easttree directed CJ to a spot near the door. He lay down and watched us to see what we might do next.

"This is my last drinking night," Easttree said. "So let's make it a good one. I've been at it since she left. Tonight, I toast the great miracle of detox." He gave a smile, and lifted his glass.

"The miracle we can't give away on the street."

"That's right," he laughed softly. "Everybody wants it, but there's always tomorrow."

"We can go easy, you know." I said.

"True. But that wouldn't be any fun, would it? You know, Axel, it's very tempting to just say 'fuck it,' and slide downhill for a while. I've considered it. But, alas, we know how that story goes."

"Yes, we do. Which is why you won't do that. Tonight, let me suggest that we drink in honor of doing something strong. In your case, that means getting back to the gym, or climbing your wall again. Like you were telling me you would." I raised my glass and he knocked his against it. "To being strong," I said.

"Yes," he said. "To being strong." He leaned back and sighed. "Jesus, Axel. I have two wonderful children and a beautiful wife. I have meaningful work, even with the burn-out factor. I'm going to have to address that if I'm going to stay in this business, though." He took another deep breath. "Thank god when I bought this house, it was cheap. We don't have any money issues. So what the fuck am I doing? Maybe I'm having that mid-life crisis they warn everyone about."

"No, it's not that."

"I don't know," he said. "After Frank Murphy, with his maggot infested foot, Sylvia dying under a bridge, I think it was all too much and it hit me over the head. Hell, I was starting to have visions of Jane Winslow in a bikini on the deck of a toy sailboat."

"That's not burned out, that's completely understandable."

"You know the crazy part? I almost feel like I deserved to get wasted and have sex in the back of my car with a twenty-year-old. That's pretty fucked up."

"Sabrina's twenty-three."

"Whatever."

"Look, Tree. It's heavy stuff, the work you do. We do. The frustration has to go somewhere, be dealt with in some way."

He leaned back and put his feet up on the table. "I shouldn't have done it that way."

"We all get toasted on this kind of work, man. And burned out or not, it's not easy to resist a beautiful woman like Sabrina. Even a good man like yourself, Tree. I doubt I could have."

"You're not married," he said.

"No, I'm not. But if she came on to me in a bar one night, and the situation was…"

"You're not married," he repeated.

"Yeah, I guess you're right."

Easttree's cell phone rang. When he recognized the number, he frowned and pointed at the stereo. I quickly got to my feet and almost spilled my drink. He made a frantic gesture toward the shelves on the other side of the room. I couldn't find the volume control, so I turned it off.

"This is Easttree," he said.

I looked through his books while he took the call. He had a vast collection of textbooks by psychologists, psychiatrists, therapists, all related to his work. He also had a lot of fiction. Hemingway, Steinbeck, Faulkner, and some writers I'd never heard of, like Andrew Vachss and Charlie Huston.

"I'm home watching the kids," I heard him say. "Rebecca's been sick all week, and I was praying there wouldn't be any major emergencies." He listened, and uttered a series of 'yeah's' and 'no's' and 'uh-huh's.' I pulled down a book titled *Blue Belle* by Vachss and took it back to my chair. Easttree was saying that he would see if he could find another clinician to cover for him, and he'd call them back in a few minutes.

"Of all the fucking nights," he muttered, and tossed his cell phone on to the table. "There was an altercation in the Wilder tonight. One of my guys. I'm second on call. Anderson's got food poisoning or some shit."

"What happened?"

"Rose Sullivan was admitted a few days ago with a bad cut on her leg. Frank Murphy was already there, as well as Rose's new man, Dennis McFarley."

"Perfect storm."

"Right. Murphy found them making out in a broom closet. Later, McFarley went out for a smoke in the courtyard, and Murphy cold-cocked him. Broke his nose. They might have to transfer one of them to the Jones Center, and they want a clinician to make the call. I'm going to see if Ted Watkins can cover it. He owes me one." Easttree picked up the phone again, went over to his desk, and punched in a number. I poured another shot into my glass. As Easttree spoke on the phone, I wandered around the room, and ended up in front of his CDs. I picked out a Muddy Waters collection, then changed my mind and went for Stevie Ray Vaughan. I inserted the disk, found the right buttons, and put it on pause. I stepped over CJ and went outside to smoke a cigarette. The night was clear and I could make out a few stars. After a few minutes, Easttree joined me.

"Ted's going to cover it for me," he said. "Thank god."

He was in no condition to handle anything right now, I realized.

We looked out over his front yard. "Listen, you know what I was just thinking about? That note from Sylvia. You know what Bernie said about her?"

"That she was a hell of a fuck?" Easttree was clearly over his limit. "Sorry, that was bad. Really bad." He paused, and closed his eyes. "Yeah, I remember. I still have her note. 'Nothing to stand on but smoke,' or something like that. Talking of smoking..." He had a funny grin.

"I was just going to suggest that. But listen, man. I think there's something important there, in what she was saying."

We went back in and as I rolled a number, he turned on the music and kicked up the volume. We passed the joint back and forth and listened as Stevie Ray sang his version of Stevie Wonder's "Superstitious." After a little while, Easttree opened a drawer in his desk and pulled out the note. He looked at it, and passed it to me.

"'Do something,'" he said, reading the words on the back. "That's about as direct as it gets. That's the whole thing, right there. Can you really 'Do something' for another person, especially when that person won't budge? You know what I mean? You tell me, Axel, you've seen what's going on out there on the streets, with these people. I was never a pessimistic person by nature, but I think this job has just about squeezed the last drops of hope out of me. So, tell me what do you think is important about this note?"

"It reminds me of that story about the doctor at New England Medical. The one who finally committed Wayne Diggs to the program at the Shattuck Hospital. Remember that one? The doc had seen Diggs in the ER so many times he began reviewing the records. Added up the cost of admitting Diggs to the hospital over a one year period – over a hundred times, I heard – and filed for a long-term treatment program for him. Being brought in by ambulances is a costly business. I hear that Diggs is still at the Shattuck, and seems to like it. He has a little job cleaning up their hallways, and he's working out in the gym. But he had to be forced in. That's the thing. He never would have chosen it for himself. Maybe that's what Syliva meant by 'Do Something.'"

"There you go," he said. "I always believed there was some kind of solution, however small. But with these kinds of people, Sylvia, Diggs, Frank Murphy, maybe it takes something bigger. There's something totally wrong with the world when a woman dies under the bridge that goes from Boston to Cambridge, with the illustrious MIT University on one side and Boston University on the other, while the world's top scholars are busy figuring out what's going on in space, and whatever happened in Germany sixty fucking years ago."

He slumped back into his leather chair and we lapsed into another silence. He was toasted. He poured the rest of the bourbon into our glasses, put on some Jimi Hendrix, and we talked about the Red Sox. Then he got up and motioned for me to follow him. We went downstairs and passed through the kitchen. He decided to have a little of the vodka that was chilled in the freezer. I steered him into the living room, and he pulled two chairs over in front of the big sliding glass doors that looked on to the backyard. We stared at the thirty foot granite wall that rose up behind the house.

"Isn't that a thing of beauty?" he said, swirling the icy vodka around in his glass. "Now that damn thing is something solid to stand on, I'll tell you that. That rock is real, and it has been there forever. Solid as a motherfucker!"

He slammed his fist down on the arm of the chair, causing CJ to jump. "Why does a sixty-year-old lady die under a bridge like that, and leave a note, Axel, that says to do something? Jesus, is it that fucking simple?"

I went over to the sliding doors and looked at the giant black wall outside. "Bernie said he saw her every day that last week. For weeks, actually. His conclusion was that she was done with this life. With the way it was for her. She couldn't make the choice to change for herself, though, just like Wayne Diggs couldn't. It had to be made for him." I watched the wind blow the limbs of the apple tree in the back yard. Easttree had planted it when he first bought the place.

"Force them in, that's it," Easttree muttered. "Maybe it was her time to go. Who knows. Imagine if that was your mother, or grandmother, under that bridge."

"I heard she had some children in New York," I said. "Two kids, that's all I know."

"Well, they'll probably never even find out how their mother died, and maybe that's for the best."

"Yeah. Maybe."

The branches of the apple tree danced in the strong wind. The sky looked cloudy. Rain would come soon.

Easttree stood up. "Come on, let's go take a closer look at that rock."

"Just promise me you won't start climbing it."

"Don't worry, my friend, we're just going to look." He opened the door and stumbled out on to the deck, grabbing the railing. CJ squeezed through his legs and shot out into the yard, disappearing into the night. "Look," he said, and pointed to the top of the granite wall. He moved back to the door, flipped a switch, and a light came on at the top. A rope was tied to a tree up there and hung down to the ground. It was his climbing rope, thick and heavy with knots every couple of feet. "The great serpent," he laughed. "Freud and Jung would've had a great time scaling that wall."

"Or analyzing why anyone would do it."

Easttree laughed and moved to the end of the deck. "What would those bastards do with street people, Axel? You ever wonder about that? What could Carl Rogers and his 'client-centered therapy' do on the street?"

"Hmm. Sometimes I wonder what Socrates and Plato might recommend."

"Probably that with a little discourse, one would naturally reach the conclusion that there's nothing left to do but stand on smoke." He started laughing, and made a run for the wall. CJ came bounding from around the side of the house, barking as Easttree grabbed hold of the rope and began climbing.

I got to him before he could get more than a few feet off the ground, and pulled on his legs. "Oh no you don't, Tree. I want to go up first. Come on down, man. I want you to get me some gloves from the house first. I'm not going up that thing bare-handed."

"Alright, alright," he let go of the rope and landed on the ground heavily. "Let's go in and get some gloves."

I herded him back into the living room, and steered him to the couch. "Let's smoke a little more first." I knew it would knock him out.

"Let CJ in, will you?" He stretched out on the couch.

I opened the door and yelled for the dog. He came running in and flopped down on the floor next to Easttree. I lit the rest of the joint. We passed it back and forth and stared out the window at the light at the top of the wall.

"Jesus, Axel, I've gotta get my shit together this week," he said. "Or I could end up under a damn bridge." He laughed to himself.

"You know what they say, Tree. Bad always comes with good. Somewhere, even in the worst of times, there's usually a little bit of light that…"

He was already asleep. I lifted his legs, took off his shoes, and gently placed a cushion under his head. CJ looked up at me.

"Take care of him tonight, old buddy," I said.

I went back up to the den, closed the balcony doors, and grabbed the book by Vachss. On my way down the stairs, I stopped to look at the family picture again. Easttree was right: what a difference a year makes.

STREET LOGIC

Chapter 10

June 8, 2004 – Noon

I left Bernie behind the library, sorting through his carriage of bottles and cans. I bought a coffee and found a good spot on the benches alongside the library, in the sun, facing Copley Plaza, and closed my eyes. I drifted south for a few minutes, alone with my thoughts. It didn't last long. Swaggert's sharp, hoarse voice rang out in the park.

"I hosed the dude!"

I put my sunglasses on and shaded my eyes. Across Dartmouth Street, on the corner of the grass, Brad Swaggert was posing in front of a small band of kids playing hooky from school. He was demonstrating for them with his legs spread wide what he'd done to the man they called TLFuckYou.

"Yeah, boy!" one of the punks hollered.

As dealer, mischief maker, and all around street guide, Swaggert was the king of Copley's lost and confused youth. There were ten of them, maybe, lounging on benches or on the grass, looking to score dope of one kind or another, or just to escape boredom. A girl jumped up and started dancing to the hip-hop blasting from a boom-box. She worked the line of people standing in front of the theatre-ticket kiosk, pushing her hips out, doing a few spin moves, shaking what she had. When she finished and went up the line holding her hat out, nobody gave her anything. The kid with the boom-box turned the volume to max and the dancer mooned the crowd. Then the music shut off. Peace in the plaza was restored.

One of the young bloods laid out on the grass yelled, "Yeah, boy, my ass! TL gonna be all up yours, Swag!"

Swaggert strutted over and looked down at the kid. "Oh yeah? He can try and whoop my ass if he wants!" He stood over the kid for a minute, then laughed loudly and hauled up a girl with spiked hair and kissed her. He pulled her after him, and they walked over to a bench and sat down.

The story I'd heard from Bernie was that there had been a little party last night behind the shooting gallery wall at Horseshoe Park. TL had passed out on his mattress. After TL's boys had all wandered off to their own spots, Swaggert and a few of his cohorts had stumbled upon the unconscious TL, and had placed bets on who had the balls to piss on the big man. None of the kids dared, so it was left to the king.

It was almost noon by now. The sun was shining through a gap in the clouds, and I had to squint to see the small, lone figure crossing the street in front of the Hancock Tower. What caught my eye was the long white hair and nearly dwarf-like appearance. He had the look of a hobbit. He wore a backpack with a sleeping bag tied on to it, a rope dangling from the pack and trailing behind him as he crossed the grass of the plaza. I didn't recognize him. When he reached an empty bench near the kids, he set his backpack on the ground and spent a moment looking around the plaza. Then he began searching through the pockets of his jacket.

Two of the kids on the grass laughed, and stood up. Their pants fell halfway down their asses as they chain-stepped slowly toward the backpacker, who was still standing, fumbling with something in his hands. When the kids got to within five feet, I sat up. One of them pulled the pockets of his jeans out and began gesturing with his hands to the old guy. When he ignored them, they stepped closer. I gave a short, loud whistle. Swaggert looked over from his bench and saw me. I pointed toward his boys and used my forefingers to make an X, shaking my head. He shrugged his shoulders. Five seconds later he barked out a name and the two kids froze. They looked back at him.

"Now!" Swaggert yelled.

The two slowly shuffled back to the group.

It had amazed me at first that Brad Swaggert, a skinny white guy in his late twenties with no muscle at all, commanded these younger, bigger, stronger teenagers like they were sheep. When I got to know him better, I understood. I told him he could make it in the real world with those skills, if he could learn to tame himself a little. He'd just laughed at that, and reminded me that his world was the true, real world. One where tame was the same as lame.

I gave Swaggert the peace sign. He hollered across the street at me, "You owe me one!"

Dark clouds moved across the sun. I stood and stretched. The weather report had been right today, predicting thunder and lightning and heavy rain for the afternoon. The Red Sox day game had already been rescheduled for tonight, weather permitting. I called Tina.

"I'm on the waterfront," she said. "Here with Tony. He's a mess, but at least he's conscious. He's been telling us about the time he met Ted Williams."

"Ask him about his encounter with Babe Ruth. You need any help?"

"No. Ripley's here. We're going to try to get him into the clinic. He's thinking about it."

"OK. I'm going to wander around Back Bay before the rain starts. Any idea where Bette is?"

"She's at South Station, having hot chocolate with Stella. Why, you got a psych case?"

"Little old guy with long white hair, big backpack. Ring any bells?"

"No."

"Hobbit?"

"What?"

"Nothing. Good luck with the old fisherman."

I walked across Dartmouth Street. Swaggert broke away from his girlfriend and approached me. He looked over his shoulder and lowered his voice. "You hear about that TL threat, man?" His eyes were red and he didn't sound cocky anymore. "Saying he's going to throw my ass in the river!"

"I heard." I stepped back a foot so I had a view of the old guy. "We should talk about that."

Swaggert was sweating and the veins on the sides of his forehead bulged. "Talk? Shit, man, that motherfucker could..."

"Maybe you made a tactical mistake this time."

"Tactical fucking whatever. All I know is I was really fucked up last night, man. Shit." All traces of bravado had vanished.

"Listen," I said. "I'll talk to him. No promises, though. You know how he is. But in the meantime, my advice is to lay low." I scribbled a note on the back of one of my cards and handed it to him. "Take this down to the shelter. Give it to any counselor at the front desk. If they have any questions, tell them to call me."

Swaggert looked at the card, flipped it over and read it. "Damn, Axel. I hate that stinking place." His voice was flat. "I don't think I can."

"Yes you can, unless you have somewhere better to disappear for a while. Plus, TL never goes down to the shelter. It may take me a few days to find him."

"Shit." He scanned the plaza. "I don't know."

The little old guy on the bench had a pipe and was trying to light it. The young punks were watching him, making jokes, but they stayed away.

"Alright, Brad, you do what you think is best. That card will get you a bed and you can even stay in during the day. Think about it. I'll see if I can find TL today. I'll look for you this afternoon, around five o'clock, down at the shelter. Let you know if I have any luck."

Swaggert's face tightened. "Fuck it," he swore under his breath. "You do owe me one, right?" He held the card between his fingers, as if he was weighing it. I nodded back. "Alright, then," he said. "I'll go nuts down there, man, any more than a day."

"I know."

"Tell him I'll make it up to him somehow." He shook my hand.

"Good. I will. Listen, ever seen that guy before? The old guy with the backpack?"

"Never."

"Thanks for calling your boys off. See what I've been telling you? You've got the stuff, man. The world needs good leaders."

He made a jester's face at me. "Yeah, right." He spit on some flowers and turned back to his girl.

"Don't forget," I said. "They have a good program at the shelter, for anybody who wants job training…"

"Axel, you ever fucking give up?"

"I try not to."

The little guy had his pipe going strong. He was sitting on one end of the bench, tossing cracker crumbs to the pigeons. I took a seat at the other end.

"They're talking about rain," I said.

He turned and inspected me through a pair of thick glasses, which made his eyes look larger than they were. One bow was attached by a piece of clear tape. I noticed some blood on the back of the hand he held the pipe with, and a few open sores.

"Those clouds are coming in fast," I continued, looking at the sky.

He looked away and puffed on his pipe.

"My name's Axel Hazzard. I was just wondering if…"

He raised his left hand to halt me. A small cloud of smoke rose from his pipe as he stared straight ahead. "Not interested," he said, in a high-pitched voice.

I let a few minutes pass while he smoked. Finally I said, "Looks like you're traveling."

"You're not one of those he-she's, are you?" he asked, still staring out at the grass. I almost laughed, but he was serious. "Because if you are, I'm not interested."

"Well, no," I said, and sat up straight. "I can assure you that I'm not a he-she, or a she-he. I'm a social worker, actually, of sorts. It's just that I noticed you seem to be camping. I've done a fair bit of backpacking myself. Nothing wrong with traveling."

He tapped out his pipe on the ground and put it in his coat pocket. Then he stood up, muttering something to himself. Before he left, he eyed me again, carefully. He walked past Swaggert and his gang as if they weren't there. They all watched him. Someone made a joke and they laughed. I got up and followed him as he headed toward the library. As I passed Swaggert, he said, "No luck, huh?"

"Gotta start somewhere."

He laughed. His cocky attitude was back. He slapped me on the shoulder. "You're alright, Axel. Even if you are an outreach worker."

"Thanks. Watch yourself."

I followed the hobbit at a distance. He went in the Boylston entrance of the library and past the security guards. Irene, the head of security, acknowledged me with a smile. I raised my eyebrows and nodded toward the little backpacker, who was walking directly toward the bank of elevators. She shook her head no. She hadn't seen him before. He stepped on the elevator when the doors opened. I waited to see what floor he was going to, and took the stairway to the basement level.

In the men's room, his pack was already off and stood next to the two sinks. He was examining his face in the mirror. I went over and stood at one of the urinals, watching him out of the corner of my eye. There were three other people in the bathroom, two in the stalls and one at the other sink.

He dug a plastic bag out of his pack that contained a can of shaving cream and a razor. Next he tied his hair back into a ponytail, and removed his glasses, putting them carefully in his shirt pocket. Then he splashed water on to his face, lathered up, and began shaving. I walked over when the other sink was free and slowly began washing my hands. He ignored me, intent on his shaving. When I started whistling a show tune from *West Side Story*, he paused in mid-stroke with the razor halfway down his cheek.

"I know that one," he said.

He rinsed the blade off and contorted his face as he shaved under his nose. "The kid wanted to be a Shark," he said.

"That's right, the Sharks. I was just a kid when I saw it, but now and then it pops into my head."

The precision of his blade work was impressive. He finished and rinsed his face off with water, patting it dry with a paper towel. I dried and re-dried my hands under the hand-blower.

"I saw it in another life time," he said, inspecting his face in the mirror. "When I had a different head. Different eyes, too." He put his shaving cream and razor back into the plastic bag, and stored them in his pack.

"I had a smaller head too, back then," I said. "I must have been eight years old when I first saw it."

He put his glasses back on. His grey eyebrows were enormous. Big, bushy, unruly, spiky ones. Under them, his cloudy blue eyes stared at me, large and serious. "I mean," he said, his high voice rising, "that I had a different head than this one. They replaced it. And the same with my arms, and my legs. I don't know how they got away with it, but they did." He hoisted the backpack on his narrow frame, and turned once more toward me.

"And for your information, I'm not interested."

On my way out of the library, I saw him sitting at a table in the newspaper section, flipping through the *Boston Globe*. I walked back to Copley Plaza and sat on a bench near the kiosk, watching the storm clouds gather. Swaggert was gone now, and so were the kids. I called Easttree and told him about the backpacker. He didn't know anyone who fit that description. Before I could hang up, he told me Frank Murphy was back on the street again.

"How's his foot?"

"The wound is healed pretty well. Almost had him on a van to the program out at the Island. But he got the last minute jitters."

"If I see him, I'll give him your regards."

"He wasn't very happy with me when he left. You might want to keep my name out of it."

"What happened?"

"I couldn't find him a pair of Levi's," Easttree said. "He had to settle for Wranglers."

I laughed. "Speaking of cowboys, Tree, how are things at the ranch?"

He said they were better, but he'd have to fill me in later. He had a client standing at his door.

The sky was deep purple now. I was thinking about going to Horseshoe Park to look for TL and start the peace negotiations when I saw another new face working the plaza.

He was on the other side of the park, wandering from trash can to trash can and digging through each with a stick. He didn't look homeless. He was too clean. The baggy black designer jeans, black jean jacket, and black student's backpack, along with his youth, indicated a student. But still, he was digging through trash. So I watched for another few minutes. My main concern at the moment was the darkness of the clouds reflected in the Hancock Tower behind him. I'd wanted to get to Kenmore before the rain started coming down, but he was coming my way now. I could see his face better. Clean, good-looking features. Could even be in high school. Reminded me a little of that Basquiat character in the movie about the artist. I hoped that he was a student at MassArt and working on a project with recycled materials or something.

It was a tree branch in his hand. While he searched the trash can next to me, I noticed that he was wearing a black t-shirt under the jacket and had a black bandana tied around his neck. Everything was black, down to his unlaced boots. His skin was the color of dark chocolate and even without the sun, it seemed to shine. Almost six feet tall, with the Afro. He had a slight build. As he pulled out a crumpled Wendy's bag and slowly examined its contents, I had a good chance to examine his face. Something registered, but I didn't know from where. Maybe I'd seen him in the shelter.

Apparently satisfied, he stuffed the bag into his backpack and dug some more, coming out with one from Burger King. Didn't like what he saw and threw it back. The entire time he never looked around him. I saw no trace of hunger or desperation, or street, in his blank, nearly peaceful expression.

The clouds were getting darker. I waited until he had finished going through another two trash cans and had sat down with his findings, before I made my approach. At the end of his bench I sat down, stretched my legs out in front of me, and started looking at my notebook. He went through everything he'd collected, pulling out leftover bites of burgers and French fries. When he finished eating, he meticulously cleaned his hands with napkins, wiping his fingers one at a time.

"Looks like a thunder storm coming in, huh?" I said.

He kept working on his hands, ignoring me.

"They say it's going to get hotter this week, too," I went on. "Maybe into the nineties." I pulled out a pack of cigarettes. "Care for a smoke?"

He turned his head this time and stared directly at me. His mouth opened as if he were going to say something, but instead he just looked at me, his eyes unblinking, showing nothing, the way a baby looks at people. I kept the smile on my face and held·out the pack to him. He slowly stood up. Still looking at me, he slung the pack over his shoulder and tossed the now empty junk food bags into the trash. Then he walked away.

I watched him cross the plaza and head toward the library. It was the second one of the day I'd managed to chase into the BPL. A Hobbit with new body parts, and the Silent One. He stopped before crossing Dartmouth and looked back at me. I had that same feeling that I'd seen him before. Then he continued across the street and up the steps, and disappeared inside the library. I let it go, and headed toward Horseshoe Park before the rain let loose.

STREET LOGIC

Chapter 11

June 8, 2004 - 3:00p.m.

I took the Green Line train to Kenmore Square. As I was walking the block to the park, the rain began to fall in light drops. I ducked under the bridge overpass as it started to really pour, and saw them gathered around the bench in front of the shooting gallery wall. TL and a few of his posse. I glanced across Commonwealth to the other side of the shoe, hoping to see Bernie's orange coat. But that bench was empty. They all watched my approach, except for TL, who had his head down. When I was within range, I stopped.

"Hey, TL." The four youngbloods who surrounded him checked me out. I checked out the craftsmanship of the block wall.

"I see you there," TL finally said. He was busy rolling a fattie on top of a magazine. Without raising his head, he swung his eyes up and locked them on mine. Cold and hard. Then his face relaxed, his big smile showing off straight, white teeth. "What up, Axel Hazzard?"

I walked forward and put my hand out. He stuck out his elbow so he could keep rolling. I knocked my fist against it, lightly. Felt like steel. "He just in time, right, boys?" They didn't look like they agreed, but I knew they'd follow TL's lead.

"So, how's things?" I said.

"I'm chilling." He finished with the joint and licked the paper. "Before the slaughter."

"I thought maybe we could talk about that."

TL eyed me for a moment before he pulled out a lighter and lit the monster-sized doobie.

"This here be Axel Hazzard, boys," he said, blowing the smoke out through his flared nostrils. "Don't keep staring at him like that, he ain't gonna bite," he laughed, and passed the joint to a big kid with a baby face. They quit checking me out and focused on sharing the smoke. "Even in this cold-hearted world we be living in, Mister Axel Hazzard still out here running around trying to do something right. Ain't that

131

something. Damn, this be some good shit, my man. Tastes like Jesus himself. Want a hit?"

"Smells good, TL, but I'm working. Speaking of which, maybe when you're done with that we can have a little talk."

His posse passed it around a few times. TL didn't say anything while he sorted through one of his pockets. Finally he stood up, and put his big arm around my shoulders. "You and me pals, Axe. You never bullshit me before. 'Course I'll talk with you." He took what was left of the joint and had a last hit, then ate it. He squeezed my shoulder like it was a pebble in his hand.

"Alright, let's go do a little walk and talk, Axe." He turned to his gang. "You all can suck down some of that beer while I talking. But leave half for me, now, you hear." His laughter echoed under the bridge.

We moved away from the bench and stayed under the bridge where it was dry, avoiding the heavy downpour from the drainage spouts. "I love the rain." TL put his big arm around my shoulder. "Reminds me of the island."

"You still got a little Haitian thunder in that laugh of yours, TL."

"I am the thunder," he said, smiling. "Black thunder, my man." The water from the drainage spouts was forming puddles, and we moved past them to a dry spot on the sidewalk of Commonweath. I stopped and faced him. He took his arm off my shoulder.

"I heard about that incident with Swaggert. Talked to him this morning. He said he wants to make peace."

TL's face was impassive. Cars passed us, spraying water in our direction. We stepped back and found a safer spot.

"That skinny little fuck," TL said, shaking his head. "He knows what I'm gonna do. If he's smarter than he acts, he's gonna disappear."

"He knows he fucked up, TL. Says he wants to make it up to you."

"I don't know how that motherfucking home-slice is gonna do that, except to take his beating. I got a rep out here to take care of, Axe." TL smiled at me as if it were plain and simple.

I burned some time by pulling out my pack of cigarettes. "Smoke?"

"Sure, man," he said, taking one. "Look, Axe. Word on the street is that he made a fool of me. I can't let that slide. Dude must've been high as a kite to make that kind of move."

"Everybody screws up sometime, TL. You got to do what you think is right for you. I'm just saying that there's a way to solve this without Swaggert landing in the river."

He lit the cigarette and blew the smoke out his nostrils. "I already know the solution."

"That's what I'm talking about. I don't want to see you get into any trouble for something you didn't start."

"What kind of trouble you talking about? Won't take me but a couple minutes to haul his ass out to the middle of the bridge and toss him in. Hope the motherfucker knows how to swim. Don't want to kill him, just teach him."

We smoked for a minute, quiet. He stared at the rain, coming in torrents now.

"How's your kids doing, TL?"

He turned and looked at me. "What's that got to do with this?"

"Just wondering. Listen," I said, pausing, thinking. "I heard something you might want to know. Could impact things out here."

He took a drag on his cigarette and looked over my head at the traffic slogging through the wet street. A few months ago, I'd been sitting with him in Horseshoe Park when his girlfriend showed up. With his two kids, a six year-old girl and a four year-old boy he called little TL. In their presence, Big TL had transformed from a street beast to a proud father. While he played with them I spoke to the young woman. She was raising them and working at the same time in a community health center as a nurse. They had met in high school, his first year in the States. She ended up going to community college and TL worked at a moving company. A year ago something happened between them. He had taken off, and hooked up with his gang and gone back to the only business he knew. He gave her money to support the kids. A lot, she'd said. She surprised me, not because she went for someone like him, or because she was a natural blond but because she had no fear whatsoever of TL.

"Alright," he said. "What you got?"

"You know Dudley, right? The street cop who works the beat around Kenmore Square?"

He nodded.

"I know for a fact," I said, which I didn't, "that they're planning on doing a sweep of this area soon. They know there's a lot of drug action here. I shouldn't even be telling you this, but they've put more undercover cops out here. Dudley told me if he finds you with so much as a joint, he's going to lock you up. As ridiculous as that is, it's the way things are. If you're still hoping to get back with your kids, and your woman, doing time in jail isn't going to help." I paused.

"So?"

"They're also making a big effort to stop violence on the street. They find you with anything..." I stopped. "Listen, you might want to move whatever you have, is what I'm saying. They're going to be searching people's camps. And if you end up whaling on Swaggert, they could get you on assault. Especially this close to B.U. When Ricky Monroe was knifed last month under the bridge..."

"I had nothing to do with that."

"I believe you. But Dudley has his suspicions," I said, carefully. "They'd like to connect it to somebody. Assaulting Swaggert could give them a reason to try."

TL smiled and shook his head at me.

"That's all you got?"

"I know, it isn't much. But maybe it's enough. They nail you for throwing Swaggert in the river..." A police cruiser with its siren wailing sped past us, TL stood with his arms crossed, watching it until it turned on Mass Ave. "You know, TL, if you end up in jail over a fight like this, your kids lose, too."

"Police got nothing on me," he said.

I tried my last card. "Swaggert's already scared shitless, man. All you have to do is walk up to him and he's going to get down on his knees and kiss your feet. Your rep is safe. Shows you don't even need to use your fists. Like I said, getting into it with him only puts you at risk. You're too smart for that, TL."

It was pretty weak, but I didn't know what else to do than to appeal to what mattered to him. For a moment, he watched the rain fall and stayed silent. It gave me time to wonder what the hell I was doing. TL gave me a gangster frown and then clapped his arm around my shoulder again, laughing.

"I know what you're doing," he said. "And I appreciate the concern. Especially about my kids. And the heads-up about the cops. Tell you what I'm gonna do. I'm gonna have a little talk with Swaggert, like you say. And if that motherfucker gets down on his knees in front of me, in front of his own gang of punks, and kisses my boots, then I'll let it go. But if he ever fucks with me again," his smile widened, "I'm gonna bury his ass."

"You know what, TL?"

"What?"

"You should get a job working with teenagers. You'd scare them straight. And get paid clean money for it."

He laughed quietly, his arm shaking me. "You're good, Axe. I don't believe a word of what you saying, but I hear what you meaning. Shit, I ain't heard no white boy talk shit like you and make it shine, except maybe that rapper from *8 Mile* in Detroit."

I had to laugh. "I don't have much of a rap, TL. But I am serious. You've got two beautiful kids, not to mention a beautiful woman."

I'd said it all, and probably too much, by the glare he gave me when I mentioned his woman. Then he broke out in a big smile, playing with me again.

"Don't you worry, Axe. You tell Swaggert I be looking for him. And when he sees me, he better know how to kneel."

"I'll tell him. Thanks, TL."

He pulled his arm away, and we faced each other. The big man looked down at me, curiously, shaking his head and then smiling. "Why you do this shit, man? This outreach stuff."

"I ask myself the same question sometimes."

He just laughed. "Alright, man. We're cool."

"Hey," I said before he left. "What's the TL stand for?"

He put his hand over his heart and looked upward. "My momma named me Terrence Lloyd," he said. "But she always called me True Love." He lowered his gaze to meet mine. "Now don't you be saying nothing about that out here, alright?"

"You got my word."

I watched him saunter slowly back to the wall. The part about Dudley was half-true. They were going to sweep the area, but mostly to run off some guys who'd moved in a few months ago under one of the bridges. Their camp had couches and tables. They were getting too comfortable.

I turned and walked through the rain to Kenmore Square.

In the B.U. bookstore, I flipped through magazines and dried off. When my phone rang, I didn't recognize the number.

"Hi Axel." It was a young woman's voice. "I don't know if you remember me, but we met in the Blue Hills."

I set the magazine back on the rack. "Holiday Golightly. Sure, I remember. With the two beasts."

She laughed. "I hope you don't mind, I called your office and Bette gave me your cell phone number."

"Oh, that's alright. So, you still camping?"

"That's what I'm calling you about."

Chapter 12

June 15, 2004

Easttree stopped the car across from St. Cecilia's park. We sat a few minutes without talking. Maybe he was changing his mind, but it had been his idea in the first place. He stared out the window for another minute while I listened to some voice messages on my phone. Finally, he opened his door. I flipped the cell shut and stepped out to the sidewalk. There was the statue of the Virgin, standing eternally with the same gracious smile. No voices came from behind her today.

"Well, it's lock and load time," I said. "You ready to do this?"

"No," Easttree said. "Duck and run is how I feel. But let's go before I change my mind."

Outside Bukowski's, he hesitated once more. When a customer pushed open the door to exit and held it for him, he let out a deep breath and nodded at me, and then walked in. I followed. She was standing at the far end of the bar, talking on the phone and playing with her hair. It was a symbolic thing Tree wanted to do, perhaps not even necessary. I knew from Wendy that her sister hadn't taken it personal that he'd never called her back. But he wanted to clear the air. It was only a few weeks since that night, but it had changed Easttree's life.

"Good luck," I offered. He advanced down the bar as she noticed him, giving him a cool stare that was hard to read. She ended her call and stuck her phone in her back pocket. Her expression shifted to a pout, and then her lips formed into a kiss. She had on a white tank-top that fit well. I felt bad for him. A tiny smile had formed at the corner of her lips. He stopped across the bar from her. Her mouth was slightly open and the silver stud glistened on her tongue. I headed for a table. As I passed them I heard her say, "So, how's things, stranger?"

I sat down. For a moment, she stared at him without saying anything more. Then she put her hands on the bar and raised herself up, coming half-way across it. Before he could react, she pulled him by his shirt toward her and kissed him. She held on to him for a long moment.

Easttree raised his hands and gently removed hers from his shoulders, placing them on the bar. I looked away, as Wendy came out of the kitchen. She sat down across from me. "Poor Easttree," she said, smiling. "He's a nice guy."

"He's a great guy," I said. "Even great guys make mistakes."

She looked at me cautiously. "Mistake?"

"He's married."

"Don't say it," she said. "You're married, too, I suppose. Separated. Just didn't want to tell me."

"I sense a sisterly-bond thing at work here," I said. "And if you forgot already, you talked about your kids last night until I finally had to shut you up."

She put her mouth next to my ear, her breath warm and smelling of strawberry lip gloss. "That was play and you know it," she said. "To tell you the truth, Axel, I never expected anything from you, not really." This was from out of the blue. Maybe they were in cahoots, and were going to dump both of us simultaneously before Tree had a chance to clear things up.

Easttree came over and sat down. Wendy gave him a look between the evil eye and a flirtatious killer smile. Things were happening outside my control, I sensed. She stood up and turned her eyes to me. I saw the story before she could say it.

"We'll talk," she said, and crossed her arms under her breasts. Teasing me before she turned away. After a few steps, she stopped and looked back over her shoulder. As if to burn her image into my brain. Then she sashayed slowly down to the other end of the bar.

"What was that about?" Easttree said.

"I don't know," I said. "How about with you? Sabrina take it alright?"

He snorted. "She beat me to the punch," he said. "Told me no worries, it was no big thing. That she wouldn't stalk me. 'Course, she did that same move, crossed her arms and pushed her tits at me, and added, 'Unless you want me to'. With that smile. Jesus."

"Sisters," I said.

"I don't think I'll be able to come in here anymore."

"She didn't seem upset," I said.

"No. She was cool." He shook his head. "Damn. She looks better now than the other night."

"Keep your focus, man. Rebecca's back, right?"

"Yeah," he said. "Yeah."

We ordered dollar burgers from Wendy, who didn't stick around to talk this time. While we waited for our food, I reminded him that he was doing the right thing, that it's better when you level with people. Easttree just nodded. I was wondering if the axe was coming down for me, and realized that I really wasn't concerned.

I read out loud from my notes as Easttree listened, keeping his eyes on the television screen so he wouldn't be tempted to look toward the bar. "OK. Sixty-something white male, little over five feet tall, wears thick glasses held together by duct tape, long white hair, high pitched voice, wild, whacky eyebrows..."

"Whacky eyebrows?"

"Yeah, it's a defining characteristic. Just listen. First spotted a week ago in Copley Plaza, with a full backpack and sleeping bag. Guarded speech, psychotic content, gives only vague details of his situation, other than that he was camping out behind his house, and..."

"Here you go," Wendy said, setting the plates on the table. "Burgers and fries, medium for you, Axel. And well-done for you, right?" She shot Easttree a false smile.

"That's right," Easttree said.

"I didn't know you were a burnt-meat kind of guy," I said, when she left.

"Today I am." Easttree looked up at the television again.

"Animals, Tree. We're just advanced animals trying to survive, all of us looking for warmth wherever we can find it. And when a man has something special like that in the palms of his hands, it isn't easy to say no." I pushed my notebook to the side and picked up the burger. "Hey. So, really, how's everything at home?"

"We're working it out."

"And?"

"Slow going. Stopped drinking."

"That's always good."

"I'm not sure I can eat this thing." He poked at the blackened burger with his fork, then lifted it to his mouth and took a bite. "Do you think it's poisoned?"

I laughed. "I've known worse stunts than that pulled by rejected lovers. I think she really liked you, man, but she's no fool. She's young and having fun. She's not going to hold a grudge. A burnt burger is kind of funny, though, if you think about it."

Easttree shook his head and started eating. We didn't talk, both of us watching the sports news until we were done. He ate all of it, and wiped up the last remnants of the mashed potatoes, leaving the plate clean. "That'll show her," he said.

Wendy took our plates, and asked if we wanted coffee.

"As long as it's fresh," I said. She spun away and returned a few minutes later with two mugs.

"So," I said, "this guy we're looking for is living at the end of a dirt-lined alleyway that runs between the backyards of two brownstones. In the South End, just off of Washington Street. High rent district. A woman living in the building noticed him, and called our office to see if we could do something. I checked it out, but he wasn't there. He's pretty much invisible from the street. Even has a hidden door that leads into the alley. I had a hard time finding it."

"It's him?" Easttree said.

"I'm pretty sure it's the same guy, from her description of him. Short older guy with glasses and white hair. She saw him once in front of her building on the sidewalk. She even noticed the whacky eyebrows. See? It's all in the details, Tree."

Easttree smiled genuinely, for the first time in a long time. "You said that he's been telling you he's camping out behind 'his' house?"

"That's what he said. I've only talked to him a few times. Said he was camping out in the woods behind his house in Milton, and then something happened. I'm thinking maybe he lived there at one point. Told me someone invaded it."

"Did he elaborate?"

"No. That's how he put it. Anyway, now's he in Back Bay. He doesn't have any dirt on him. No record in the shelter, nobody from the department of mental health recognizes the description, none of the staff at the Wilder know him. All I've got is his first name, Pete. He talks about replaced body parts, he-she's, she-he's, implants that can track his movements, all that. And whoever invaded his house even commandeered the air rights above it – which is illegal, did you know?"

"The air rights, huh? Never heard that one."

"Me neither. You want more coffee?"

"I think that would be pushing our luck." He looked toward the bar.

"Let's go. I'll pay and meet you outside, if you want."

Easttree put some money on the table and stood up. I went and paid. Sabrina took my money and large tip. "It's alright, Axel. No big thing. As far as I'm concerned, you can both still come in and eat anytime."

"Gee, thanks," I said.

"Jesus," Easttree said as we walked up Boylston. "If I were only twenty-five again."

"By the way, well done."

"Funny."

"Sabrina thinks you're a class act."

"Bullshit."

"I think she appreciated your honesty."

People were hurrying along the sidewalk because of the storm clouds. A light rain was already coming down. By the time we reached the library, it had started to pour. Inside the front entrance, we dried off and watched the rain fall. Irene spotted us and came hustling over from the information desk.

"Hi, Axel, hey Tree," she said. "If you're looking for that young kid, the one dressed all in black, he was just here. But he left right before the rain started."

"Bad timing. He say anything to you yet?"

"Not a word. I've been saying hi to him, even offered him a sandwich from the café, but he refused it. Maybe he just doesn't speak."

"Is that the young man you told me about, Axel?" Easttree said.

"Code name The Silent One. Another excellent distinguishing characteristic to identify the nameless."

"So this Silent One won't say word one?"

"Zip," Irene said. "Not even a sound, come to think of it. You know how a lot of the kids just grunt their answers at you."

"Uh," I said.

"Like that," she laughed.

"And what about Pete? The little old guy with the backpack? Has he been in today?"

"Earlier. Saw him leave about an hour ago."

We thanked her and walked from the new section of the library through the outdoor courtyard, pausing to study the statue in the fountain, of the mother holding her child.

"That one's my favorite," I said.

"I still like the Virgin at St. Cecilia's," Easttree said.

"But look at that figure. It doesn't compare."

"She's too young for you."

"That's what I want, Tree. A young woman full of joy. I might even think about having kids then."

"What about Wendy? She's young."

"Yeah, she is. But I don't think she's the one. Too dark. That's why she's a poet, I guess. Plus, I read her today. I think she's ready to move on."

We left the courtyard and exited from the original entrance, facing Copley Plaza. The rain had lightened up, but the skies were still dark.

"It's about ten minutes from here," I said. "Maybe he went back to his spot. You want to check it out? You should see his set-up anyway, for your professional enhancement as a clinician."

"Just as long as we don't find another dead body."

"Don't jinx us, man. You know there's no guarantees in this business, Tree."

We found the side street where Pete lived just as the rain began to let loose again. I led us to the tall wooden fence that separated the cobblestone sidewalk from the backyards of the brownstones. "Watch this." I took hold of the small wire that stuck out between a crack in the fence, and pulled it until I heard a click. "*Voilà*. Welcome to the other side."

The door creaked open on rusty hinges, revealing a short set of stairs that led to a narrow path of wet grass and mud that ran about a hundred feet in, before stopping at a concrete wall. "There it is." I stepped down the wooden stairs. At the far wall, stretched between two fences, hung a blue tarp. A clear plastic sheet spread across the opening, flapping in the wind. "Let's check it out."

"Lead the way," Easttree said. A series of planks ran down the middle of the path. We stepped carefully from one to the next, past the small, empty backyards of the brownstones. I glanced toward a lit window in one of the basement units, and saw a man sitting at a kitchen table in a t-shirt and shorts, working on a laptop. He watched us for a moment before going back to his computer.

At the end of the path, I turned around. "I don't see anybody, unless he's lying down under those blankets and sleeping bag. It's hard to tell. Hey, Pete! Are you here?"

There was no answer. The sleeping bag lay on top of a layer of blankets, with cardboard and another tarp underneath. The clear plastic shower curtain served as the entrance. The blue tarp overhead had been tightly secured by rope to the tops of the opposing fence-posts. Inside the makeshift tent were a few bags stuffed with canned food and clothing, and there were bags of newspapers stacked along the back wall.

"Nice, huh?" I said. "Dry as a bone in there, too. When you meet this guy, you're going to think he must be somebody's eccentric grandfather."

"Don't even want to think about my grandfather living like this," Easttree said, glancing up at the wall behind the blue tarp. "That would be a good wall to climb."

"You been climbing lately?"

"I've been climbing alright. Out of a deep hole."

"I meant your rock-climbing wall."

"Every night."

"At night?"

"I have the lights out back. Part of my training."

"Nice."

"You should try it sometime," Easttree said.

"Someday. Come on, let's get out of this rain. Sorry for bringing you all the way out here for nothing."

"It's never for nothing."

As we navigated our way along the planks, the man from the condo came out, wearing a long yellow raincoat. He waved and walked out to meet us.

"You looking for the little guy?" the man said, peering at us from under his hood. "Kind of looks like a hobbit?"

"We are," I said. "Know him?"

The man studied us for a moment. "Mind if I ask what you want with him?"

"Not at all. Name's Axel Hazzard, this here is Ken Easttree. I work for the Evergreen Shelter."

"Social workers?"

"Good guess," Easttree said, extending his hand to the man. He reached over the fence and shook both of ours.

"I'm glad somebody's checking up on him." The man relaxed. "Guy seems too old for this kind of thing."

"Have you seen him today?" I asked.

"I saw him early this morning. He's been set up here for a couple weeks. Doesn't seem to bother anybody, but still. Can't have somebody using your backyard for a bathroom, know what I mean?"

"Yeah," Easttree said. "We'd like to get to know him. See if we can figure out a better arrangement for him than this."

"I talked to him once. Guy doesn't make a lot of sense, but he's likable enough."

I closed the wooden door behind us as we left the alley. "Well, we didn't learn much there, other than we know for sure it's his spot. How many hobbits can there be on the street? Want to grab a coffee?"

"Sounds good."

There was a café nearby on Washington Street and we sat at a table next to the windows, watching the rain. I listened to some messages on my phone, while Easttree called Rebecca. The waitress brought us coffee.

"You're not going to believe this one," I said.

"What?"

"A message from Underwood, about this girl we met last winter. I told you about that time we went on this wild goose chase in the Blue Hills, right. Well, she called me last week."

"And?"

"She wanted to know if I knew any cheap places to rent."

"You didn't."

I kept looking at the rain. "I did."

"Is she homeless?"

"Not like the ones we're working with. More like Thoreau, Walden, you know."

Easttree gave me a puzzled look.

"She's a student at UMass," I said. "Her folks lost their house and had to move out of the Boston area. She wanted to finish her degree here. Thing is, she actually seemed to enjoy camping out."

"During that cold spell?"

"Like Thoreau."

"Oh, com'on. You're pulling my leg."

"No, I'm telling you straight, man. At first, I thought she was in trouble of some kind."

"What's her name?"

I smiled. "Calls herself Holiday Golightly."

"I read that one. A literary type?"

"Seemed to be. When we told her who we were, why we were there, and asked her if she needed shelter, she laughed and called us Rescue Rangers. She said homeless people should live somewhere beautiful, out in nature. Not in shelters."

"Got a point there. So what did you do?"

"Already did it. That was Underwood on my message, saying that she's moving in to his attic studio. I guess I can put it on our stats as a 'housing placement'."

"How many you got so far?"

"Housing placements? Are you kidding me?"

"That bad?"

"Shit, man, I think two, maybe three. That's the whole outreach team I'm talking about."

"I guess you do need to fatten the stat sheet a little."

I stared at the rain, beginning to let up again. "What do you think of Pete's camp site?"

"I'd say the hobbit is up against the wall."

"I thought the same thing."

"Sorry, bad joke. At least he knows how to use a tarp. Does he have any medical issues?"

"He has a nasty looking sore on one of his hands. Talks about having implants in his body."

"Is he digging at them?"

"Could be."

The waitress came and filled our coffee mugs again. She was cute, and Easttree gave me a look after she left. "They're everywhere," he said. "Well, if the hobbit is digging into his body like that, it could be enough to have him evaluated."

"I need to get a better look at it."

"Doesn't sound good, either way. When you find him, give me a call. I'll try to get out here and meet him."

Easttree put his notebook and phone in his jacket pocket and stood up.

"I gotta roll, man. I'm taking the rest of the afternoon off. A little quality time at home with the woman."

He dropped a five dollar bill on the table. I picked it up and handed it back to him. "On me, Tree. Buy Rebecca some flowers."

Easttree smiled. "Hey, by the way. I never really thanked you for keeping me off the wall last weekend."

"That's what friends are for, bro."

"God, I was wasted. Guess I needed to blow it out, good, before reining in the demons."

"I know what you mean. Say hi to the kids and wife."

I left the café and walked toward Back Bay Station in the light rain, pulling my hood over my head. On Clarendon Street, next to the Hard Rock Café, I saw Howard Bingham stemming at his usual spot near the restaurant's entrance. I crossed the street and walked up to him.

"Hey Axel, my man! What's going on?" Howard said. "Listen, brother, you gotta help me out with Jack! He won't listen to me anymore, won't listen to anybody! It's your job, man!"

Howard Bingham had a history of histrionics. His method of stemming was charming people with his passionate speeches. He sincerely wanted to get off the street. He sincerely wanted to help other street people. He sincerely was willing to work, if only he could find a job. Sometimes people hired him, too, he'd told me, to paint their apartments, clean out basements, yard work. I'd noticed that the people who stopped and talked to him usually gave him a few bucks. Bingham was in his early fifties, a short, heavy-set guy. He claimed to have a couple of kids he still had to keep an eye on. One was in a psychiatric group-home and he was the guardian. The other was a troubled kid still living with his ex-wife. I never knew what to believe.

"It's my job alright, Howard."

I sat on the wall next to him and listened for the next ten minutes to the latest story of Jack Irons, father of Jimmie Irons. Jack suffered from some kind of mental illness that nobody was able to diagnose, compounded by his alcoholism.

"He's spent his whole check drinking and eating and now he's trying to hit me up for money! I can't do it, Axel! I love the guy, but I can't keep supporting that!"

"When are you going to give it up, Howard?"

"Give it up? What, give up on Jack? Is that your advice? What Jack needs is the right kind of talk from the right kind of person! Someone to listen to him and develop his trust, and work with him. And get him into housing. Am I right?"

People passing us gave us a quick look and kept going.

"Howard, you know better than I do that Jack likes to spend his monthly social security on other things than housing. He's been doing it for how long? Years, right? He would qualify for housing, but every time I talk to him about it, he says he doesn't want to go through the process. Part of me can't blame him if he wants to spend his money as he likes. Did you ever consider that maybe he needs the street?"

"Needs the street? Needs the street? Are you crazy? Nobody needs the street! Jesus, Axel, you call yourself an outreach worker? I could do a better job than that. At least I'm trying, aren't I? You know how Jack is, he won't listen to anybody unless they have money and he's after it. Listen to this."

He lowered his voice and looked up and down the sidewalk.

"He goes over to Southie with those two fucking goons, right, Dickey what's his name and his brother, Tommy, to use the bathhouse. Two weeks ago, right. They said they had money to go drinking up at the L-Street Tavern afterwards, for cheap beers and whiskey. So Jack says alright. He'd just cashed his check, and they knew it. So, like the big old dummy he is, Jack goes along with these clowns, these good for nothing scumbags!" He spit on the sidewalk. "Over to the bathhouse. And while he's in the sauna or the steam bath, I don't know which, what do you think happens?"

Howard stared at me, waiting for me to say something. I shook my head.

"That's right! They steal all his money out of his locker. How do you like that? Then Jack comes to me with his sob story, 'Oh, Howard, you have to help me!' All that shit, excuse my language. And on top of that, he wants me to buy him some booze! Give him twenty bucks. I told him no. I said, listen here, Jack, I'll buy you something to eat, but that's it. No booze. You have to wait until you have your own money for that. So he says OK, and we go to Pizzeria Uno, right? We sit down and order the large pizza special, and I go to use the bathroom. When I get back, Jack's ordered drinks. What do you think he ordered?"

"It wasn't a Shirley Temple."

"You're damn right it wasn't! He ordered Johnny Walker. Not just one, but two. I told him to get the hell out, that I wasn't paying for him to drink." Howard paused to catch his breath. "He got pissed off at me and started yelling. That's right. Of course they called the police. He drank those two shots in about three seconds and then left before the cops arrived. I had to explain it to them, and they almost took me in! I had to pay for the whole damn thing, fifteen bucks for the pizza, the same for his booze. No, I'm not helping him out anymore with money."

Howard stopped talking as a woman put a five dollar bill in his hand. He lowered his voice, smiled, and they talked about the next church dinner. The woman said she might have a job for him, from one of the church patrons. Howard thanked her profusely, blessing her, taking her hand as she said goodbye. Then as he slipped the money into his coat pocket, he grinned at me.

"See, I have the gift," he said. "Now back to Jack. I should give up, but sometimes I think it's my fate, Axel. I can't just let the guy starve. So I buy bread and meat and make sandwiches and give him three each day, and he gets stuff from the soup kitchens. When his next check comes, he'll lose that one too before he can pay me back. "

"You're a good man, Howard."

"I should be doing your job. I'd get these people some help."

I watched Howard work the crowd for a while, trading talk with a few of his regular donors about the Red Sox. Howard had charisma and a good word for everybody. I shook his hand and told him to keep up the good work.

I wandered toward Copley Plaza, saw it was empty and kept on going down Clarendon Street. The alley that runs off Clarendon, parallel to Boylston Street, was named Rat Alley by the homeless. It stretches from the Public Gardens at Arlington Street to the fire station on Hereford Street, a long eight blocks between wealthy townhouses, expensive stores, and the backs of restaurants. In the winter, the wind cut through it like ice picks. In the summer, it was a popular hangout. But with the rain like it was today, it usually emptied out and was about as private a place as you could find. I cut up Rat Alley off Exeter and felt for the matchbox in my pocket. I was looking for privacy.

A half-block in, I saw the Ninja's bike parked up against one of the restaurant dumpsters. A chain was wrapped around it, securing it to a fire-escape ladder. A pair of boots sat next to the bike, partially covered by a blanket. No sign of the Ninja himself. I walked on down the alley, pulled out the matchbox and opened it.

"Hey, Axel."

The voice came from a small, recessed parking spot. I closed the matchbox and put it in my pocket. Phil Carter raised his bottle toward me and waved me over. His partner, Jimmy Jay, sat next to him on a milk crate. They had a deal with the condo owners, guarding the cars from other alley rats. They even kept the place tidy.

Phil was a fifty-year-old depressed alcoholic with the kind of face you see in the movies, playing the sad sack sitting alone at the end of the bar. One of those guys who's always frowning. I had tried to picture him in the real world, if he were pulled off the street and forced to dry out long enough to do something. But I never could. He nursed a quart bottle of beer and scowled at me.

"You hear what happened?" he said in his raspy voice.

"Not yet. Tell me, Phil. I could use a good story."

"Well, now you got one." For a split second, he almost grinned. "They came and took the Ninja last night."

I didn't say anything, just nodded my head.

"JJ said he saw the whole goddamn thing," he went on. "It was just like the Ninja said. Someday they would come and get him."

I looked from Phil to Jimmy. "Who came and took the Ninja?"

Jimmy straightened up and shook his head. He was younger than Phil by twenty years, and preferred to drink Listerine. When he didn't say anything right away, Phil blurted out, "They just came, a bunch of 'em, and they were…"

"You didn't see shit," Jimmy finally said.

"OK, smart-ass, you tell it."

Jimmy Jay poked Phil in the side and winked at me. "Take it easy, old timer." Phil pushed Jimmy's arm away and lifted his bottle.

"I wouldn't have seen anything," Jimmy said, "except for I had to get up and take a piss in the middle of the night."

"Get a drink, more like," Phil muttered.

"You gonna let me talk or what?"

"Go on then."

Jimmy ran a hand across his sunburned face and continued. "They were quiet as mice. I never would've heard nothing, but after I got up to 'relieve' myself," he shot a look at Phil, who rolled his eyes, "I looked over my shoulder, like something was telling me I had company, right? And there they was, all standing around his tent. Looked like goddamned demons if you ask me. Spooky as hell…"

"Get on with it," Phil muttered.

I looked at Phil and put a finger across my lips. He frowned, and hoisted his bottle.

"Six of 'em, I even counted them all," Jimmy said. "A half-dozen goblins, it seemed, all wearing these dark hooded robes. Maybe they were, like, monks or something. So I was standing there, with my patriot missile in my hand, frozen in mid-launch…"

"Jesus Christ, JJ, tell the story!" Phil sputtered, beer dribbling down his chin.

"So I stuffed my rocket back in my pants, right, and stood as still as a bird. Minutes went by, I don't know how long, my legs were shaking and I still had to piss. They were conversating about something, I couldn't make out any of it. And then the Ninja came out of his tent. Went through his whole damn ritual, bowing to the east and the west like he always does. And just when I thought I was going to bust a main line, they all started walking down the alley, and he just walked off with them. Just like that. All quiet-like. Haven't seen him since."

I looked back and forth from Jimmy to Phil, to see if they were joking. Phil was shaking his head, like he didn't buy it. Jimmy Jay picked up his bottle and took a drink.

"I'm not shittin' ya, Axel," he said. "They fucking came just like the Ninja was saying all along! That someday they were going to need him back."

"Aw, get the fuck outta here!" Phil erupted. "I think you were shit-faced and hallucinating."

Jimmy turned and barked, "You were asleep! I saw what I saw, man. It was like I said, a bunch of demons came and took him. And the Ninja just walked away with them!"

The Ninja. Self-proclaimed billionaire, songwriter, rock star, martial artist, licensed to kill. He showed up last summer riding a bike, all geared out with camping equipment. He was a loner, at first. Fairly young, late twenties. His proclamation of his 'license to kill' was the red flag. His right as a ninja, he'd told me. I pegged him as a bipolar with schizoid qualities thrown in, and too many episodes of *Samurai Jack*.

"Gone, just like that?" I said.

"I'm telling ya the goddamn truth," Jimmy said. "On my mother's grave. I thought he was talking shit all the time, about that ninja training and those billions of dollars, and everything else, and then, bingo, they come and get him!"

"What do you think, Axel?" Phil looked up.

"Could be," I said. "I saw some of his Ninja moves. But who knows."

Phil snorted but didn't say anything. He was eyeing the Ninja's tent and bicycle.

The Ninja had told me many stories. Like the time he was giving a concert with his band, the Black Devil Ninjas, in California, and the authorities had to shut down the whole show because girls were rioting and jumping on stage. Clawing at his clothes, he said. Like how his father was a multibillionaire, and he himself had a billion stashed in the bank on Clarendon Street. Like how he'd almost killed a girl when she didn't give him a light for his cigarette, but he'd restrained himself.

STREET LOGIC

I sat down on an empty milk-crate Phil pushed toward me. The rain had stopped again. Somehow, the Ninja's being taken by some order of robe-wearing members of a 'sect of lunatics', as Phil proceeded to call them, didn't sit well with either of the two Rat Alley stalwarts. Jimmy produced a cheap pack of cigars from inside his jacket and spent several minutes working to get one lighted.

"Phil," I said. "What do you know about this?"

Phil grunted. "Ninja, my ass." Jimmy had the cigar going and grinned at me through the smoke, and then nodded at Phil. Phil was staring straight ahead and taking short drinks from a bottle of vodka now.

"Aw, com'on, Phil. Tell Axel what you saw."

A look of irritation passed across Phil's heavily lined face.

"Oh, what the hell," Phil growled. "But give me a minute to group my thoughts."

Phil took another pull on the vodka, then capped it and straightened his back against the wall, closing his eyes.

Jimmy stood up and muttered, "Oh, sweet Jesus, here he goes. His meditational trance, or whatever." He walked over to the Ninja's camp, puffing away on his cigar. There were pieces of an old tent, a few large garbage bags, and a tarp stretched out under a fire escape.

"Alright," Phil began. "I saw them, too. But it wasn't last night."

He kept his eyes closed as he spoke. Jimmy was kicking something around behind the tent.

"Three nights ago," Phil started, "they came and spoke to him. JJ of course was passed out like a piece of wood. I was the one taking a piss in the middle of the night. I was just zipping up when I heard a low voice. I thought it was JJ at first, then I recognized it was the Ninja. I figured he was talking to himself like he sometimes does, right? I snuck up a little closer, over there by the dumpster. Then I'll be damned, but the wind blew open the front of his tent, and I saw him sitting in there with a hood on, a candle burning, and another guy with a hood. Just the two of them. They kept on talking for a while but I couldn't make out anything they were saying. Then, you know what happened? The headlights of the outreach van shone down the alley. And that hooded

153

guy was gone in an instant, took off in the other direction. I got some soup and coffee with the Ninja from the van, and afterwards we stayed up the whole night until dawn, drinking the rest of my vodka. All he said was that it was one of his brothers. And they wanted him to come back. I asked him why, and he said they needed him. Can you believe that shit?"

I didn't, but then again, these guys didn't usually make up stories like this. A gust of wind swept up the alley and a flapping noise came from the Ninja's tent. Jimmy stepped over and peered inside. He crouched down and whistled. "Check this out!" he said.

Jimmy held a playing card up to us. It was a game card with a picture of a green turtle on it. "Teenage mutant ninja turtles," he said. "Kid's stuff. There's cards all over the damn place, must be hundreds."

He started picking them up.

"Fucking mutant ninjas," Phil muttered.

The first time I met the Ninja was in the Commonwealth Avenue mall in March, three months ago. He was sitting cross-legged on a bench, in a meditation posture, with his hands on his knees, palms upward, eyes closed. He had a short, squat Buddha kind of shape. As I walked past him, he suddenly jumped to his feet.

"Got a cigarette?"

He planted himself squarely in front of me. I stepped back a foot. He countered by stepping toward me a foot.

"I might," I said. I moved back another foot, and when he tried to match my step, I went forward. He pulled back just before our noses would have hit. Then I stepped back and stood there, reached into my pocket and pulled out my pack. I shook a cigarette loose from the box and offered it to him.

He was close enough for me to smell his breath. Peppermint flavored, unusual for a street guy unless he was drinking flavored mouthwash. But it didn't have that antiseptic smell. His round face had been recently shaved, and his hair was shaved close to his skull. In his eyes, I could see a kind of euphoria going on. In one swift motion, he plucked the cigarette out of the box and stuck it between his straight white teeth. Evenly spaced and clean. Incredibly clean.

"Just kidding," he said, grinning. "I have some cigarettes. You want to try one of mine?"

He stepped closer, I stepped back. Boundary issues, evidently. If his features were a tad more one way or the other, the guy might have been considered handsome. But the nose was too small, bordering on a pug nose, and his tiny, round ears didn't fit his large face. Something was off center about the chin.

His hand shot out quickly with a pack of roll your own tobacco. "Smell this."

"Name's Axel," I said, thinking he would reply with his own.

He gripped my hand and performed a series of complicated handshake maneuvers that ended up in a soul-brother hand grip. But he didn't offer his name. He smiled again with those white teeth and opened the pouch. It was a clear, Ziploc bag, and the tobacco smelled rich, with a reddish tint to it. He rolled a fast, perfect cigarette and handed it to me. A specialty tobacco, he said. Only available in Harvard Square.

He lit his Zippo lighter, holding it out. I got the cigarette going, but kept the smoke in my mouth and exhaled through my nose, tasting it first. Pure tobacco. Then I stepped back and waved my hand in the smoke, a pretext to get a few feet away from the guy. He stepped forward anyway.

"Thanks," I said.

"No problem."

"Looks like you're on some kind of bike tour, with all that gear there?" I gestured at the new-looking mountain bike, and the packs, tent, and sleeping bag lying on the ground.

"Camping."

"Nice time of the year for it."

"Yeah it is." It sounded like a Maine accent. He started humming a tune, tapping out the rhythm on his bike seat. "Almost as nice as Cali is."

"Oh," I said. "You from out there?"

He shook his head. "But they kicked me out of the state, after that last show."

"Kicked you out of the state?"

"That's right. They can't handle me. The girls go nuts out there at my concerts. They jump up on stage and rip their shirts off, that kind of thing. And I'm just trying to entertain people, right? Hey, you want to hear my new song? I just finished composing it today."

There seemed to be no saying no. I considered making a quick getaway, saying I was late for something. But I wasn't, and a part of me wanted to see where this was going. "Sure."

"I wrote it for a level thirteen," he said, getting excited. "That's the highest octave possible. Do you know how high that is?"

"No, I can't say that I do."

He came closer and lowered his voice.

"The highest octave, Axel," he said, as if imparting ancient wisdom, "is a ten. Anything over ten, forget about it. Even the best singers have trouble hitting an eight or nine, let alone a ten. I wrote this song in a thirteen. I'm the only one who can sing it. Steven Tyler can't even touch this."

He showed his teeth again as he smiled, and then cleared his throat several times as he paced around in front of me. I sat on the bench and waited to see what a thirteen sounded like.

He sang it in soprano. At times he built it up to an extraordinarily high pitch, a piercing, sharp sound. The lyrics concerned a girlfriend who leaves her guy for another man. He sang with increasing emotion, his chest heaving at times, and when he finished, his voice achieving that trembling, fluttering sound that opera singers do, I felt that I'd witnessed a man possessed by something. He wiped his brow and sat down on the bench next to me, catching his breath.

"Did you hear that thirteen, man?"

"Oh yeah," I said. "Incredible."

The song wasn't that bad, and even in the high voice, he'd managed to pull it off.

"Nobody, I mean nobody, not even Michael when he was with the J-Five, has ever been able to reach that octave. Ever. I'm the only one who can reach it."

I could only nod.

"You ever heard of anyone singing a thirteen?"

"No. I never even heard of such a thing."

"Well, now you have," he grinned. "And there's more where that came from."

He stood back up and cleared his throat again, and gestured at me with his forefinger to wait and listen. Then he launched into an entire collection of songs that he introduced as his latest CD. They were fairly elaborate, emotional, a little crazy, but they were complete, finished songs.

I tried to get away after the third song, but he corralled me into listening to just one more. Then another, and then another. Finally, he finished with a number about his most recent ex-girlfriend. She had tattoos and piercings all over her body because an old boyfriend had forced her to get them. The Ninja's lyrics detailed the pain she endured in order to gain the man's love.

"What do you think?" he said, sitting down.

"Kind of sad, that last one. So what ever happened with the band?"

"Had to quit. The other guys in the band couldn't handle all the attention I was getting. Our last concert was shut down by the police because one girl jumped on stage and ripped her shirt off. It would have been alright, but all the others followed. The guys in the band were jealous. So I said to hell with that, I'm going solo."

I never learned his real name. The first couple of months, he stuck to himself, camping somewhere along the river at night. He wouldn't give me much information, other than his exploits in martial arts and rock n' roll. Never needed any of our services. After a few months, he settled down in Rat Alley, got to know the locals like Phil and Jimmy Jay, and began accepting food and blankets. Until last night, apparently.

I left Phil and Jimmy Jay still poking around the Ninja's tent and wandered up Rat Alley. The rain fell lightly. I didn't see any of the other regulars, most of them likely in the BPL or under cover somewhere else. It was three-thirty, and there was one more place I wanted to check out before calling it a day.

At Gloucester Street, I emerged and took a right, crossed Newbury, and down the stairs to Morrison's convenience store. The small, ground level courtyard had a hidden passageway that led behind the store to the larger alley. No wider than four feet, and maybe forty feet long, it was virtually invisible. I was looking for a guy who reportedly had set up camp in the recessed area under the fire escape.

Stepping over puddles, I reached the fire escape and saw that it was empty. The person must have moved on. From where I stood, nobody could see me. Seemed like the right place. And now it was quitting time. I removed the half-joint from the matchbox and lit it, watching the smoke rise. The soft sound of raindrops falling into puddles, the occasional car, the faint jazz music coming from an apartment. In the city, there aren't many places where no one can see you. You have to seek them out. This was one of the most private, right in the middle of the action of Newbury Street. I looked at my watch and saw it was four o'clock.

A slight scraping noise came from around the corner. I snuffed the joint out, put it back in the matchbox. Then I heard a deep cough. I stepped slowly out from my hiding spot and peeked down the tiny alley. Coming out from behind an air-conditioning unit was a man crawling on his hands and knees, coming out feet first, wearing what looked like a full-length black leather coat. He couldn't see me. I moved quietly out of the alley in the direction of Morisson's courtyard. When I reached the end and stepped around the corner, I heard a loud laugh. I waited in front of the store to see if he would come out.

A few minutes passed and he didn't appear. I ducked into Morrison's and asked the Indian man behind the counter if the man he'd called us about wore a long black coat. He confirmed it.

"Any name?" I asked him.

"No, just John."

158

"Friendly or...?"

He grunted. "Sometimes."

I went up the steps to Gloucester and walked half a block to the main alley, figuring I'd see him there. When I reached the edge of the apartment building and turned the corner, he stood in front of me. He was of medium height, but seemed double his size because of the coat. His beard, matted and long and hanging down to his chest, also gave him a sense of being larger than he was. He glared at me with one eye, his other one almost entirely closed, his face screwed up in a semi-grimace, semi-grin. "I smelled you out," he said, in a deep, scraping voice. When I didn't respond right away, he stepped closer. "You're the one smoking in the alley, aren't you?"

"Well, you got me," I said.

"Yeah, I smelled you out, alright," he said again. In a tone of voice that held an edge of desperation and aggression, he added, "You got any cigarettes?"

"Sure," I said. I gave him one and then lit it for him with my lighter. He stepped back and inhaled deeply. He wore leather pants and a leather vest as well. Some scuff marks covered the coat and part of the pants, but otherwise they looked new. I lit a cigarette for myself.

"Nice threads," I said.

He nodded his head rapidly, busy inhaling as much smoke as he could. "Genuine rawhide," he said, between puffs.

I took three more cigarettes out of the pack and handed them to him. His bad eye opened halfway. "Well, thanks," he said. "Mighty nice of you alright." His face relaxed and the fierceness was replaced with a likable grin.

"No problem. Sorry I disturbed you back there."

"Can't hear anything with the air conditioner running, but I can smell things. No sir, I can't blame a man for needing privacy. No sir."

"I guess so."

He finished the cigarette and lit the next one from the butt. Once he had it going, he shuffled around a little on his feet, staring at the sky, smoking furiously. Under his beard, I could see his face scowling again.

"Ain't nowhere safe," he grumbled. "Not with all that radar and high-tech surveillance they got. They're watching and listening to everything! I'm telling you, pal, you gotta watch yourself and be careful! They know where you are all the time." He winked with his good eye. "Even in that alley back there. I'm just telling you, that's all."

I nodded my head. I didn't want to get on his bad list, so I pulled out my pack of cigarettes and offered him the pack. "Take these, pardner. I have another."

His face lit up in a huge smile. "Well, that's mighty friendly of you. Mighty friendly, I must say. Not many friendly people out here, but I meet some. Thank you, I appreciate it." He looked to see how many were left in the pack, and then slipped it into his vest pocket.

"Name's Axel," I said, taking a chance and putting my hand out. He stared at it warily, then laughed, and gave it a quick shake.

"John," he said. He glanced around him, then repeated, "No, not many friendly people out here."

"Been around here long?"

The guarded look returned to his face. "Why do you want to know?"

"It's just that I'm out here on the street a lot, and I haven't seen you around before."

He eyed me closely with his good eye. "Got to be careful what you tell people these days," he said.

"That's the truth." The rain started falling harder, and I pulled my hood back on. "Well, listen pardner," I said. "I'm going to get out of this rain. You take care. Maybe I'll see you around."

His face turned up toward the sky as I started to move away.

"Wait a minute!" he said.

I stopped and turned back.

"There aren't many safe places left," he said. "Remember that. I'm just telling you, that's all."

"I will, John. Take it easy."

I walked back up Gloucester to Newbury and crossed the street. Turning around, I saw him standing in the same spot, looking toward the sky and the tops of the buildings. I followed his gaze to the towers of antennae.

STREET LOGIC

Chapter 13

July 2, 2004

It was a Friday night, before the long weekend. I sat on the outdoor deck over the garage, staring up through the tree tops, searching for stars. A few were visible. Inside, through the kitchen windows, Underwood was opening a bottle of wine. A string of year-round Christmas lights blinked behind him from the hallway. I kicked my feet up on the railing of the deck and lit a cigarette. Peering upward again, I saw the light from her room in the attic studio.

"Here we go," Paul said, opening the screen door. "Great night, good wine, new housemate to welcome. And the Red Sox are still hot." He carried a tray with three wine glasses and the bottle, and set them in the middle of the table.

"She's coming?" I said, looking at the third glass.

"Of course. I invite everybody when they move in. Only way to know someone. I've hardly seen her since she arrived, but this morning we talked for a while, and I told her she had to join us. She said she would."

He poured wine into two glasses and set the third in front of the empty chair next to me.

"How does she, uh, seem to you?"

"What do you mean?" he said. "Besides being gorgeous and friendly?"

"Well, she was living in the woods last I saw her. I only talked to her on the phone for about five minutes."

Paul laughed and raised his glass. We toasted the arrival of hot summer days. "And to all things beautiful," he added.

I glanced up at her window again and saw the light go off.

"I gave her the lowest rent I could," Paul said. "She seems sincere, responsible, a hard-working young woman doing the best she can with what she's got. And she's got a lot, pal. Smart, too. Knows her literature and music."

"Well, good," I said, raising my glass toward him. "For taking a chance. And giving her your rent special."

"Hey, we'll see. Don't forget, man, I gave you a good rent, too," he laughed.

"You better have. I helped your ass out a few times too, now, don't forget that, pal."

Underwood smiled. "I haven't."

We drank some wine, listening to the game on the radio. "What I was getting at, actually," I said, "was that not many people will brave it out like that, in winter, going to college every day. I mean, I can relate to living outside the mainstream, I had my years in various vans in the Keys. Remember that mini school bus all painted up?"

"Christ have fucking mercy, dude, how could I forget? What ever happened with that thing?"

"Donated to a junk-yard."

"What did you do with that awful collection of true-life short stories you wrote down there, about living with that chick in the bus…?"

We heard a noise from inside. Holiday was coming through the hallway, past the flashing Christmas lights. She saw us through the window and waved, moving with a light bounce in her step.

"What's up, guys?" She pushed the screen door open. "Great night, huh?" She kissed both of us on the cheek, her eyes bright, almost mischievous.

"Absolutely," Paul said. "We have to enjoy it while we can."

"That's for sure," she said, sitting in the chair beside me. "So, what were you guys talking about, before I interrupted you?"

Paul poured some wine into her glass. "You're not interrupting anything, don't worry. But we were talking about Axel's vagabond years," he said, winking at me. "Searching for the lost ideals of man."

"Are you serious?" Holiday said, amused. "A searcher? I thought they were almost an extinct species." She lifted her glass in the air. "To the searchers."

"I don't know if I'd want to be living in the Ancient Greeks' time myself," Paul said. "I'll take my gas heat, supermarkets, and junk food."

"Wouldn't you rather live in nature?" she said.

"This is as much nature as I need," he said, gesturing at the trees and sky. "Right next to the kitchen."

She laughed again, a spontaneous, playful laugh. Her hair, long and wavy and golden brown, hung loose over her shoulders. An almond smell came off her.

"Yeah, I know what you mean," she said. "Living in the woods was a trip, and I wouldn't trade that experience for anything. But I wouldn't want to do it again. Not unless I'm just camping for fun. But hey," she said, looking at me, "at least I got to meet you, and then Paul. Strange how things happen."

Her eyes were wide and alert, and alive. Fully alive. A smile played at the corners of her mouth as she drank from her glass.

"At least Thoreau had a little cabin," I said.

"Now that's the way to do it," Holiday said. "Next time."

We drank the first bottle slowly, talking about various camping adventures. I told one about nearly falling off a cliff in Chaco Canyon as the Navajo spirits chased me and an old traveling mate of mine, Eddie Rivers.

"It was almost dark, and we were running through the high desert toward these cliffs, where the path down to the parking lot was. I couldn't see Eddie anymore, I could only hear him scrabbling through the rocks ahead of me. Suddenly, for some reason, I just stopped. I lit a cigarette, and from the light of the match, I realized that I was two feet away from a fifty foot drop-off."

"The great spirit stopped you," Paul said.

"And just in time," Holiday said.

"Something did, for sure. I was right on the edge of that damn cliff."

"In more ways than one," Paul laughed. He remembered that Eddie and I had been high on peyote at the time.

Paul told the story about the night he spent in the White Mountains, with only a poncho, trapped by a sudden snowstorm. He'd survived because he knew the mountain weather could change fast. Instead of panicking like a lot of hikers do, and trying to keep going, he'd found a place among some boulders and waited it out.

"It was being able to build a fire that saved me, I think," he said. "I had just enough time to get some wood and find that rock shelter. But an entire winter in the Blue Hills? You've outdone both of us."

"It wasn't that risky," she said.

"I'm going to get another bottle." Paul got up. "To drink to survival."

Holiday shifted in her chair and faced me. She was easy to look at.

"So," she said. "Here we are. Funny how things work out. You and your Rescue Rangers were so nice, coming out there in the snow, in all that cold, seeing if I wanted shelter. And now I have it. Thanks to you."

I took a drink of wine and found myself staring. "I'm glad you survived it."

She went on, her voice more serious. "I remember your question, before you left. About my father. Got me thinking."

I sat back, took another sip of wine. "Well, you know, I didn't mean to be prying. I guess that I was just concerned that maybe you were on the run from somebody."

"That's OK," she said. "I just, well, I guess I was kind of surprised, that somebody would care enough to ask a personal question like that. Not that you should have been in my tent, you know," she added, with a smile.

"I apologize for that. And as I recall, your book was open, I couldn't miss it, right there, under your hanging socks and…"

She laughed again, and waved a finger in my face. "OK, OK. I know what you were really looking at in my tent."

"I was impressed with your book collection," I said.

"Uh-huh," she said. "I'll bet."

"Speaking of books," I said, shifting in my seat. "How's things at UMass?"

"I'm taking a lot of different classes," she said. "Next year, I'll focus on my major, archaeology. But now I'm into philosophy and literature, mostly."

"They say there's no future in archaeology," I said.

"Ha-ha," she said, smiling. "There's no future anyway, as far as I can see. Everything's right now."

"Sounds like you like the literature of the Sixties."

"Of course," she said, playing with her hair. "Kesey was ahead of his time. So was Kerouac, but he flamed out. His message lived on, though."

"I thought there was no future?"

"Ah, I sense a comedian inside that social worker's mind," she said. "I guess explorers have to be a little ahead of the times."

"The times, they are a changing," Paul sang as he came back with a fresh bottle of wine.

Holiday was curious about the street people. She wanted to know what their options were. I told her that it was a maze for these people to work through, and that it takes time, years even, for them to get housing.

"Really?" she said. "I thought there were shelters, halfway houses, subsidized housing, all that? You mean there's a long waiting list to get in?"

"For housing, there is. They can stay in temporary places until they're placed. Thing is, a lot of the people on the street aren't looking for housing, necessarily. Most of them aren't in any kind of condition to even go through the process."

"What about the elderly? Must be something for them that's easier, isn't there?"

Underwood was giving me the eye, directing me to her legs. I shook him off, turning back to her. "There are some programs for them. And subsidized housing. But they have to spend most of their disability check, or social security, just to pay the rent. Unless they stay in the shelters. Mental health issues get in the way, addictions, too."

"Hmm," she nodded. She held the wine glass in front of her, staring off at the trees in the yard. Underwood kicked me under the table. Again he shifted his eyes to her thighs, which were bare, and beautiful. Her short cut-off jeans rose up high. She crossed her legs and caught me staring at them.

"So they're basically stuck, is that what you're saying?" she said.

"They seem to be. Sometimes it gets bad enough, and they go in somewhere for a little while. Permanent solutions, housing-wise, are hard for some of them to find, or keep."

Underwood kicked me again. I ignored him.

"Well, whatever their problems are," she said, "I think they should have a place to go, far from the city streets. Somewhere in the country. A farm, maybe, where they can live and try to get healthy again. The kind of place where there's nothing but nature to look at, with things for them to do. An organic, working farm."

"With a spa?" Paul said.

"Why not?" Holiday laughed.

"Well, Plan A doesn't seem to be working," I said.

"What's that?" she asked.

"What I'm doing. Getting to know them, building a relationship, trying to steer them in somewhere."

"And Plan B?" she said.

"Sectioning them. That's not a pretty option either, but it's the last resort."

"Sectioning them? Sounds Orwellian."

Paul laughed and poured more wine.

"It means they're legally taken in for an evaluation," I said. "When they're considered to be a danger to themselves, or others, the law comes in. Unable to care for themselves, basically, unable to eat, accept food, or clothe themselves. Or they're really ill and won't accept medical help. Then a doctor evaluates them, and they can keep them for a week or two. After that, it's up to doctors and judges to decide whether to keep them longer or not."

"What about the really crazy ones?" she asked.

"Well, if you can survive, you can stay out there. As long as you don't cause a public disturbance, or bother people, you can be as crazy as hell. There's just not enough good treatment programs."

"No cures either," Underwood said. "Meds stabilize people, but they can have those nasty side effects."

The night was hot, with hardly any breeze. The street seemed a long way from the deck we were sitting on. Holiday seemed to be contemplating something. Underwood got up and lit some candles.

"There should be a farm out in the country where they can do all that," she said, tying her hair in a ponytail. "Try different treatments, maybe some natural ones too. In a good, healthy environment."

"That would be Plan F, then?" Underwood grinned at her.

She laughed, raising her glass. "Sure, why not? Here's to Plan F. The Farm."

"Send 'em to the health farm," he said.

We finished the second bottle. Underwood said he'd get another if we wanted, but he was going to bed early so he could drive up to Vermont in the morning.

"Maybe just a little," Holiday said.

He brought us another and said goodnight.

"Thanks, Paul," she said. "For everything." She pointed up toward the attic, smiling at him.

"Glad it worked out," he said.

The wind picked up and blew out some of the candles. Holiday re-lit them.

"He's really nice. He gave me a student rate, he called it."

"Yeah, Paul's a good guy. He gave me the social worker's rate."

She laughed and held her glass out. "I don't usually drink much, but this is great wine."

We sat and listened to the breeze through the trees. She untied her ponytail, running her hands through her hair. "You want to go inside?" she said. "I can show you my studio, now that's it set up."

"Sure."

Her room was three flights up. I carried the bottle of wine, watching her move on the stairs in front of me. She walked on her toes, stepping lightly. On the landing outside her door, she lit a candle sitting on a small table and picked it up, and pushed open the door.

"Watch your head," she said. "The ceiling's low in places."

I followed her into the room. The candle cast shadows on the low, V-shaped ceiling. She turned on a small lamp set on a table next to a futon mattress, which was covered with pillows of different colors. A low bookcase sat next to it. Her desk was a thick piece of wood balanced on two filing cabinets. The room was simple and smelled like lavender.

"Not bad," I said.

"I don't have any chairs, except the desk chair. It's more comfortable to sit on the futon," she said, moving some pillows around to make room. She lit another candle on the bookcase. "Chill out. I need to use the bathroom."

I sat on the corner of the futon. Her collection of books ranged from Tom Robbins to D.H. Lawrence to Paul Bowles. Several of Anaïs Nin's diaries were stacked alongside college textbooks on philosophy, environmental science, and wire-bound notebookoks. There were a few pictures of her and the dogs, and some wooden boxes and pottery bowls. One photo had been taken on the beach. She was knee-deep in the water, in a red bikini. Another one appeared to be of the Blue Hills in autumn. I picked up the beach shot, and brought it under the light. The bathroom door opened.

"Martha's Vineyard," she said, coming over to the futon and sitting next to me. "Last summer. You know the beach with the clay cliffs?"

"Sure. Back when you could still climb up them and sit in the pools," I said, putting the photo back in its place. "Nice picture. You could always get work as a swimsuit model. Reckon it would be a great way to make a living, standing around and looking good."

She smiled, shyly for a change. "Thanks," she said. "If things get tight again, I'll keep it in mind." I liked that she didn't try to deny it.

She leaned past me, rubbing against my arm, and took one of the small clay bowls off the shelf, along with some incense sticks. Her hair smelled sweet, an oil of some kind. It shone. She set the bowl on the floor and lit one of the sticks, waving it in the air to get it going. "Where did you grow up?"

"I'm an Ohio boy," I said. "Outside of Columbus about thirty miles. Ever heard of the Great Circle Earthworks?"

Her look was skeptical, but amused. "No. Sounds, um, indigenous?"

"They call them the Moundbuilders. The Hopewell Indians, two thousand years ago, built the largest system of connected geometric earthworks anywhere in the world. Just a little history for you. In my town, Newark, there's a golfcourse now built around some of the mounds."

"Yuk. Sacriligious."

"We used to sneak out there at night, light a few ceremonial candles on the putting greens, pass the peace pipe. It was a great place to grow up. We had woods behind the house that went for miles. Our dogs never needed leashed."

"That sounds like the Blue Hills. We lived right next to it. It's nice to have nature out your back door, and the city nearby." She reached across me again and picked up a small wooden box. "Hey, you look like the kind of guy who likes to smoke. You want to try a little of this stuff? A friend of mine gave me this big, fat bud. Kind bud."

"I'm a big fan. One of mother nature's finest products. Sure."

She laughed, and opened the box.

"My friend grew it in his closet. He's got a real green thumb. Does it with all the lights, the whole works."

"Fire it up," I said.

"You know," she said, putting part of the bud in a pipe. "You seem pretty cool for a social worker."

"Thanks. I'll take any compliments I can get."

"I can't give you one about being a swimsuit model yet," she grinned. "Until I've seen the goods."

As she inhaled, she closed her eyes momentarily. Her face was very young. High cheekbones, a slightly large mouth, full lips that curved up naturally, a soft looking, round chin. Even her nose was sexy. She opened her eyes playfully wide and rolled them around as she slowly exhaled. "Watch out. It's really strong. Here." She passed me the pipe.

We smoked for a while in silence. The window was open and I heard the hum of the Amtrak commuter train. She was comfortable

171

with not talking. I poured wine into both our glasses. "Thanks again for hooking me up with Paul," she said. Then she brushed my arm as she reached past me one more time to pick up her portable music player. Her skin felt warm and soft.

"You like Billie Holiday?"

"She's got that sweet voice, but she's sad."

"That's her gift."

"True. She's the real thing."

"What do you think of the kind bud?"

"Your friend grows the real thing, too."

We listened to the queen of the blues from two small speakers that sat on a shelf above the futon. Holiday leaned back against some pillows, folding her hands across her stomach. I stayed sitting cross-legged, sipping the wine. When I turned my head to look at her, her eyes were closed.

"I liked living out there in the woods," she said after a while. "Was good for me. That's why I think they should build farms for the homeless. Nature cures."

"Did you need to be cured?"

She didn't answer. I didn't say anything more. The music drifted over us, and I looked out the window at the leaves of the oak trees, blowing in the summer breeze. Soon, I felt her hand on mine.

The sun woke me up. It streamed through her attic window, falling across the futon. It shone on her face as she slept. Her lips were slightly parted, and I could hear her soft, shallow breathing. Hair covered half of her face, but I could see her eyelids, trembling now and then from dreams.

When Tuesday morning came, and with it the end of the long weekend, I awoke again to the sun from the attic window. Holiday was already up and in the shower. She worked in a coffee house on Centre Street in JP. I lay there on the futon, and looked at the clock. It was six-thirty. I stared out the window, and listened to her singing. Wondering what I was doing.

Finally, I got up and got dressed, and stuck my head through the open bathroom door. I could see her through the clear plastic shower curtain.

"Hey, I gotta go," I said. "Back to the jungle. See you later, I hope."

She slid aside the curtain of the tiny, stand-up shower, and stood there for a full minute, washing the front of herself with soap, the water running down her shoulders and some splashing on the towel on the floor.

I walked in and kissed her. "I believe," I said into her ear, water hitting me, "that what I'm seeing right now, in this moment, is the most extraordinary specimen of nature that I've seen in, say, at least the past hundred years."

She pulled away from me and splashed me with water. "You're not that old."

"Not yet. Have a good one out there today. See you."

"I know where you live," she said, turning her back to me.

I went downstairs to the studio and stepped into my own shower. A cold shower. Then hot. Then cold. I closed my eyes and saw her washing her small, perfectly shaped breasts with soap. I was out of my league, or age range, or something, but it had happened, and it had felt alright.

Thirty minutes later, I stepped out the back door. Underwood was up on the deck, drinking coffee. He came to the railing and grinned down at me. "Thank god it was a long weekend," he said, and glanced up at the third floor attic window. "Somebody had too much fun, I can see."

"There's no such thing as too much fun." I pulled the door closed behind me.

"Especially when you're on, dare I say it – Holiday," he said.

"Nice one, chief," I locked the door. When I looked up at him, he was beaming.

"Couldn't resist." He saluted.

STREET LOGIC

Chapter 14

July 21, 2004

It was lunchtime. He was working his way around the plaza, collecting the nine-to-fivers' leftovers. I was working a different approach. I had positioned myself on a bench in between the statue of Thomas Copley and a trash can that he hadn't searched yet, with a bag of fast food, uneaten except for a few French fries, sitting next to me.

A few homeless guys had gone for a swim in the shallow fountain, forced out of the water by a couple of cops who had to get their feet wet. As my guy neared the trash can next to me, I stood and dropped the bag of fast food on top of the rest of the garbage. Then I sat to watch.

His stick-hand was protected by a white plastic bag. He wore the same black jeans, jacket and t-shirt, and his backpack hung over one shoulder. Examining the contents of the nearly full trash can, his facial features showed nothing, as if he hadn't a care in the world. After a few minutes, it appeared that he wasn't going to take my offering.

His Afro had grown in the last month, or maybe he had picked it out. Today it seemed twice as large, almost billowing out of control. When the wind shifted, I noticed a strong body odor coming off him that I could smell from my spot ten feet away. As he straightened up and was ready to move on, without my lunch, I got up and walked over to him.

"Hey, there's a burger and a bunch of fries in that one. Just bought it, but my stomach doesn't feel right. Might as well take it if you want. I didn't even touch it."

He stopped and stared at me, wordlessly. Not a single indication that he had understood me. In fact, nothing showed on his face. The Vegas poker pros would have no clue what kind of hand this kid was holding. Neither did I. All I knew was that he wasn't holding my bag of lunch.

"Well, I guess that Double Whopper with cheese and large fries will have to go to waste," I said. "Too bad. Should have listened to my stomach, but it smelled so damn good."

Maybe he didn't understand English. He started to move off. I felt again that I'd seen him somewhere other than the street.

"By the way," I said. "There's a good lunch served at the Arlington Street church, just up the street. Every day at noon. Everybody's welcome. You know about it?"

I could have been talking to the statue of Thomas Copley. His stare didn't waver from mine. He was as still as the ten-foot-tall sculpture of the famous Bostonian standing on the marble pedestal beside us. Finally, he turned and went on to the next trash can. I looked longingly at the wasted food, but left it there.

I crossed the grassy plaza and sat on a bench across from the Copley Fairmont Hotel. He was going through the cans on the other side of the park, next to the ticket kiosk. I wanted to see if he would go back for my lunch. That would, at the very least, rule out the kind of paranoia that I was beginning to suspect. It was possible, too, that he had recently suffered a schizophrenic break, and the psychosis was setting in. It might explain his muteness and refusal to accept a simple offering like a bag of food. I was assessing his capacity for self-care, starting at the bottom of Maslov's hierarchy of needs. Acceptance of sustenance. Paranoia might prevent him from taking something from strangers. Safer to take leftovers that weren't intended for him, maybe. But the first requirement of the street is to survive. So why turn down the exact thing that you're looking for? On the other hand, maybe there was such an abundance of fast food leftovers out here that he didn't need mine. Maybe he just didn't like my long hair.

He finished his circuit without returning to the trash can that held my Double Whopper and fries. My stomach growled. I watched him sit down and start sorting through his findings. I sat in the square until he left for the library, just to see if he'd go back to the trash can by the fountain. But he must have been satisfied with what he found.

Chapter 15

August 3, 2004

"This one time they dropped me over the line into enemy territory. I was supposed to go into the jungle and find their camp. They gave me a whole new set after that, and never replaced them with my old ones. Did it more than once, too. They said they'd put them back, and never did. Left me with these."

"You asked them about it?" I said.

"What do you think?"

"I don't know."

"You don't just ask for your head and arms back! They deny ever taking them!" Pete rose from his chair and excused himself to use the restroom. I looked at Easttree and shrugged my shoulders.

"You see what I mean?"

"He's feisty," Easttree said. "That means there's something to work with."

"What do you think he means by all that?"

We were sitting in Starbucks on Boylston. Easttree scratched his head, giving the matter some thought.

"Probably that he doesn't like the head he has," Easttree said. "The one that thinks all those thoughts about body parts, he-she's, and lord knows what else. Could mean that he just wants his original, pre-psychotic head back. Or, it's just his own delusional way of explaining what happened to him."

"Which is?"

"Psychosis."

"I knew that. What about the military part? You think he served?"

"Maybe his break happened while he was in the service. Or else he never served, but his brain needs to blame somebody. Maybe he's read about mind experiments conducted in the military, brainwashing, all that. 'Enemy territory' could be the place his mind went."

"As bad as being in real enemy territory."

"For him, it is the real thing." Easttree checked his watch.

"Any thoughts on whether it's true?" I asked him. "You know, I hear this kind of stuff, in various forms, from all kinds of people out here. Gets me to thinking how the military did a lot of shit to people that we're probably never going to know about."

Easttree grinned. "Axel, maybe we need to schedule you for a little evaluation."

"Oh, com'on Tree. You know they did some experimenting. I had an uncle who said the navy…"

Pete came back and sat down, a piece of toilet paper sticking out of his ear.

"So, Pete," Easttree said. "Axel tells me that you spend some time in Milton. Is that where you grew up?"

Pete looked at Easttree for a moment through his thick glasses. "Why do you want to know?"

"Oh, just asking. I grew up in Quincy," Easttree offered.

Pete took his glasses off and set them on the table. "The lady who answered the door was somebody from the ship, I think," he said, picking up his coffee and taking a drink. "I don't know how she got clearance to be there."

I glanced at Easttree. His expression was the same as if he were listening to his son tell him about his day. Interested and patient. Like he wanted to hear more. He gave Pete an encouraging smile.

"She said it was her house," Pete went on. "Oh, I told her about the air-space rights, but she didn't want to hear it. Then she went to feed the baby or something, and the police came, and well, then we went for a little ride."

Easttree stopped smiling and flashed me a quick look. There was something truthful sounding about the police part. Usually Pete's delusions were much grander than going for a ride in a police car.

"That must have been scary," Easttree said. "Where did they take you?"

Pete stared out from behind his thick lenses. "To the station, of course."

"The police station?"

"Where else do you think? Put me in custody for five hours."

"What happened there?"

"They asked me what I was doing at the house. They didn't believe me."

"You mean they didn't believe it was your house?"

Pete started coughing and grabbed a napkin. It took him a few minutes of hacking and gasping for breath, until he finally sat back and picked up his coffee cup. Easttree kicked my foot and put a finger in his own chest.

"You alright there, Pete?" I said.

He nodded his head, and then reached into his jacket pocket and produced a small nip of whiskey.

"Care for a little?" he said, looking from Easttree to me.

"No, thanks, Pete," Easttree said.

"Me, neither," I said. "But thanks for the offer."

Pete poured about a tablespoonful into his coffee. Then he stuck the bottle back into an inside pocket. Under the lightweight, blue jacket was a brown button-down shirt with a striped tie. There were a few stains on the tie. His leg stuck out to the side of the table, his brown trousers rising high above his ankles, revealing white socks and scuffed, worn down leather dress shoes.

Pete drank some of his Irish coffee and sighed, leaning back in the chair. "Phew," he smiled, holding up his cup. "I needed that." Then he turned his eyes on Easttree. "What exactly is your duty again, Mr Easttree? I get it confused with what these other reach-out people are doing."

Easttree maintained his sincere expression. "Well, I work with people who don't have a place of their own. I come out to the street, with other, uh, reach-outs, like Axel. To see if there's anything I can do to help."

"Can you help me find a new pair of feet?" he said, a little smile on his face. "Because I sure could use some."

"I know some good foot-doctors," Easttree said. "We could even go today, if you want. Doctor Huffman, a colleague of mine, is working in the medical clinic this morning. I'm sure he'd be happy to take a look at your feet."

Pete sipped his coffee, studying Easttree. "He can fix my feet?"

"He could offer some suggestions."

For a moment, Pete held his gaze, and seemed to consider it. Then he set his coffee down and rubbed the back of his hand. The open sore he had when I first met him was a little bigger.

"He could see about that wound on your hand, as well," I said. "What happened there, Pete?"

He pulled the sleeve down to cover it.

"Looks sore," Easttree said.

"Well, it is," Pete said. "I've got no choice. I have to get those things out of there."

"What things?" Easttree said.

"Those things they put in there! Haven't you been listening? Tells them where you are at any time, in case they want to bring you in."

He pulled the sleeve up and dug at the wound with a long fingernail. Easttree caught my eye and pushed his chair back, stood up, and asked Pete if he wanted anything to eat.

He stopped digging at the wound and covered it with a napkin. "Now that you mention it, I am a little hungry. A cookie, if they have it."

"Chocolate chip OK?"

"Sure," Pete smiled. He dabbed at the blood on his hand with the napkin.

"Be right back."

Pete and I chatted about the Red Sox until Easttree returned with some bagels and a chocolate chip cookie.

"Must be my lucky day," Pete grinned.

"Why not?" Easttree said. "Everybody deserves a lucky day now and then."

Pete laughed in his high-pitched voice. "My sentiments exactly. Gee, this is a pretty big cookie," he said, holding it up. "It's the size of this plate." He took a bite, leaving a few crumbs at the corner of his mouth, and chewed slowly.

Once we'd all said our goodbyes, I walked with Easttree along Boylston to where his car was parked.

"Likable guy," Easttree said.

"What do you think about the house story?"

"Maybe he grew up there. The police part sounded true. We'll have to keep an eye on that sore he's digging at. I'll talk to Huffman about it. If it gets worse, or even stays the same, could have him evaluated."

"Danger to self. I'm keeping an eye on it, I see him almost every day." We turned on Hereford and Easttree slowed down in front of the alley where Frank Murphy had been holed up last winter.

"That the spot?"

"Frostbite alley. Seems harmless in the summer, doesn't it?"

Easttree looked down the alley, shaking his head. "All these people with feet problems. We need to open a foot-care clinic."

We were at his car. "So how's things with Rebecca these days."

"Slow going. But it's been repairing little by little, you know. All summer."

"Glad to hear that."

He opened the door of his car and slid into the driver's seat. "And you? How's Miss Golightly?"

"Remember that statue in the library fountain? I think I found her, in the flesh."

"Mercy," he grinned. "With a baby in her arms?"

"Slow down, Tree. You know, just enjoying the newness of it all."

"I hear that. Keep it real, man."

I took the subway to Park Street Station and rode the escalator up to the plaza at the base of the Commons. The 23-carat golden dome of the State House shone brightly in the sun, high above the poor bastards crowded around the fountain at the bottom of the hill, waiting in line to get lunch from Food Not Bombs. A roof of gold, when some people don't have a roof at all. I passed the gang of regular drinkers who lined the benches, hoping none of them would corral me into a long story, but they were preoccupied with their business. I started into the park. Took the sidewalk past the frog pond, full of kids splashing around in the two-foot deep water, screaming with joy and an occasional curse at one another. Then I hiked up the short hill to the monument, where I stopped and looked out over the sloping green toward the Public Gardens. About fifty feet below me sat John Leather Pants, his back against the base of his surveillance tree, dark in his leather gear. He was scanning the Back Bay skyline through a pair of binoculars.

I walked down the hill and approached him from the front. The only name he'd given me so far was John. Since we had a lot of John Does on our radar, coming up with a tag for this one was easy.

"They have air conditioners up there," he said, still peering through the binoculars. "And those radars I was telling you about? They're watching everything. Listening, too. Networkers. Can't find privacy anywhere. Here, wanna take a look?"

He lowered the hi-tech binoculars and held them out.

"That's OK, John. Nice looking glasses."

"Go on, look!" He thrust them forcefully toward me. "See for yourself. I'm just trying to tell you something, that's all." His good eye zeroed in on me, his face in a scowl.

"Alright, let me have a look," I said, taking them from his rough hands. "Where? On top of the Hancock?"

"Look anywhere! Anywhere! The tall ones, that's where most of the heavy action is. The signals are coming in and out from there. Just look, you'll see them!"

The August sun was bright, the skies clear. The sweat from Leather Pant's hands covered the grips of the expensive looking binoculars. I always wondered where he got the money from. My guess was a disability check with a retroactive lump-sum payment on top of it. All that leather - the pants, the black cowboy boots, black leather vest, and the full-length black leather coat lying next to him on the grass - had to cost some serious change.

"Aw, if you're not going to look, just give em' back to me," he growled.

"OK, I'm looking." I raised the glasses to my eyes. The tops of the Hancock and Prudential came into view, crystal clear.

"They're up there doing whatever they want, and I know it!" He spat the words out from deep in his chest. I had run into John L.P. every once in a while after our first encounter. Lately he'd been coming here to the Commons. Sometimes I saw him in the small courtyard outside of Morisson's convenience store, drinking coffee and smoking. But I stayed clear of his air-conditioned lair in the tiny alley. I didn't want to get trapped back there with just him. I peered through the lenses at the Hancock, using the automatic focus button. "Wow, these glasses are beauties, John. I can see the flies in those office windows."

"Not there! Look up! Up there where those elevator shacks are, on top! See all that?"

I aimed the glasses at the top of the two big buildings in Back Bay. It was a veritable cluster-fuck of transmission towers, cables, wires, satellite dishes, and other weird, oval looking things. I gained a new insight, or at least appreciation, of what John's world must look like to him. I scanned along the skyline slowly, seeing the vast array of technology sitting on tops of other smaller buildings.

"Jeez, John, you're right. There sure is a bunch of stuff up there."

"See what I'm saying? Look for the air conditioners! That's where they hide the special detectors. That's why I stay where I stay. They can't detect me there because…" His voice halted, then trailed off into something unintelligible.

Leather Pants wasn't the only one who noticed these things. I'd encountered others who had similar ideas. Pete had the implants, which gave them his exact location. Steve Winston wore duct tape around his shoes and a hard hat wrapped in tin foil to ward off the beams from other galaxies. Leather Pants believed that cowhide kept him safe from their getting a good read on him. They were an unconnected tribe of street people who specialized in electronic surveillance awareness. ESA, I called it. After a while, I decided it wasn't for me to dispute their claims. And after 9-11, I almost started to believe them.

"Now you see what I'm telling ya?" John said.

"That is quite a display of electrical capacity up there, alright." I lowered the glasses.

"Quite a display? That's all you see?"

"Well, I mean…"

"That's how they know everything!" His voice ratcheted up a few notches. "There's tracking devices on top of those super-towers, there's supersonic transmitters, titanium beams, microwaves, it's all there, they're listening and watching everything! I can hear them listening! I'm just trying to tell you, that's all!"

He suddenly sat bolt upright. I stepped backwards. He surprised me, and lunged forward to grab for the binoculars at the same time as he tried to rise from the ground.

"Gimme those, they're mine!"

I reacted, and lofted them in the air toward him. They floated in a high arc, the strap looping upward in a circle, in a perfect toss. He didn't even have to move. They landed in his hands, the strap nearly falling over his head. An amazed look ran across his face as he fell back against the tree, staring at me. He examined the binoculars closely, muttering under his mustache. Then he raised them to his eyes and looked out.

His grumbling intensified. Something was wrong. He stabbed at the focus button.

"Now you've done it!" he cried. The veins on his hands stood out as he squeezed the grips. "I never shoulda let you use them! The focus is broken. Why'd you have to go and throw them like that?"

I knew why. He'd scared the shit out of me. "I'm sorry, John. I don't know. Are you sure they're not working?"

He shook his head violently back and forth, and then did the same with the binoculars. He tried them again. "Goddammit!" he bellowed. He banged them against his leg and looked through them again. His face got redder, his jaw clenching and unclenching. I stepped back a few feet. Finally, he threw the glasses on the grass and glared at me.

"You broke them," he said quietly. "You broke my protection."

Chapter 16

August 13, 2004

"This is my second favorite spot," she said, hanging upside down. Her loose t-shirt had fallen over her face, her hair cascading in a golden-brown wave toward the ground. I sat perched on another branch, admiring Holiday's tan stomach and the whiteness where her bikini top usually was. It was Friday the thirteenth, and for luck I'd called in sick. Holiday had the day off as well, and after a long breakfast in bed we'd roused ourselves to walk over to the arboretum. I was showing her one of my favorite trees, a small Japanese pine in the middle of the park. The branches were like arms and legs, and within the curtain of green was a round, hollow space. From outside, nobody could see you. There was an opening in the top of the tree that let the sun in. "I'll show you my most favorite place," she said, pulling her shirt away from her face so she could see me, "if you'll answer me one question."

"Uh-oh."

She smiled, which looked like a frown from upside-down. "You don't have to answer it, if you don't want to. But then," she made a pouting expression that appeared to smile at me, "you might miss out on seeing something really great." She dropped her arms and the t-shirt fell again. "Anyway, it's no big thing. Just curiosity."

I shifted on the branch so I could hang upside down opposite her. I lifted the shirt from her face. Our faces were level with each other. "OK, I'm ready. Fire away."

Grinning, she tucked the bottom of her shirt into her cut-off shorts. "I wanted to verify if my instincts were accurate." She reached over and pushed me a little, swinging me backwards. "You slept with her, didn't you? Maybe not many times, but you had something."

I knew who she meant. Last week, Holiday came with me to a party that Adrian and her partner, Janice, had in their new apartment. Holiday had connected immediately with Adrian and they'd spent a good amount of time talking. For some reason, I had never told Holiday about my boss. Didn't feel it was necessary, I guess. But now, my long-held belief in women's abilities to divine these kinds of things, intuitively, was being confirmed yet again. Because I knew for a fact Adrian wouldn't have told her.

"I met Adrian while I was still living in Maine, way before I started the job," I told her. "Kind of just happened. I think it was a last fling for her, in a way, while she was still working out some things. She met her partner around the same time. Maybe I helped her figure something out. It's never been an issue, if that's what you're getting at."

Holiday swung forward and grabbed my hands, pulling me toward her. She took a long, deep look into my eyes, and I felt the vulnerability in hers as much as saw it. "Well, at least she had a good man before she settled down."

"I noticed you did say 'good'." I reached toward her face and brushed the hair aside. She pushed me again, laughing, and I swung backwards hard so I could flip down to the ground. I just barely landed on my feet. She grabbed my shoulders and let herself down, standing in front of me. Her question answered, she tugged on my hand. "Come on, I'll show you my favorite place." Her teasing humor was back. "You earned it."

Her hideout was tucked away in the hilly area beyond the small cliff that overlooks the city. Boulders and trees kept us out of view of any hikers, and in any case, we were way off any of the park trails. We unrolled the blanket I'd brought and ate some cheese and bread, with some wine. "This spot is perfect in the afternoon," she said, looking up toward an opening in the trees where the sun shone through. Soon, Holiday was in just her underwear, tanning herself. I joined her.

Later, we wandered out of the park to a cafe across from the Forest Hills train station. I called Easttree to see if he was finished with work. He said he'd been playing hooky today as well, and invited us over for dinner. "I'll be cooking in the back-yard, or we might still be working out, but just come find us," he said. He sounded good.

Rebecca, five years younger than Easttree, slim and athletic, had always been in great shape, ever since I'd met her. She'd played field-hockey in high school and college. Looked like she had never stopped training. An English teacher at Boston Latin for five years, she quit after having Sophie, and now she stayed at home with Eric until he could start elementary school. From the kitchen, she glanced again toward me, as I lounged on the couch. I caught something in her look, subtle, but it was there. I hadn't seen her for a while, since before the night at Bukowski's when Tree hadn't come home.

"You want to help me make some drinks?" she said. Holiday and Tree were in the backyard getting the fire going. I hauled myself up and started mixing Kool-Aid for the kids in a large plastic pitcher she handed me.

"She's really great, Axel. Older than her years."

"I know. She's young, but seems more mature than me sometimes."

Rebecca laughed as she got some ice from the freezer. "By the way, I don't hold you responsible for what he did. He's a grown man. Still," she turned toward the window and looked out at the smoke now surrounding Tree and Holiday, "you were there... I guess, that's all I'm saying."

I stopped stirring and put the spoon in the sink. "I've known him a long time, Becca," I said. "He's crazy about you. Always has been. I'd never seen him so upset with himself."

She turned back to me and now her expression was softer. "I know. It just scared me."

"I'm sure it did."

After we cooked out, and Rebecca was helping the kids with their baths and showers, Tree took us up to his den.

"I want to read you guys something," he said. Holiday and I sat in the leather armchairs while Tree searched through his papers. "Here it is. Part of a longer article."

We listened as he read out loud: "What is happening on the street sometimes appears to be the equivalent of a blood sport. One with no rules and that makes no sense. When assessing each individual's struggle to avoid facing the hole they are in, it's clear that the denial factor can be lethal. They will lose half a foot rather than feel the pain of the life they're trapped in. They disregard their health in the name of some kind of psychic survival that's invisible to the rest of us. They live under the radar, but out in the open, in a constant battle to make it to the next day, surrounded by loneliness, thievery, strange but fierce friendships, violence, and death. It is an otherworldly place they inhabit, most of all. They subsist, unnoticed, as we pass them daily on the street corner. We see them, but possessed of our own strange denial, we walk past. Because to see them clearly would mean to do something, to try something. So we say to ourselves, they're free to make bad decisions. In the end, their rejection of our efforts to help pushes our own capacity to understand, and to feel compassion for them, to new places." He stopped and looked up. "I have to work out the rest of it."

"I like it," Holiday said. "Denial on many levels. I guess we all do it sometimes."

Easttree looked from Holiday to me, then back to her. "What did you say you were studying?"

Holiday smiled at him. "Human nature. What else?"

Chapter 17

October 13, 2004

"I know this might sound a little callous," I said, looking around the conference table, "but I can't agree with the sponge-baths. We're not working in a leper colony in the middle of the jungle, or an AIDS community in Africa. We're in one of the most medically advanced cities in the world. We have options. We're not missionaries here, without resources."

Ripley smiled, but Adrian's frown kept the rest in check. Bette Malloy was busy looking at her notes. I already knew her thoughts on this. Tina glared at me, her lips compressed. Perfectly expressing her opinion.

"Axel," Adrian said, "I want everybody's best thinking here, and I want a game-plan before we break. Something we can live with. We're supposed to be the professionals. And we know Tony as well, if not better, than anybody working with him. It's not war, it's not Africa, I agree. It's social work. So let me hear everybody's best shot."

"No pun intended, right?" Ripley said.

Adrian gave him a tight-lipped smile. "No, we're not going to shoot Tony Ruffo, Ripley. No matter how frustrating he can be." She glanced around the room. Nobody said anything. "One more thing I want to make clear," she said. "We support any and every effort being made to help this man. I don't care who is doing it, or how they're doing it, as long it doesn't hurt him. And that includes the Medical Care nurse's 'sponge-bobbing' of him in the back of our van, as you like to put it, Axel."

Bette suppressed a laugh. Tina looked out the window.

"I just meant," I said, "that we had a good plan that day. To take him into the shelter clinic for the scrub-down and new set of duds, so a doc could see him. Specifically, we'd all agreed to not clean him up that day until he came into the clinic. To set a limit, basically. It just doesn't make any sense to me to keep cleaning him up on the street.

We have to push him a little, and the clinic is better than the van, professionally speaking. He's never going to move if he knows he can get everything he wants sitting there on his milk crate on Atlantic Ave."

Adrian just stared at me. We'd had this argument before, about the difference between helping and enabling. It was an old debate that we never solved. I shook my head and looked away.

"We're not going to change Tony Ruffo," Tina said. "And we're not going to change the beliefs of other people who are trying to help him. Plus, they are nurses. They did an informal physical of him that day, there in the van. I propose we support them."

Ripley cleared his throat. "Ethically speaking," he gave me a sympathetic look, "I think Tina's right. We have a duty to treat him with compassion, at the very least. Let's just help make this guy's life more comfortable, whatever form that takes. That doesn't mean I'm going to personally give him a sponge-bath in the van, but I don't care if someone better than me wants to do it."

Bette nodded her head.

"However," he went on, "there's always the good old section route. Get a doctor to sign the papers, take him off the street for a few weeks and get him into a hospital. It's strong-arming him, but at this point I'm on board with that. Although I know Dr Phil doesn't believe it works."

"Because it generally flops," Adrian said. "To Phil's credit, he's committed a lot of people over the years. Most judges throw them back to the street. But Phil told me last week he's willing to support us, if we present a compelling case."

That led to another silence. I picked at the callouses on my hands. I'd started lifting weights again a month ago. I couldn't imagine a more compelling case than Ruffo's, but I kept my thoughts to myself.

Bette flipped through the pages of her notebook, her lips moving as she read something to herself. She looked at me, then Adrian, Ripley and finally Tina.

"I have to agree with Tina," Bette said, looking at me. "Who cares if someone else is cleaning his wounds and sponging him down in our van? We should applaud those nurses."

I gave Ripley a subtle shake of my head. He almost choked on his coffee and ended up spilling some on the table before he could set it down. Adrian handed him a napkin. "Steady there, Rip," she said.

"Sorry about that," he said. He glanced at Bette. "Were you finished?" he asked her.

"Sure, go ahead."

"I guess this is the way I see it," he continued. "This thing just seems way more than we can really handle. We see Tony nearly every day. It's clear that he's not going to decide on his own to get any help. So whether we're talking about sponge-baths or whatever, we have to remember that this is a man's life we're talking about. The tail end, too." He paused. "Let's look at it like this. How would any of us want a group of city outreach workers to treat us, if we were in Tony's position? Or if someone in our own family was in his shape, on the street? I mean, he can't even get to a bathroom now. He barely makes it to the bushes behind the bank. This is a guy who used to be able to take care of his basic needs, but not now. So, if some nurses sponge him down, at least they're doing something, preserving his dignity a little longer. I don't think I could do what they're doing. So," he gave me a quick look, "I say, hats off to the good nurses. But the bottom line is, it's not going to get this man off the street."

He stared down at his hands, as if examining them for an answer.

My eyes went around the group, and saw they were all staring at their hands, except for Adrian. She was staring at me. No matter how much she disliked my attitude, she knew the logic of what I was saying made sense. She knew I had tried with Ruffo, many times, just as we all had. She understood that I was asking him to try.

"I wish there was something we could do besides sitting next to him on the sidewalk and talking about impossible football heroics and big fish stories," Bette said. "I feel like that's all I'm doing. I know on some level that's probably what he likes the best. An audience, someone to listen to him, to accompany him."

I was almost beginning to wonder if my own barnacle-encrusted heart had lost faith in the most simple acts of kindness. But I had given this a lot of thought.

"Let's not forget Sylvia Thompson," I finally said. "I don't want to see that happen again."

If it had been silent earlier, now it felt like the air had been sucked out of the room. I waited for a minute, considered leaving it at that. But I couldn't.

"I feel like I should've noticed that she was getting sicker. All I'm saying here is that Tony Ruffo isn't moving around much either, just like Sylvia during that last month. It's a bad sign, and in those circumstances, just cleaning him up doesn't work for me."

I was done. I could feel everyone in the room watching me. I gave Adrian and Tina a brief glance, and then stared back at my notebook.

As the boss, it was Adrian's job to keep us on track. "Listen, Axel," she said. "You've got a point there. But let's try to focus on what might work. As hard as that sometimes can be, in this job."

"Sure," I said. "I'll be right back. Keep going." I didn't need to use the restroom, but I needed a rest from this conversation.

When I returned, Ripley was in mid-speech.

"Just listening to his stories, the boat business, the restaurant in Marblehead, the beach houses, the list of cars. And, my personal favorite," I could see the humor in Ripley's eyes, indicating that his serious speech was finished, "the time he single-handedly decimated a squad of gooks in Vietnam, or Korea, depending on which day you're talking to him – and then marched twenty miles through the jungle carrying a wounded Marine on his shoulders to safety."

He stopped. Smiles started going around the table. Then Ripley suddenly slapped the conference table. Everybody jumped, including me.

"I've got it!" he announced. "We'll kidnap him, and he can live with Bette!"

That broke the tension. We still had no solution, but the meeting lightened up after that. We went through the list of people we were most worried about. I gave an update on Lamar Cleveland and his worsening leg infection. I told them about Phil and Jimmy Jay's testimony on the disappearance of the Ninja. Pete and his implant. The binocular incident with John Leather Pants worried some people, and

Bette chipped in that, clinically speaking, this man gave her the impression of a killer.

"I don't know about that, but he gives me the creeps too," Tina said. "Although when he's in a good mood, he's kind of, well, charming in a way."

"Charming?" I said. She didn't respond. Still pissed at me for my hard line stance on Ruffo.

"What made you throw the binoculars?" Adrian asked me.

"It was a knee-jerk reaction. He kind of freaked me out for a second."

"Hmm," she said. "Well, anyway, we're going to have to get some people from Medical Care down there to see him. That air conditioning unit he's living behind is the most disgusting spot I've ever seen. That alone should qualify him for an evaluation."

"Oh!" Bette said, her face lighting up. "He's getting his monthly social security check from someone at the Department of Mental Health."

"How'd you learn that?" Adrian said.

"An old contact at DMH."

"So we have a real name for him now?" Adrian said, a slight tone of annoyance in her voice at hearing this development now, and not sooner.

"Not exactly," Bette said. "I was leaving their offices and saw him coming in. I'm not sure who he saw, and I didn't get his name. But I'm working on it."

"Who's your contact?" Adrian said.

"Well, actually, I was just there visiting a friend. She's going to find out for me."

Adrian maintained her composure, the way she always did, by putting her hands behind her head and leaning back.

"That would be nice," she said. "Now, what about the Silent One? Has anybody been able to make any progress with him?"

Nobody had.

"Well, it's October already," Adrian went on, "it's going to get colder, and we have to start talking to people about their winter plans.

For now, he's sleeping on the grates in front of the library, according to the crew on the outreach van. He's begun to accept soup and blankets from them. That's the only positive sign, but it's not much."

"I'm telling you," Bette said, "I think he's a young man in the midst of a psychotic break. Could even be his first break. He doesn't speak. There's a lot of literature in the field about psychotic people hearing voices telling them what to do and not to do. Maybe they're telling him not to talk to anybody. That's just my hunch. Unless he really is mute."

"But if he was just mute, wouldn't he try to communicate in other ways?" Tina said. "He'd have a little notepad or something, or use sign language. He's not communicating at all. And he does look up when I've said hello to him while he's got his head down or looking the other way. He hears me, I'm pretty sure."

"Axel," Adrian said, "after the meeting, can you go down there with Tina and see if you can meet up with Easttree? Today's one of his days on the street. It would be good to get a few more clinical opinions on him. What do you think, Bette?"

"Absolutely," Bette said.

"And maybe you can go with Ripley and see how Tony is?"

"Sure," she said.

Ripley stood up and pumped his fist. "I'll use Axel's method if I have to. 'Come on Tony! Win one for the Gipper!" He grinned at me.

"Worth a try," I said. "If it doesn't work, tell him the Patriots are interested."

Tina and I met Easttree at the Finagle A Bagel in Copley Square. She and I hadn't exchanged a word on the walk from Evergreen to Back Bay. After a quick coffee in the second-storey seats along the windows, where we could see the entire plaza, Tina finally spoke. "It's still a little early, I guess."

"The lunchtime crowd isn't out yet," I said, finishing a peanut-butter bagel. "We can go to the library and look around, and see if Pete's there, too."

"How's that implant infection?" Easttree said.

"Doesn't look any worse," I said.

While Easttree used the restroom, Tina and I waited on Boylston Street.

"Tina, listen," I started.

"No, let me say something." She faced me. "I'm sorry. I get a little too, I don't know. Overwhelmed, I guess, with what we're doing."

"You should. We all should. It's too much sometimes."

She gave me a grateful smile. "I wasn't going to say this yet," she said, as Easttree came out the door of the restaurant, "but you did have a good point there, about Sylvia."

I smelled him before I entered. His odor had become distinct in the past month, a strong, bitter, almost fecal smell. The door leading into the men's restroom was propped wide open. The rankness hit me full force as soon as I entered. There was nobody else inside. Then I heard splashing, and bent down to look under the row of three stalls. In the furthest stall, one of his bare feet was on the ground in front of the toilet. I heard more splashing sounds. Bending further, I could see clothes sticking out from behind the toilet. Someone walked in. I looked up, recognized Howard Bingham.

"Axel! What are you doing?"

I stood up and smiled at him. "Howard. How you doing?" I gestured toward the stall, then motioned for him to follow me out to the hallway.

"You've got to do something about that kid, Axel! I mean, I've smelled some pretty bad things in my time, but that? Jesus Christ, that should be against the law!"

I walked him away from the entrance. "Howard, I'm working on it. Let me ask you something. You talk to everybody on the streets, right? You ever try to talk to him?"

Howard Bingham, never one for a loss of words, opened his mouth and then shut it. He looked toward the restroom. His brow furrowed as he raised his eyebrows, then he pulled me a little further from the open door. "One time," he hissed loudly in my ear, "I tried to give him a sandwich, right? Same kind I make for Jack, ham and cheese. I went up to the kid in the plaza, saw him digging through the trash, and said, 'Hey, my man. I got a fresh ham and cheese sub here, made it myself. All yours.' And you know what he did?"

"I think so."

"He stared at me until I thought I was looking at a devil of some kind! I got the hell away from him! Something's wrong there, Axel, I'm telling you. Nobody ever looked at me like that!" Howard shook his head and turned to go. "I'm going to use the other bathroom in the old section of the library. I can't stand it in there." He looked toward the restroom. "Jesus, Axel, for the love of Christ, do something with the kid! You're outreach, not me."

I watched him get on the elevator, thinking of Sylvia Thompson's note.

"He was washing himself in the toilet?" Tina said.

"From the sounds of it, I'd say yes."

Easttree made a low whistling sound. "Three months without a shower, wearing the same clothes during a hot summer. Won't go into a shelter. Public bathroom's the only way."

Tina frowned. "Yeah, but in the toilet, not the sink? It's not good. Plus, he puts the same clothes back on. Poor kid, he's trying, though." She stuck her hands in her back pockets and pondered it. "I'm going over to the Old South Church to get some clothes. Let's try to give him some."

"Alright, go for it," I said.

Easttree and I waited near the elevators, with a view toward the stairs in case he came up. Irene from security spotted us.

"I can't kick anyone out for smelling bad," she said, when we told her our plan. "Not yet, anyway."

"Have you ever had to?" Easttree asked.

"Ask someone to leave because of their odor? Only once. He was a mental patient from New York. He was lying on the floor upstairs, way in the back, sleeping. When I asked him if he needed any help, he tried to kick me. They got him," she said. "Took him back to New York, I heard."

"Try with this kid yet?"

She gave Easttree a look.

"I see," he smiled back.

"Irene, any sign of Pete today?" I said.

"Hal, from maintenance, told me he hasn't seen Pete for the last few days. He usually comes in every day. Kind of strange. I hope he's alright."

Tina returned, carrying a shopping bag with a pair of jeans, a black t-shirt, and a hooded sweatshirt. "Hi, Irene. So, Axel, did he come out yet?"

"No, but Howard Bingham did. Tree, let's you and I go," I said, taking the bag from her.

"Howard?" Tina said.

"Said the kid was the devil."

"Right," Tina said. "So what are you going to do? Just give the bag to him?"

"I don't know yet," I said. "We'll figure something out."

"Well, good luck," Irene said.

Easttree and I took the stairs back down to the basement level. Outside the restroom, Easttree stopped, his face screwing up. "I see what you mean. How do you want to handle this?"

"I'm going to leave the clothes in plain view, in the bag, on top of the trash can. Then get out."

"Why not just ask him if he needs them?"

"I've tried giving him things. He's never taken anything from me. He's a trash picker. Seems to need to find it himself. The direct approach doesn't seem to work."

"OK. He's your guy." He pinched his nose and turned toward the open door. "In the name of social work," he said.

"Outreach work," I said.

"Whatever." Easttree walked into the restroom. I gave him ten seconds to experience it himself.

Easttree stood near the urinals. We were the only other ones in there, besides the Silent One, who was still splashing around. I motioned to Easttree with my hand to look under the stalls. Shaking his head, he nonetheless bent down and peeked toward the last stall. I went to the trash can and left the bag of clothes sitting on top. Then I pulled the jeans and t-shirt out, hanging them from the side of the trash can where he couldn't miss seeing them.

We left the restroom and walked toward the auditorium. There was a long table and a chair, and Easttree sat down. "Wow," he said. "That's, well, just incredibly potent."

I watched the entrance to the restroom. "It's one thing to stink," I said. "But even in the shelter, they won't let anybody get that ripe, not even the lobby vets."

"You know," Easttree said after a few minutes, "I've had a few cases, with psychotic patients, where they don't seem to smell their own odor. I want to try to talk to this kid when he comes out."

"We don't call him the Silent One for nothing, Tree. Kid won't say a word. But you can try."

"I just want to see how he responds. The look in his face. Might not tell me anything, but sometimes a person in the midst of a psychotic break shows it in their eyes. Sometimes. What's Bette's take?"

"She thinks he's having his first break."

"And the sanitary thing," he said. "If he's washing himself in the toilet, there's a qualifier to build the case for an evaluation. There's no law against body odor, but with feces and hepatitis transfer, it's a health hazard."

"See, that's why you get the big bucks."

He laughed. We discussed the playoff series with the Yankees. Ten minutes later, the Silent One still hadn't come out yet. I peeked in the can once, and saw him still in the back stall. The clothes were in the same spot I'd left them.

"No luck so far," I told Easttree.

We went upstairs to meet Tina and stood where we could see both the stairs and the elevator.

"Here he comes," Tina said, a minute later.

He was wearing his same clothes, the black jeans and t-shirt, with his jean jacket draped over one shoulder and his black bag on the other.

"Maybe he put them in his backpack," she said.

"Well, Tree, now's your chance," I said. "Go get him. I'm going to run down and see if the clothes are gone."

I took the stairs to the lower level. The restroom smelled like he was still in there. The clothes were untouched. I put them back in the shopping bag. Upstairs, Tina and Easttree were standing in front of the Silent One. Easttree was talking to him. I stood off to the side and watched.

Thirty seconds later, the Silent One turned away and walked toward the exit.

"By my calculations, Tree, you may have broken the record," I joined them. "Any luck?"

"My guess is Bette is right. He's psychotic. Doesn't appear to be deaf. I dropped my keys on the floor and he looked down. The main thing is he doesn't attempt to communicate at all. Autism maybe. But I don't think so. The lack of any affect – the blank face, the direct stare, the non-speaking – we're talking psychiatric hospitalization to find out what's going on with him exactly".

We left the library and wandered up Boylston Street to show Easttree where John Leather Pants was living. Easttree hadn't met him yet.

"First, I want to see if he's back there," I said, as we stood in front of Morrison's. "Wait here a minute." I went down Gloucester and took the main alley, stopped at the short stairway. The air conditioner sat just a few feet from the bottom step. I had to get next to the adjacent building in order to see if he was there. It was dark behind the a-c unit, and I couldn't see very well, but it seemed empty.

"I don't think he's there," I told Tina and Easttree. "But you have to see his spot, Tree. Adrian thinks it's a health hazard."

Tina had seen it before. Easttree followed me into the alley from the courtyard entrance. The air-conditioning unit, built under a partial overhang of the building, was at the other end. Half-way in, I stopped him and pointed.

"He's got a little cave in there," Easttree said. "Looks like a nice place for rats, too."

"It is. Let's go. I don't want to run into him here, he was pretty pissed off at me last time I saw him."

Easttree crept closer to the lair and crouched down. I watched both ends of the alley. When he was satisfied, we walked back to the lower level courtyard outside Morrison's. Tina was talking to Leather Pants by the stairway, his back to us. She saw us, and we ducked back into the alley.

"Let's go out the other way," I said. "We'll come around to them from the street side."

"Are you sure that you're not the paranoid one here, Axel?" he grinned.

"Trust me, Tree. It's better to keep a clear boundary with this guy."

We went back through the alley, then down Gloucester to Newbury. At the top of the stairs, we saw them. Easttree poked me in the side. "Now I know why you don't want to get caught back there. He looks like Hellboy. You seen that movie yet?"

"No. I was thinking Captain Hook."

We descended the steps to the courtyard and approached them.

"Hey, John," I said.

He jerked his head around. "Oh, it's you. They still don't work," he growled. "Just so you know."

"I'm sorry about that, John. This is Ken Easttree, a friend of ours."

Leather Pants looked Easttree over.

"Good to meet you, John," Easttree said, extending his hand. John stared at it for a long moment, then stuck his own hand out and shook. "You know, I always liked leather. I had some pants like that once, believe it or not, but they were too hot for me. Temperature-wise, I mean. How do you like them?"

"Oh, these," John grinned. "Yes sir, they're good for all seasons, I'll tell you that. Have to wash them out once in a while, they need that, you know."

I offered him a cigarette. He took it, still scowling, and accepted a light. He wasn't going to forget the binoculars incident. Easttree worked the conversation, as non-threatening and non-intrusive as possible. Light subjects, like tobacco preferences, leather cleaning products, anything but the fact of his living behind an air-conditioning unit. Finally, Easttree gave me a quick look.

"So, John, it must be difficult to be living out here, on the street. Is there anything I, we, could do to help you?"

"It's too bad he threw 'em," John looked at me. "Those were the best high-powered glasses I could find. Now the focus is all messed up."

Tina spoke up before I could respond.

"John, you know what? We have a pair of good binoculars down at the shelter, a donation from last year. Nobody ever uses them. Would you like to try them? I can bring them out next time."

He grilled me with his eyes for another minute, then turned his head to Tina. "Well, if it's no trouble, sure, that would be mighty nice of you. If you want, that is."

"I'll bring them out," Tina said.

He smoked the cigarette down to the butt and pitched it on the ground.

"You know," he said, looking at Easttree. "They keep close track of people like me."

"Must make you feel nervous, I'd imagine."

Leather Pants stared up at the sky. "That's why it's good to watch them back," he said. "So I know what they're up to. They don't think people know what they're doing, but I do." He squinted with his good eye toward the convention center on Boylston. "They have them everywhere, too."

"What do they have?" Easttree said.

Leather Pants made a snorting sound and stared back at Easttree.

"They have equipment that keeps track of everybody. Even you."

Easttree nodded, saying nothing. It seemed like a good time to leave.

"Well, John," I said. "We have to get going. You want another smoke?"

I gave him a couple. He mumbled under his breath as I handed them to him. He grudgingly accepted them, and even shook my hand as we left.

At Starbucks on Newbury we all went in to wash our hands.

"See, Axel," Tina said. "You need me around when you're dealing with him."

"You're a natural, Tina. I've always told you that."

"I think you owe me a donut."

Chapter 18

November 16, 2004

The Silent One came out of the library from the Dartmouth entrance. Thirty degrees on a grey, mid-November, ugly day. "What's he wearing?" Tina jabbed me in my shoulder with her finger. I looked up from the sports section. From our bench, we were a hundred yards away, but it was clear that he'd changed his clothes. At least on the upper body. "That's not what I think it is, is it?"

"I can't tell." I folded the paper and stuffed it in my backpack. "A wind-breaker, maybe."

Earlier in the day, we were down on the waterfront talking to Tony Ruffo. He'd needed a shower, new clothes, new shoes, the works. But he didn't want to go into the shelter with us to get them. Jimmie Irons was spending an occasional night in the shelter as it grew colder, usually transported late at night by the outreach van. Stella Simpson had relocated to a parking garage near the Fleet Center.

We sat on the bench in the cold wind with cups of coffee, and watched the Silent One as he crossed Dartmouth Street. "It's definitely plastic," Tina said.

A few people were gathered around Swaggert, and they didn't even bother to look at the Silent One as he searched the trash can near them. Swaggert waved at Tina and me, and shouted "Nice day, huh!" The negotiation between him and TL had gone smooth enough. Nobody was hurt. TL had decided it was too cold to be camping out, anyway, and had moved back in with the mother of his kids. After he'd finished the three-week drug treatment program in Lowell. Last I'd heard he was working with the furniture moving company again.

Tina jabbed me again, this time in my ribs with her elbow. "My god, Axel, he is, he's wearing a trash bag! Look!"

"I think you're right."

He moved from trash can to trash can in his slow, methodical routine, picking through leftover fast food bags. It was slim pickings with the cold weather, as most people were eating indoors. A large black garbage bag was pulled over his upper body. His arms were bare.

"Well, now we're talking business," I said. "The inability-to-care-for-self rule. I don't see the jacket he had on yesterday. Could he have washed it and left it to dry somewhere?"

Tina stood up and dug into her backpack, coming out with a sweatshirt. "I don't care, it's too damn cold out for that. I'm going to try to give him this."

"Good luck. I'll watch from here."

She walked straight up to him. His head was down, but he looked up at Tina's approach. She held out the sweatshirt to him. She held it out there for what must have been a good thirty seconds. I could see she was talking to him. When he wouldn't take it, she dropped it on the ground. I got up and walked over.

"I'm not playing anymore," she was saying to the Silent One. "Axel," she turned to me, "I told him he better accept some help from people before he freezes to death. I told him about people getting frostbite and losing fingers, toes, feet, hands." She looked back at him. "And I'm pretty sure you hear me. Maybe there's a reason you won't say anything or take any help, but it's going to get deadly cold out here soon."

He stared at her for just a few seconds, and then walked away. "Bye," Tina said. To me, she gave a bright smile. "Get me out of here before I scream, will you."

"Is it donut time?"

"Stop with the donuts, will you!" But she was smiling. "I'm thinking bagels, maybe brownies afterwards."

"Good idea. By the way, that was a hell of an effort. I think we're talking action-time, and maybe soon. If he doesn't accept clothing and the van sees him tonight and he won't take blankets…"

"I know. Shall we call Easttree, just to let him know we may be needing his help?"

"I'll call him."

We left the plaza as the Silent One continued his rounds. He still hadn't picked up the sweatshirt. We left it there, and went into the library. Pete was reading the *Globe*, and told us he was feeling a little sick. "Want to go somewhere?" I asked. "The hospital or the shelter clinic?" He stared at me through his thick lenses. "No thanks," he said, his voice sounding weak. "I'll live."

Lamar Cleveland was still holding court on Mass Ave at the bus stop. His legs were swollen badly and bleeding. He said he wanted to go to Saint Elizabeth's tomorrow. "Ten o'clock," he said.

Horseshoe Park was empty except for Saint Bernard. He was ready for winter. His elevated fort under the Storrow Drive bridge was high and dry, and he'd reinforced it with some Styrofoam insulation that some construction guys gave him. He was the only one all set for winter.

STREET LOGIC

Chapter 19

November 25, 2004

Thanksgiving was the biggest day of the year at the shelter, as far as the public was concerned. Volunteers started showing up at seven in the morning to set up tables and bring donations, and share some conversation with the guys. By noon, hundreds of turkey dinners would be ready to be served. The Mayor would arrive and make his rounds, shaking hands and sharing a few laughs. Made the guys in the shelter feel good. Made me want to hit the street.

Ripley and I stood in one corner of the lobby, watching the action. "There's more volunteers than homeless in here," he said. "I've seen this so many times now, but it still amazes me."

"What's it been? Ten years, right?"

"Including the time I worked at Fort Point? Must be a few more than that."

"Ever feel like working inside again?"

He shook his head and grunted. "You?"

"Nope."

A group of high school volunteers came into the lobby, crowded tightly together, looking lost. "See the expressions on their faces?" Ripley said. "That's what I love to see. There's nothing like that first visual of the lobby."

"Scared the shit out of me the first time."

Ripley laughed. "Was working the dinner line, wintertime. Messy, I recall."

"Standing room only. Hey, there's AD." I nudged him in the side. "We're being summoned."

"Time for the Turkey Run," he said. We started toward the stairwell where AD was waving at us.

"Tell you the truth, I'd rather go out on foot. Feel like walking?"

"In this snow?"

The tradition was that we all went out in the van, inviting people to come in for the feast. There were always the hardcore holdouts, guys like Phil and Jimmy Jay, Murphy, Lamar Cleveland, who wouldn't make the trek to the shelter, or couldn't, but might take a ride. Riding with a bunch of drunk guys crowded in the van didn't appeal to me this morning. I wanted to check out a few spots. And with the snow that fell last night, I knew it would be beautiful on the street.

"You shouldn't go solo, but what the heck," Adrian said. We were having another cup of coffee before hitting the road. Bette had the 'flu, so it was just the four of us. "Don't go anywhere dangerous," she added.

Tina was filling a large trash bag with the gifts that had been donated, socks, hats, scarves, to be passed out to whoever they ran into. She pulled a black ski-mask down over her face and pointed her fingers at us like guns. "Stop right there," she said, trying to sound like a gangster. "Get on the van and come eat turkey, or else."

"There you have it, AD," I said. "I'm telling you, Tina's the most dangerous one out there. I'm safer on my own." Tina dropped the bag of gifts and rushed across the room, punching me in the shoulder.

"See what I mean?" I said. "Nobody out there has ever punched me."

"Go on then, tough guy," Adrian said. "But don't call us when you find yourself cornered in an alley."

"Hit 911," Ripley said.

The place was crawling with volunteers by the time they drove out of the alley. I cut through the staff parking lot and came out on Berkely Street. I heard voices coming from inside Foley's Bar on the corner. It was 7:00a.m. A little early maybe, but it was Thanksgiving.

The snow was four inches deep, fluffy, not wet. I had my insulated Red Wing hiking boots on, my all-weather parka, gloves and hat, and was making tracks through the ball-field at Everett Park when I saw blood in the snow. Dark red drops that began at the playground and ran all the way to the small stand of trees behind the jungle gym. There was nobody around. Just some birds, making a lot of noise.

I followed the drops through the playground. There were footsteps next to the blood. The trail disappeared into the thicket of bushes and trees that lined one end of the park. Loud voices came from inside the snow covered grove. Then someone howled, and another voice laughed. I recognized the laugh of Jack Irons. I moved around to where I could see through the branches. Jack was sitting in a lawn chair in a small clearing, drinking from a quart-sized bottle of what looked like Diamond brand vodka. Next to him, on a milk crate, sat Jimmie Irons, his bloodied hand stuck out in front of him. Squatting in front of a small fire was Howard Bingham, breaking a wooden crate apart.

Jack poured some of the vodka on to Jimmie's hand.

"Shit!" Jimmie cried out, then laughed. "Forget that, I'd rather drink it! I thought you said you were a goddamn medic!"

Jack roared with laughter and staggered to his feet. "One more pull of this and I will be a goddamn medic!" He tilted his head back and took a long swallow, and then held his hand out to Howard. "Steady as a rock, ain't it, Bing?" Howard broke a piece of the crate over his knee and tossed it in the fire.

"Quit talking and just do it," Howard said. "Before you're too shit-faced to see straight."

Alright, goddammit!" the elder Irons barked. "Don't tell me what to do!" He turned to Jimmie. "Now sit still and don't move."

Jimmie held his hand out again. Jack doused it with more vodka, then stuck the bottle in the snow. Jimmie's face screwed up in a tight grimace, but he didn't make a sound. Jack fumbled in his pockets and came out with a box of Band-Aids and some white tape. He went to work. "Ouch!" Jimmie cried out.

"Shut up and take it like a man!" his father ordered. "It's only a goddamn scratch." He finished up, using strips of cloth to wrap the hand. As a final measure, Jack secured the bandage by wrapping a t-shirt around his son's hand, using a shoestring from one of his own boots to tie it in place. "There," he said. He pulled the bottle out of the snow and nearly fell over getting back in his chair.

Howard had the small fire going and had started cooking hot dogs with a stick. "Medic my ass," he said. "Professional goof-up, more like it."

"I was a goddamned medic!" Jack erupted. "Don't forget, I patched you up once! Keep your whining up and I'll kick your ass from here to Bridgewater!" He belted the words out, and then broke out laughing and passed the bottle to Howard. "Here, you little pipsqueak hot dog vendor, take a drink, will ya? You're making me nervous, going cold turkey on Turkey Day." He thrust the bottle out. Howard looked at it for a moment, then grabbed it out of his hands.

"Alright, big shot," Howard said. "Let me remind you of something you forget. You walked out on me a hundred times, leaving me to pay the bill. So I don't owe you anything." He took the hot dog stick from the fire and held it out. "And you should know better than to offend the cook. I might spit on your dog. So quit being an asshole, Jack. You always do this when you drink. Relax for once, will you?"

Jack laughed loudly, and poked his boot in the fire. "Alright, alright, let's just enjoy the goddamn snow, the booze, the good company," he gestured at Jimmie and Howard, "and those goddamn hot dogs! There's turkey at the shelter, and we're having a weenie roast." He roared again with laughter.

"You said you didn't want to be jammed in the crowd there, so we're here!" Howard jeered. Then he took a small drink and handed it to Jimmie. "Jesus, Jack, make up your mind."

I heard a few more shrieks of laughter from their camp as I left.

The silent, cobblestoned sidewalks of the South End were empty. It seemed like a perfect morning to enjoy my lone wolf status. I pulled out my matchbox and took a few tokes, then lit a cigarette.

My first stop was Pete's camp. I lifted the latch that hid the neighbor's back alley, and peered down the snowy path. The blue tarp was covered in white, and there were no footsteps. Either he was in there, or he had slept somewhere else. I went carefully down the slippery stairs. Half-way in, I stopped to listen. But there was only the sound of wind. The front flap was blowing and the camp looked deserted. I kept going, and looked inside the tent. It was abandoned.

There was no sign of recent activity, no sleeping bag and blankets. Just a pile of wet cardboard and some bags that contained trash.

I walked from there to Back Bay Station. Only the guy selling newspapers was there. I walked through Copley Square, and saw a few drinkers sitting on benches, guys from the shelter, laughing. They said they were going back to eat later. Behind the library, where Frank Murphy had been staying again, I found nobody. The heating vents in front of the library, where the Silent One usually spent the night, were empty as well. I kept moving and walked up Boylston toward Mass Ave. I called Adrian to update her.

Lamar Cleveland was sitting in his spot, under the roof of the bus stop. He was sleeping. "Hey Lamar. Happy Thanksgiving."

He moved, and slowly opened his eyes. As he focused, his scowl grew. "Happy Thanksgiving, my ass," he said, and closed his eyes again. He shifted his body on the bench, moaning as he tried to straighten his back. He finally opened his eyes and looked at me properly.

"Axel," he said. "What the hell are you doing out here on Thanksgiving? Ain't I told you, what you need is a vacation with pay, and a good woman to take with you. Not out here talking to an old fool like me."

"I couldn't think of a better thing to be doing, Lamar."

He smiled. "I don't believe that."

"Where is everyone this morning?"

Shrugging his shoulders, he just shook his head.

"You want to go eat a great dinner and get your legs looked at by some pretty nurses?"

He gave me that wide, loopy grin. "See, Axel, you think I don't know what you're doing. But I do."

"They're serving a great lunch, in a few hours. How's the leg, anyway?"

He reached into his coat and pulled out a bottle. "It ain't that bad."

We talked a little while, then I moved on. Newbury Street was dead. Nothing was open yet. At Gloucester, I turned up the alley and looked down the steps toward the air conditioner. There were tracks all through the alley. I walked back around to the front entrance of the convenience store. There was John Leather Pants, drinking a coffee and smoking a cigarette, talking. There was nobody else around. I walked down the steps and stopped about ten feet away.

"Hey, John." He looked up, his mouth still muttering. I smiled, and gestured at the snow. "Early this year, huh?"

"I don't know," he said, his voice agitated. "They want me to stay quiet, I'll stay quiet."

He shifted around on his feet, smoking rapidly. He finished one cigarette and lit another.

"Well, just wanted to let you know there's a big turkey lunch being served at Evergreen. If you're interested, I could see if the van can give you a ride there." He paced and smoked, muttering in his agitated way. He seemed aware of me, but didn't look my way or say anything else. After a few minutes, I started back up the steps. "I'll see you later, John. Take care."

He muttered a little louder, but I couldn't catch what he'd said. As I left, he was shaking his head in sudden jerky movements, scowling at the skyline.

I went down Rat Alley. Phil and Jimmy Jay were sleeping under the tarp left by the Ninja. They had strung it up over their spot in the back of the parking lot. I left them sleeping. The plaza at Copley was still quiet, though there were some people out now looking at the snow. A couple of kids were making snow angels in the middle of the park. I walked over to the bagel shop. They were selling turkey on a bagel, but I got my usual, peanut butter on wholewheat. I took the coffee and bagel and the newspaper upstairs, and sat in front of the windows. It was a perfect view of the entire plaza.

Halfway through the sports section, I looked up and saw the Silent One on the far side of the plaza poking through trash cans, as he always did. He was too far away for me to see if he still had the trash bag on his upper body. It was black, that's all I could tell. Something seemed odd about his pants, though. They were flapping in the wind. I needed to go take a closer look.

"Hey, Tina," I said into my phone, crossing Boylston toward the plaza. "How's the turkey transport going?"

"Well, believe it or not, we're taking Tony Ruffo in for a shower," she said, to sounds of laughter in the background. "And then he's going to have Thanksgiving dinner with the family of the bank manager, again. Remember last year?"

"You're busting my balls."

"No, he's in the van with us right now. Want to say hi?"

"Not now. Well, OK. Put him on."

She must have held the phone up to his ear. "Just talk, Tony," I heard Tina's voice say, nearby. "It's Axel."

Ruffo's gruff voice came through the phone. "Axel, you there?"

"Hey, pardner. I hear you got plans."

"Yeah. My friend at the bank."

"Nice to have friends like that," I said. "Maybe you'll get to watch the Lions lose another Thanksgiving Day game."

"They always shit the bed on Turkey Day." He started to laugh, then began coughing and hacking.

"Don't instigate him!" Tina said. "And you know what else?" she went on, her voice amused. "Guess what he's wearing to dinner?"

"Hopefully not what he's wearing now," I stopped in front of the fountain. I could see the Silent One better now. Some kind of shorts flapped around his knees.

"Tim from the dry cleaners gave him one of the suits from his collection of never collected clothes. The banker's family is picking him up at the shelter in a little while."

"Incredible. Hope they have another sweat suit ready."

"So what's with you, any action down there?"

"Leather Pants is talking to himself, Lamar is snoozing at the bus stop. Haven't seen many people. Just now spotted the Silent One. Listen," I said. "Let me call you back. Something looks a little funny about his outfit."

"Still wearing the bag jacket?"

"Could be a matching suit."

"Uh-oh," she said. Ruffo was talking again. "I got to go. After we drop Tony off, we'll head over your way. See you soon."

I walked past the statue of Thomas Copley and aimed for the far corner of the park near Dartmouth Street. The kid was walking between trash cans. The thing on his legs appeared to be cut-off shorts, but cut down the sides as well. I passed the ticket kiosk when he looked up and saw me. I gave him a friendly nod, and he gave me his standard no expression look. He had fashioned a pair of shorts out of a heavy-duty trash bag, the same kind he was wearing on top. The jeans were gone. The top didn't have any sleeves, and his arms were exposed to the cold. The shorts came down to his knees. He still wore the black boots, no laces, no socks.

I stopped and stared. He had to be freezing. As I began walking towards him, I greeted him, not expecting any response. "Good morning," I said, halting a few feet from him.

He looked up. "That's a pretty creative design there, with the bags." I watched his face for something, anything, but got nothing. It did seem he was shivering a bit. "But aren't you cold?" He turned away and began looking in the trash. "I can get you some clothes, if you want. Some good, warm gear. What do you say? Sound good?" He kept digging.

"Tell you what," I said. "Keep doing what you're doing there, and when the clothes arrive you can come over and take a look. There's some hot soup and coffee and sandwiches on the van as well. Think about it, OK?"

Whether he did, or could, I'll never know. Before I left, I took a close look at his legs and arms, and could see they were shaking. I walked toward the Fairmont Hotel as I called Adrian.

"He's wearing garbage bags, AD. Top and bottom. His arms and legs are exposed. Still has shoes but no socks. Didn't say a word, as usual, but I told him there would be a van with clothes down here soon."

"Calm down, Axel," Adrian said, "you sound a little stressed. I assume we're talking about the Silent One. Is he still there, within sight?"

"Just across the street from me."

"We're coming right now," she said. "Where are you?"

"Inside the Fairmont Hotel entrance. The one with the lions."

"We'll be there soon."

I hung up, and watched through the windows as he moved towards Trinity Church. I dialed another number.

"Happy Thanksgiving," I said as soon as he muttered a hello. "Did I wake you up?"

"Yeah, you did. What time is it?"

"About nine o'clock. Sorry to bother you, but I need a consultation – it won't take more than two minutes."

"I doubt that," Easttree said. "Hold on a second." I heard him say something to Rebecca, followed by a long pause, then a click. "I got it!" he yelled. "OK, what's up?"

"It's the Silent One. He's wearing garbage bags. It's below freezing with four inches of snow, if you haven't looked out your window yet. Shoes, no socks. Shivering like hell. I'm waiting for the van to get here with clothes, see if now he'll take some."

"Say anything?"

"Of course not."

"Anything else?"

"What else do we need?"

"Nothing. That should do it," he said. "Want me to call now?"

"Yeah. And can you call Phil, too?"

"Don't know if I can reach him, but I'll try. He's in Vermont, but he always has his cell." He paused. "Remember, Axel, if he ends up accepting clothes from you guys, he's going to appear to be able to clothe himself appropriately. To take care of himself out there. Know what I mean? So before I call Huffman, I want to know that the kid's refused a direct offer of clothes. I'd rather have him evaluated in garbage bags, to tell you the truth."

"Exactly."

"Call me as soon as that offer gets refused."

"Thanks, Tree. Talk soon."

"Oh, yeah," he said. "Happy Thanksgiving."

I went out the revolving doors and stood by the twin golden lions. No sign of him. I hurried across the street, and headed toward Trinity. If I lost him now, the whole opportunity could fall through.

He was on the other side of the church, still rummaging through empty trash cans. The outreach van turned down Boylston and pulled over at the bagel shop across the street from us. Tina saw me, and waved through the window. I walked up to the Silent One and cleared my throat.

"Hi. It's me again." He ignored me. "The clothes are here," I went on, "in the van across the street. Do you want to check them out, and get something to eat, too?"

I stood there another minute. Part of me was relieved he had refused. The shivering had intensified in his legs. I felt like I'd tried everything short of throwing a blanket on him. I left him and walked across the street to the van, turning a few times to keep him in sight.

The side door slid open. Tina stood there with a cup of coffee in her hand. "Here," she said, handing it to me. "So how did it go?"

I climbed on board and sat down where I could see out the windows. "You should see the shorts he's made."

Adrian turned around from the driver's seat. "Did he refuse clothing?"

"Yes."

"We can take some clothes out there and offer them to him," Tina said. "If he doesn't take them now, in this weather, we did everything we could." Tina glanced at me. "Although, if he goes into an evaluation dressed as he is, in those bags, it's better odds they'll keep him."

"I was thinking the same thing," I said.

Adrian looked at us both, then stared out the front window. He was still next to Trinity, his shorts flapping in the wind. "I know," Adrian said. "Still, we have to give it a shot. I'm more of a stranger to him than you two. If he won't take it, we call it in."

"I already did," I said.

"You already spoke to Emergency Services?"

"No, I called Easttree. He's going to alert them. Tell them what's happening. And he's willing to call Huffman in Vermont as soon as we know he's refused clothing."

"Good work," she said, opening her door. "Pass me that black coat and a pair of those black sweatpants, will you?"

We sat in the front seats and watched her cross the street, the clothes in her arms.

"What happened to Ripley?" I said.

"He's got Tony Ruffo duty. Dressing him up for dinner at the banker's house."

"Poor Rip."

"That's what I thought," she said.

I called Easttree. "Adrian's approaching him as we speak," I told him. "To make a final offer."

"I hope she doesn't try to force-clothe him," Easttree said. "Strike that. I just want to make the best case we can."

"We'll know in a few minutes. What about Emergency Services?"

"They're alerted. They're waiting to hear from us."

"Good. You want the play-by-play?"

"Give it to me," he said.

"Adrian's twenty feet away, the kid's head is in the trash can. Ten feet now. She's talking to him. He's looking at her. Now she's holding out the clothes. He's staring at her, she's still got them out there, he's still just staring, and, and, and…"

"And what?"

"No go. He didn't take them. She's coming back."

"Let me talk with her, make it official."

I rolled the window down as Adrian walked up, and held the phone out to her. She passed me the clothes. "Easttree?"

"Yeah," I said. She grabbed the phone out of my hand. She spoke for a few minutes, then walked around the van and climbed in the side door. "We need to keep him in eye contact. Easttree's calling Emergency Services to say it's a go. He's giving them my number so they can call for our exact location."

"Well," Tina said. "Finally."

We lost sight of him when he went into Trinity church.

"Shit." I slid the door open and jumped out of the van. "I'll go in. You guys can watch the exit."

"I'll go with you," Adrian said. "Tina, can you keep an eye on the front entrance, in case he slips out."

Adrian and I entered the church. The massive cathedral was nearly empty. I counted three people kneeling or sitting on the benches. No sign of the Silent One.

"Jesus, he's got to be in here somewhere," I said.

"I didn't know you prayed, Axel."

"One of my hidden strengths, AD."

"Good morning." A young woman came over to us from a table near the entrance. "Services start today at eleven. But of course you're free to stay."

"Hi," Adrian said. "We're actually looking for someone. My name's Adrian Dantley, this is Axel Hazzard. We work for the Evergreen Shelter. The young black man that just came in? Did you see him?"

"Why, yes," she said. "In plastic bags?"

"We're pretty concerned about him," Adrian said.

"Oh I'm so glad you're here! He's over there," she said, pointing toward a confessional box.

"Inside?" I asked.

"Yes."

"Is there a...?" Adrian started, then paused.

"No," the young woman smiled. "Confessions are heard only on Tuesdays and Saturdays."

"Mind if we sit here a while?" I said.

"Not at all." She hesitated, looking from me to Adrian. "Is he alright?"

"Not really, no," Adrian said. "There's an ambulance coming to take him to the hospital. If he's still here when they arrive, the paramedics and the police will probably have to come in here, to get him. I hope that's not going to be a problem."

The women's eyes widened. "Oh. He looks like he needs help." She seemed relieved. "I was so surprised when I saw him like that, and was just trying to figure out who to call."

We took a bench at the back of the church to wait. "I didn't think girls that young were allowed to be nuns," I whispered to Adrian. "Or that women even wanted to be nuns anymore. Maybe in Italy, but here?"

Adrian quieted me with her eyes. We settled back to watch the door of the confessional box.

About ten minutes later, he came out. He wandered slowly around the church, looking at the ceiling, the statues along the walls, and then stopped for a moment in front of the altar. We stayed put, watching him. Finally, he came up the aisle, passed us without looking, and headed out the exit. I waved at the nun as we left.

He crossed Boylston and passed in front of the van. Adrian called Tina. "Stay with him. Axel and I are going to split up and take opposite ends of the street. We can't lose him."

"I'll take Clarendon Street," I said. "You want to stay on the park side and move toward Dartmouth?"

"OK. Looks like he's heading toward Dartmouth now. If he cuts toward Newbury, go up Clarendon and watch the alley. I'll let you know if he heads that way."

I crossed Boylston. Tina trailed at about a hundred feet as he wandered up Boylston toward Dartmouth, away from me. A guy came out of the ATM on the corner of Dartmouth, and the Silent One grabbed the door and went in. Tina turned and waved at me. She joined Adrian, and they took up a post outside the Old South Church. I walked toward the ATM and stopped a few storefronts down from it.

A police car pulled up and two officers got out. I recognized one of them, Jim Dudley, who usually had the Kenmore Square beat. "Thought Copley was out of your area, Officer?"

Dudley used to play college ball and he walked like an ex-linebacker. Powerful, almost graceful, for a big man. "Just helping out." His hand swallowed mine as he shook it. "Happened to be in the neighborhood. What's up, Axel? How you been?"

"Working Turkey Day like you are. I'm doing good. Hey, by the way – TL said your little talk with him was the first time a cop ever treated him like a human being."

Dudley laughed. "Most cops are scared of a brother like TL. Just needed a little heart to heart talk, a push in the right direction, that's all."

"Most cops aren't as big as TL, or you, either, Jim," I looked at the other officer with Dudley, a short, trim, white guy in his twenties. "But size isn't everything, right? Look at me…" The little guy gave me a dry smile.

"I'm just glad he's off the street," Dudley said. "Hope he stays clean. So, what have you got for us?"

Adrian and Tina walked up and greeted Dudley. They knew him from the meetings we all attended at City Hall.

"Hello, ladies," he said. "How we doing today?"

"Doing," Adrian said. She filled him in as the ambulance arrived. One of the paramedics walked over to join us, while the other opened the rear door and pulled out the stretcher. Dudley took a quick look at the paperwork the paramedic showed him.

"Mass General, huh?" he said. "Want us to follow you?"

"No thanks, hospital security will be there."

I looked at Adrian. "Mass General?"

"Dr Phil called a buddy of his," Adrian said. "He wants to have the evaluation done there. They have a bed, too, for now."

"OK by me," I said.

"Where is he?" the lead paramedic asked.

"He's in the ATM," Adrian said.

"Can't blame him," Dudley said. "Well, gentlemen, shall we do this?" The other paramedic rolled the stretcher on to the sidewalk.

"Before you take him," Adrian addressed the paramedics, "just so you know, this young man has never spoken with us. We've been trying for months. We believe he does hear, but, well, you'll see. And," she added, "he's shown no indications of violence."

The lead paramedic stuffed the commitment papers in an outside pocket. "Report said he's wearing trash bags?"

"He had clothes, but in the last week or so he gradually lost them. Something happened," I said.

"Asking for help, sounds like," Dudley said.

"How do you think he's going to react?" the paramedic asked.

"To the police? No idea," Adrian said. "When we've approached him, he just looks at us, and walks away."

"Then we'll need you guys," the paramedic said to Dudley and his partner. "You all want to be involved?" He turned to Adrian, Tina and me.

"No," Adrian said. "We don't have any influence with him."

"OK."

Before they started for the ATM, Dudley took a credit card out of his wallet. "Police training," he smiled. "Never go to work without it."

Adrian, Tina and I crossed Dartmouth and stood near the Copley T-stop entrance. We watched Dudley insert his card and open the door. He went in first, followed by his partner, then the paramedics. They left the stretcher on the street. The Silent One must have been on the floor, because they were all looking down. It looked like Dudley was doing most of the talking. After a few minutes, we saw the Silent One stand up, gesturing with his arms, moving them up and down. Dudley's partner took a step toward the kid, but the big man put a hand out to stop him. Then the Silent One began doing jumping jacks.

"My god," Tina said. "He's showing them he's healthy."

An hour later, we were back in the office, drinking hot coffee and sitting around the conference table. We filled Ripley in on the action. Easttree called to tell us the evaluating psychiatrist decided in favor of keeping the Silent One for the maximum ten-day evaluation. After that, they would decide whether to go for a longer commitment, or release him.

"Well, that's it," Tina said. "Now they can figure out what's going on with him."

"Rogers time, I imagine," I said.

"That shouldn't be hard to get," Ripley said.

A Rogers was a legal device that gave the treating doctors the right to administer medication when they believed the patient couldn't improve without it. With or without the patient's cooperation. A judge needed to approve it.

Adrian walked in from the holiday dinner that was still going on downstairs, carrying two plates of desserts. "Here ya go," she said, setting them down on the conference table. "For a good day's work."

Tina picked up a fudge brownie and bit into it.

"How is that thing?" I asked.

"Don't start," she said, her mouth full.

"Just asking." I picked up one and tried it. "Damn, I'd say it beats out the Boston Kreme."

"Nothing beats Boston Kreme," Tina said, taking another bite.

Adrian sat down at the table, her face relaxed for the first time since we began the stake-out in Copley. She picked up one of the brownies and took a big bite out of it. "I just saw Tony leave," she said. "You should have seen him. All dressed up and sitting in the back of a Lexus Sedan. They even gave him a haircut in the clinic."

"I was the barber," Ripley said, grinning.

"Tony has a way of getting around, doesn't he?" I said. "He must have loved riding in a new Lexus."

"If he even knows what it is," Adrian said. "He always told me he liked the Cadillac Fleetwood the most."

"He told me the Lincoln Mark 4," I said. "Was he walking or did they need a wheelchair?"

"He was walking," Ripley said. "Slowly. Doing the TR shuffle like only he knows how."

I took another bite of the brownie. "What exactly are they going to do? Keep him overnight this time? Put him in the guestroom?"

"They're going to bring him back here later," Adrian said.

"I'd love to see that Thanksgiving dinner," I said. "Did you remind them he needs vodka or he might go into a seizure?"

"I did," Ripley said. "They said they were prepared."

We tried a few of the other desserts, drinking coffee and talking about weekend plans.

"I didn't see Leather Pants downstairs," Adrian said after a while.

"He was in a real state this morning, when I saw him," I said.

"Real estate?" Ripley said.

"He does live in the high-rent district. Actually, I didn't push the shelter feast on him. He was kind of unapproachable. The festivities here would probably send him over the edge."

"I think he's already there," Ripley said.

"We have to do something about him," Adrian said. "But not today. Go home and get some rest, you guys. Good work out there. And don't forget the conference, 10:00a.m. Monday at the Wilder."

I drove home listening to Stevie Ray Vaughan's "Couldn't Stand the Weather", pushing the Lincoln's speaker system to its limit. I turned it down for a quick phone call.

"Hey there. It's officially the long Holiday weekend."

"Very funny," she said. "I have the turkey in the oven already."

STREET LOGIC

Chapter 20

November 28, 2004

I spent most of that weekend at home, between my studio in the basement and Holiday's attic room. With an occasional stop midway, in Paul's kitchen or out on the deck.

"So, have you discovered her real name? Or doesn't it matter?"

We sat at his kitchen table after the wind drove us off the deck. He'd set out two small glasses and filled them with Glenlivet.

"I have. And it doesn't."

"That's all you're going to say?"

I raised the glass and felt the warmth go down my throat. "She doesn't like her given name."

"That bad?"

I looked at him over the top of the glass. "You still think I'm fooling around with a kid, don't you?"

He laughed. "Not at all, Axe. I've talked to her enough. She's more mature than most thirty-year-olds. Hey, whatever happened with Wendy?"

"Lucky for me, she fell for a biker."

"Before or after you and Holiday?"

"Does it matter?"

He raised his glass and knocked it against mine. "Damn glad for you."

"And I'm glad you rented her a room. Without a deposit or third-party guarantee."

"You're my guarantee," he smiled. "So you going to tell me?"

"Alice Grim," I said.

He held it together for about five seconds. When he was done laughing, he wiped his eyes. "Can't blame her."

The temperatures remained below freezing all weekend. But in the mornings, the sun streamed brightly through the attic window for an hour or so, directly on to the futon. Sunday morning brought clear skies.

"Almost as good as the beach," Holiday said. She was wearing the bathing suit she had on in the photo, with Walt Whitman's *Leaves of Grass* resting on her stomach. The sun lit up her entire body.

"I'd say better. No rules."

"You like that, huh? No rules."

"Depends. It's good to have rules for some things. Kids should go to school, adults shouldn't molest children, politicians should be impeached if they're lying sacks of shit. You know, simple, easy to understand rules."

"And every society should be responsible for the truly poor, sick and crazy people who can't care for themselves?"

"Whitman, I presume?"

"I'm paraphrasing."

"Take care of the poor and the crazy, I think it goes."

"'Stand up for the stupid and crazy'," she corrected me. She bent the corner of the page she was reading and closed the book, tossing it on the floor on top of a book about the Great Depression.

"What about that one? Any good advice from that on how to live?"

"The Depression? Save your money under the bed, I guess. That was pretty crazy," she said. "People lost it all, killed themselves over it. Total panic."

"Seems like we're headed for another one. And supersized."

"But to kill yourself over it? That's too much."

"They defined themselves by their losses. Probably couldn't live with themselves."

"Still, you have to go on," she said, crawling on top of me. "Money and possessions can be recovered. But not your life." She lay her head on my chest, brown eyes watching me playfully. "Right? You have to go on."

"Right," I said. I ran my hands through her hair, down her warm back. "If you can."

226

"You don't believe those people on the street can?"

"No. Some of them, no. Not on their own."

"Like the Silent One?"

I looked into Holiday's clear, hopeful eyes, at her almost tan skin. "Exactly. Like the Silent One."

I pulled her up so she was on her knees, facing me. She put her hands on my shoulders, shaking her hair loose.

"You have a beautiful face to go with that beautiful spirit," I said.

"You talk this smooth on the street, you ought to convince even the toughest ones to get some help."

"I wish it were a matter of talking."

"So you had to pull the trigger on him," she said, softly, rocking her body forward and backward.

"We had to do it," I said, reaching for her.

"Just like you might have to pull the trigger on me someday, huh?" She said it with a smile, but I caught the double meaning.

"Anybody can pull the trigger on the other, in a relationship," I said. "You could pull it on me, too."

"I suppose I could. But, for now, I think I'll just pull on this," she reached behind her neck for the string of her bikini top, and let it drop. She leaned forward, bringing her face close to mine. "You want to section me?"

"Are you going to come easy, or will I have to strap you down?"

She narrowed her eyes and started swaying from side to side, like a cobra ready to strike. "I can't guarantee that I'll come easy. Are your intentions pure?" she hissed.

"On the street, I only pull the trigger with the best of intentions."

"And in bed?"

"Same thing."

"Well then, Mister Outreach Worker," she formed her hands into pistols and pointed them at me, "I think it's trigger time for you."

STREET LOGIC

Chapter 21

November 29, 2004

On Monday morning at quarter to ten, I was sitting in my car in the parking lot of the Wilder Center. I opened the ashtray and considered what lay in it, listening to the finale of The Who's 'Won't Be Fooled Again'. Then I pushed it closed and lit a cigarette instead. Good choice. Tina's red Toyota pulled into the parking spot next to me. She jumped out and opened the passenger door of the Lincoln, sliding into the front seat. "Having a pre-game smoke, huh?"

"Breakfast of champions. How was your weekend?"

"Peaceful. I didn't go out at all, just to run and walk Sappo."

"Lucky dog, that Sappo. Cold out, but at least the sun was nice." I thought of Holiday, sunbathing on her futon.

Tina rested her head on the back of the seat and yawned. "I hope this meeting finally resolves something."

"For who? Ruffo, or everybody who gets to 'air their feelings'?"

She gave me a sarcastic smile. "Listen, after what happened with that kid last Thursday, in plastic bags, maybe there's a momentum here. Plus, I don't think cold, wet blankets are much different than bags, at this point. Speaking of Tony, did you hear?"

"No. What happened?"

"The banker's family brought him back to the shelter after Thanksgiving," she said, stretching her arms above her and yawning again. "They dropped him off at the entrance, walked him in, right, to see that he was all set. Apparently, he walked back out after they left. The overnight van found him three blocks from the shelter on their last run, took him to Evergreen. And Ripley just saw him back on Atlantic about an hour ago. But he's got a new sleeping spot. Guess where?"

"The bank president's office?"

"Hardly." Tina reached over and turned the radio station to 94.5.

"Hey, that's classic rock you're messing with," I said. "I can't handle that jam'n hip-hop stuff before noon."

"You'll live. You know the entrance to the highway, across the street from the bank? Now he's set up there, between those concrete Jersey barriers. He said he was getting mugged at night along the waterfront."

I ground out the cigarette in the ashtray. "Now he really is stuck between a rock..."

"I know," she said. "Ripley said the same thing. I hope you guys don't make those kinds of jokes in the meeting. But I have to admit," she pushed her shoulders back against the leather, rolling her neck in tiny circles, "there's definitely a need for humor sometimes."

"A little levity goes a long way in this business." I opened my door. "You ready, champ? Let's go kick some ass."

"Don't you mean win one for the Ruffo?" She straightened up. "You know, Axel, everybody's going to be in there. Some with different opinions about Tony, and not all of them as humorous as yours."

"Me, humorous? Tina," I looked straight into her deep brown eyes, "I'm serious as hell. Hey, you know what?" I paused, giving myself a few more seconds to look at those eyes. "Has anyone ever told you that you have too big a heart, not to mention too much smarts, to be doing this kind of a dirty job?"

She flashed a skeptical look at me, holding my gaze. "Nope," she said. I saw the smile before she turned and swung her leg out of the car. "But they do tell me I'm too sexy."

I laughed. "I'm sure they do. You have a lot of 'too's there, Tina." I turned off the radio and pocketed the keys. "Well, maybe we can at least agree on the best one."

She swung her head around. "Best one?"

"Best opinion. On what to do about Tony. What did you think I was talking about?"

When she stepped outside, she turned and gave me a bright smile. "My finer points, of course. I was thinking in the plural."

The conference room was on the second floor of the Wilder Center, at the end of the hall where the medical staff had their offices. An L-shaped table occupied most of the small room. The chairs crowded around the table gave people just enough room to walk behind them. I slipped behind Bette, said hello, and moved on to get a cup of coffee and a muffin from the snack table. People drifted into the room and I found a seat before they were all filled. Besides the street team from Evergreen, two other city outreach teams were in attendance, as well as the Medical Care street team.

I watched Bette Malloy as she worked on a jelly donut and spread cream cheese on a bagel at the same time. Her skills never ceased to amaze me. A little clumsy, sometimes, in her interactions on the street, but she was dead on when it came to making a clinical diagnosis. Behind her, hanging next to a window, was a painting that looked like a copy of an Andrew Wyeth. An immense green field stretching toward a white farmhouse. Tree branches scraped against the window. Another storm was forecast for later tonight. I drank my coffee, looked from the darkening sky to the painting, and tuned out the buzzing of voices.

It had never been more evident to me what I believed in. In the past year and a half, I had formed my own opinions. They weren't always popular. My legs had grown strong, but my knees were sore as hell some days. My mind was tired from the effort to find solutions to nearly impossible situations. My right Achilles ached at the end of the day. I knew that dealing with survival issues day in, day out, against bad odds, adds up. But I wasn't sure what it added up to. I didn't feel burned out. Maybe I was fooling myself, though. For now, I was going to put out whatever fires I could. My mind drifted towards the painting above Bette's head, thinking of the long conversations with Underwood and Holiday about the Farm. I'd mentioned it to everyone on the team, including Easstree, usually when things seemed the most futile. A farm with a field like the one in the painting.

I brought my mind back to Tony Ruffo's case. Despite all the varied and heroic efforts from the people in this room, Ruffo was still out there. And at the same time that he had managed to galvanize an entire network of health care nuts to discuss his future, I felt sure he was at this moment staring up at the Harper Tower clock, bottle in hand, and if he was conscious at all he'd be hearing the bells of ten o'clock ringing.

"Well, I guess we can get started," Phil Huffman said. "We all have a lot to talk about, I'm sure."

I leaned back in my chair and took a bite out of the chocolate chip muffin, and scanned the room. Smiles were at a minimum, I noticed. Adrian sat with her forearms on the table, her face neutral, her attention focused on Huffman. Ripley sat next to her. He caught my eye, gave me a subtle wink. I nodded, drank more coffee, and waited to see who'd jump into the fire first.

Nobody said anything. It was up to Dr Phil. He cleared his throat, nodded at everyone, and launched into the medical perspective. Tony suffered from alcoholism, cirrhosis of the liver, low blood counts, and neuropathy, among other things. "Alcoholic neuropathy, from damaged nerve endings," Phil said. "Specifically, limb-kinetic apraxia, gait apraxia, which makes it difficult for him to start walking, and keep walking."

"Is there any treatment for it at this stage?" Tina asked.

"In Tony's case, with thirty, forty years of drinking under his belt, the best is that the deterioration could be slowed down, maybe stabilized. He could still get around, and would probably get a little stronger without alcohol. That is, if we can just convince him to give up the bottle."

I liked Phil. He said it like it was. Then a few nurses gave their opinions. They were especially feisty as they defended their practice of giving him sponge baths in the van. It was his dignity they were protecting. It was the Hippocratic Oath they'd taken as nurses, one of them reminded us, staring at me, to care for those who needed it, whatever the situation was. I stayed quiet. They were right.

Easttree came in late and sat down next to Huffman. Phil gave him the floor, but he kept it short, saying only that Tony was one of the most vulnerable people he was working with. He deferred to Adrian. "I think outreach knows his daily situation better than I do."

Adrian gave him a courteous smile, and gave our team's point of view. How many times we saw him, on average, what condition he was in, his usual refusals to come into the shelter, even during the worst weather. Exceptions being under direct orders from the Mayor himself, she added, and Thanksgiving Day. That brought the first smiles of the meeting. "But the main thing," Adrian said, "is that we all would like to see him have a chance to live in better conditions. It's pretty apparent to us that he's stuck, unable to make any decisions about his health, and his situation."

Tina gave her side, Ripley his. Both were pretty much the same as the picture Adrian painted. Bette set her bagel aside and pitched in, saying that in her opinion, until he could address his alcoholism – or be forced to, she added – he would be risking his life out there every day. Especially with another long winter coming.

The other outreach teams presented similar stories. I glanced at the clock. Almost an hour, and still no solutions presented. Phil turned to me. "Axel, you've been quiet so far. Do you want to add anything?"

I closed my notebook and looked around the table. At all the faces of those who had tirelessly gone out there and tried to do something good. Adrian was watching me. "Sure," I said, and sat up straight. "It seems to me that we're basically down to Plan F."

Adrian closed her eyes and rubbed her temples. Tina opened hers wide, shook her head, but then sighed and gave a quick nod. Ripley was grinning, encouraging me to put it on the table. I looked at the nurses, who had curious, almost suspicious, expressions. The members of the other outreach teams and the social workers eyed me expectantly. Easttree smiled and leaned his chin on his hand.

"Perhaps, Axel," Phil said, with an amused look, "you can fill in those of us who aren't in the know about what, exactly, is Plan F."

I glanced at the Wyeth painting above Bette. "Plan F is what we don't have in place yet, actually. If it were, it might look a little like that painting, there." I pointed above Bette's head. I heard some murmuring going on among the nurses.

"I'm suggesting the ideal," I went on. The room grew quiet. "For me, when I analyze this kind of situation with Tony, as well as some of the others who are in his category of high vulnerability and severe incapacitation, I think about what should happen." I paused. It seemed even quieter. Adrian had re-opened her eyes.

"After all the various efforts that many of us in this room have made, and I commend everyone for using what they have," I glanced at the head nurse for Medical Care, "our man is still on the street. And getting worse. The good old 'Come on, Tony, you can do it' approach isn't working. I think we have to be honest about the results. It's great that he gets all the attention he does, that he gets cleaned up once in a while, that he gets invited somewhere for Thanksgiving besides the shelter. But to continue to keep doing the same things, and getting the same results, well," I looked at Bette, an ex-alcoholic, who was nodding her head, "we all know how that goes. And what I also know is that we're not in the middle of the Sahara desert, or some ideal world like in that painting. We're here in the city of Boston, where there are services available even for guys like Tony Ruffo. But Tony can't make that decision. As he's been known to say, it would kill him." I paused, shifted in my chair and looked at Phil. "There's only one law that can intervene, unfortunately, or fortunately, depending on how you look at it. So," I glanced around the table, and gave my best sincere smile, "since we don't have the country spa and farm of Plan F set up yet, we have to use the system that we have. I vote for you, Phil, to consider signing off on the commitment papers. Get him into a hospital long enough for him to dry out, and be medically evaluated. The rest of us can follow up as best as possible. Visit him, visit his docs and nurses. Work with them. And maybe, if we can convince a judge that he's not competent to care for himself on the street, we can steer him into some kind of supervised housing with medical care. At this stage, I just don't think it's right not to do something different."

The silence felt heavy, but I felt lighter. Phil looked around the room, and waited to see if anybody was going to respond. They were all looking at him.

"Well, I have to say, Axel," he said, with a smile. "Well put. As you know, a commitment with someone like Tony is a tricky piece of business. I've been doing it long enough to know that it's a tough battle. The commitment with an alcoholic, unfortunately, rarely sticks past the initial evaluation period. But," he paused, taking a look at the Wyeth painting for a moment, "given the nature of this case, and the investment of everyone in this room, I have to agree with you. Winter is here already, and he's going to need a miracle to survive another one. And we have enough witnesses to fill a court room, if it comes to that. Which it probably will, in order to get a commitment ruling for extended treatment. But that's getting too far ahead of ourselves. I'm going to need a few days to set this up. I'll let everyone know when we're ready."

It wasn't what I expected. I thought there was going to be more resistance to a legal commitment, given the failures of past efforts. Everyone started talking and the meeting was adjourned. Adrian shook her head, but couldn't hide the smile working across her face. I pushed my chair back and walked over to Phil.

"Well, Phil, congratulations. Another successful outreach meeting. Now comes the hard part. But at least we have the Hippocratic Force with us."

Phil's loud, hearty laugh, was probably one of the factors that kept him healthy. "Plan F, huh? I was waiting for you to drop the punch line, but never expected farm. I was thinking of other f-word possibilities," he grinned.

"I would never. Just a big healthy farm in the country, that's all we need. Medically staffed, of course."

"Organic, too, I hope. It's a plan ahead of its time, Axel." He lowered his voice and guided me out into the hallway. "In all seriousness, doing this thing for Ruffo is going to be a matter of a lot of little things falling into the right places. Placement being the most difficult. It's damn hard to get a judge to go for a long-term commitment without that lined up. And the costs of treatment. Unless the judge happens to be in recovery himself, or herself."

"I know. Be nice if we could arrange that," I said. "Anyway, I'll be happy to testify at the commitment hearing."

"I'm sure you will." He shook my hand. "I'll let you know as soon as we're ready to pick him up. Plan F," he chuckled. "Good one, Axel."

Adrian walked out of the room and watched Huffman wander down the hall. She poked me in the ribs. "I thought I was going to have to personally kill you." She smiled.

Chapter 22

November 30, 2004

In the library, I found Pete sitting at the newspaper table, reading the sports section of the *Globe,* as was his habit. His mouth moved a little as he followed the words. I took a chair opposite him. "How are you doing, Pete?"

"Oh, Axel." He raised his head. "So-so, I guess."

"How so-so?"

"Not so good, actually. I might be coming down with a cold."

He was more than pale, I realized, almost white. His skin normally had a Mediterranean kind of year-round tan. And his voice was raspier than usual. Almost sounded like something was caught in his lungs.

"All this cold weather doesn't help."

"That's true." His thick glasses hung near the end of his nose. He managed a weak smile. "Can't do much about that."

"Maybe you should see a doctor, Pete, if you're feeling sick."

He barely shook his head. "No, I'll be alright. It's warm in here."

"And at night?"

"I'll be alright," he said again. I knew he spent his check on a room at the Milner Hotel, in the theatre district. I'd seen him coming out of there once, accidentally, as I was driving downtown one night. I went in and gave the receptionist my card in case anything ever happened to him while he was there, and to see what I could learn. Found out he usually stayed five or six nights at the beginning of each month.

"You know something, Pete?"

"I know a few things."

"I know you do," I smiled. "A lot more than me, I'm sure. But I'm a little worried about you, pardner. Being sick, down with the cold, out in weather like this. And the long winter coming. A guy like you deserves a warm place, that's all I know."

He began to chuckle, shaking his head slowly. "Axel. I have a place. I'm trying to get it back. In the meantime, I'm alright."

"You sure you don't want some help with that?"

"What kind of help?"

"For starters, somewhere to operate from. We can get you a bed tonight, in the quiet part of the shelter. They have a nice set up. From there, you can make phone calls, receive phone calls, and there's some people who can help you track this thing down. Whatever happened with your house, it can be tracked down. And in the meantime, you're warm at night." I felt like I'd delivered this speech a hundred times.

He didn't say anything for a while. We sat there, surrounded by the quiet of the library. I pulled a section of the newspaper over and looked at a photograph of a beach in Bermuda. Checked the prices. Pete's head was down, his snoring garbled.

"It's going to be a nasty winter, Pete," I stood, aware that I was probably talking to myself. "The elder statesmen program at Evergreen is free. And it's quieter, much quieter, than the rest of the shelter."

I wandered up to Mass Ave, pulling my wool hat out of my backpack. Lamar Cleveland wasn't at the bus stop, or in the subway entrance, or down where the tracks and long benches were. I kept walking toward Kenmore. Tina called and said she was over at the Jersey barriers where Tony was hunkered down. Status quo.

"He said he might hitch-hike to Gloucester," she said.

"He's in the right spot to catch a ride. Maybe he senses the big hand of Phil about to come down."

"Don't be ridiculous."

"It's hard not to be," I said.

I talked to a lot of different people, none of whom wanted anything in particular. I looked down the alley where Leather Pants' cave was, standing safely at the edge of Morisson's courtyard. He was pacing back and forth in front of the air conditioner, talking to himself. Occasionally shouting. I kept going. I thought about Plan F. Maybe I just liked the way it sounded on Holiday's lips.

Chapter 23

December 2, 2004

"How about those Pats?" I leaned over the Jersey barrier, raising my voice against the traffic. Ruffo lay flat on his back inside the triangle of concrete, his head resting just below me on a blanket. His body was positioned in such a way that his legs, covered in blankets, were at the base of the triangle, with his head near the top angle. Pointing south, I noticed. He was still wearing the Thanksgiving Day suit and overcoat. Cradled in his arm was a quart-sized bottle of vodka. He heard me, squinting as he opened his eyes.

"Hey," he muttered. "What time is it?"

I pointed up at the clock on the Harper Tower. "Three-thirty. You got somewhere to be?" It was Thursday and I'd been here to see him twice this week, waiting for the plan to be finalized. I'd just gotten off the phone with Phil Huffman ten minutes ago. Tomorrow, everything would be set up. Phil had apologized for how long it took. Tony would be taken to Mass General for the initial evaluation, and kept until he was medically cleared for a bed in a locked-unit detox program. Generally positive, Phil had sounded annoyed at the delay.

Tony Ruffo peered up at the sky. "All I see are clouds." He didn't smell good, but he'd be getting a good long shower soon enough. He groaned and gritted his teeth, and slowly raised himself up to a sitting position with his back against one of the barriers. Once he was settled, he turned his blue eyes toward me. "The Pats," he said. "Keep winning, don't they?"

"They have a coach that would rival old Woody, don't you think?"

Ruffo made a face at me and grunted. "Woody was tougher," he said. "Knew how to handle his players."

"Like whacking them up side the head?"

"Worked, didn't it?" He tried a grin, but it came out as a grimace.

I shook my head and smiled at him. The traffic light turned green and cars sped past us up the ramp. I waited a minute. "Nowadays,

Tony," I went on, "a coach would be arrested for motivating his players like that."

"That's what I hear. Shame."

"The world's changing. Even the Buckeyes."

"How's that?"

"Well, for one thing, the new Woody they have now, looks like a grade-school principal. And the players are all about five times your size."

"Hard to believe," he said. "Axel, you ever play ball?"

We'd had this conversation many times before. "Tony, I once played in the Ohio high school championship game," I shouted, as a semi-truck started up the ramp. When it passed, he asked me the same question he always did. "How'd you do?"

"We got our asses kicked. I was on the sidelines mostly, I was only a sophomore. The one time I got in, I thought I'd been hit by Dick Butkus himself."

"The most feared man in the NFL," Tony chuckled. "How big were you?"

"Same as now. Your size, maybe, when you were in fighting shape. Small, but quick."

"That's how I managed," he said. He picked up his bottle and took a drink. "So how's Tina?"

"What, you don't care about me? Or Bette, Ripley, and Adrian?"

"OK, how's Adrian," he grinned.

"Always a ladies man, huh. She's fine. They're all fine. They keep wondering when you're going to come in out of the cold."

A few cars whipped up the ramp and drowned out any response he made, but the shaking of his head was enough. "Ripley?" he said.

"He's great. Also wants to know when you're going to get off the field and into the locker room." Tony started to laugh, then coughed for a while. When it subsided, he pulled out a pack of cigarettes. "Got a light?"

"Sure," I gave him one. "Need anything from the van tonight?"

"No, thanks. I'm all set."

"Alright, Tony. Stay warm. I'll see you tomorrow."

He raised the bottle and waved it at me, and took another drink. I left him as a car sped past, spraying loose pebbles against the Jersey barriers.

Friday morning while we were still in the office, Phil called. The hospital was expecting Tony, and Emergency Services would send an ambulance as soon as his location was verified. Adrian, Tina and I took a taxi to the waterfront and were there twenty minutes later. The driver dropped us off next to the on-ramp, giving us a strange look as we stepped out. Under the expressway, the bulldozers and dump trucks were busy on a new section of the Big Dig. Rush hour traffic was heavy.

All of his blankets, empty bottles, paper bags, everything, had been cleaned out from between the Jersey barriers. Tony wasn't there. Only some shards of broken glass sparkled in the cold morning sun.

"Maybe the construction crew finally had the police move him," I said. Adrian stared at the empty space in disbelief, her mouth forming a tight line. Tina let out an audible moan. She shaded her eyes from the sun and began scanning the area around us. "He couldn't get far," she said. "He's somewhere nearby."

We took another look at the empty triangle of concrete.

First we checked the pine tree behind the bank, and along the waterfront. Back on Atlantic, Tina went in to ask Tim if he'd seen him, and Adrian went to see if Mary was working at Dunkin' Donuts. I knocked on the door of the bank manager, and she said she hadn't seen him all week. "Could you call me if you happen to run into him?" I gave my card again.

"Goddammit," Adrian said, a rare word for her to use. We were huddled in front of the coffee shop. Neither Tim nor Mary had seen Ruffo today. When a customer came out, followed by the smell of coffee and donuts, Tina told us to wait a minute, and went in. I saw her through the window as she skipped the line and went directly up to Mary.

"What's your guess?" I said.

"I'm trying to come up with one," Adrian said. "You?"

I looked up the sidewalk and saw Jimmie Irons stagger around the corner and sit down on the sidewalk. "Police moved him off," I said. "The work is getting too close to his spot." I stared across Atlantic at the heavy action now underway near the triangle. "They wouldn't have known anything about our plans for him." Tina came out with three coffees and three donuts.

"Here," she said, passing them out. "Energy for the search. And I don't want to hear anything about it."

Adrian's face still showed her frustration and disappointment, but she took the coffee and donut without a word and started eating. I glanced at Tina. She was trying to not look like Adrian did, but wasn't succeeding. I looked again up the street at Irons, and nudged Adrian with my elbow. "Hey, why don't you start with Jimmie. Maybe he knows where Tony is."

She turned and looked down the block. "OK," she said, facing us. Her expression was almost normal. "We'll search the area until we find him. I'm going to talk to Jimmie, then go up to Columbus Park. Tina, maybe you can go up Atlantic the opposite way. The other place he could be is under the expressway, maybe he just moved spots. Stay in contact." She turned to go. "Oh, and Tina," she smiled. "How is it you always know what to do? Thanks for the snack. Alright, I'm off."

Tina gave me a skeptical look and started walking up Atlantic. I went back to the highway to search. I passed by the barriers, staring again at the empty space. A car hubcap that I hadn't noticed before was wedged in one of the corners. I leaned over and picked up a piece of the broken glass. It was thick, like from a car windshield. Not from a vodka bottle.

There were a lot of places he could have holed up under the highway, but he wasn't in any of them. I did a loop around the entire area, and then called Adrian.

"No sign of him yet," I said. "You?"

"No. Jimmie hasn't seen him, and he's been hunting, too. Tony owes him some money. I checked out Columbus Park, didn't see him there either."

"How about Tina?"

"No luck." It was silent on the phone. I could hear her breathing heavily, like she'd been running.

"You alright there, AD?"

"I'm fine. I'm pissed off, but fine." She let out a deep breath. "Shit, now I'm going to have to call Emergency Services and tell them we can't find him."

By the end of the afternoon, we hadn't found Tony Ruffo anywhere. Adrian called the other outreach teams to see if they had seen him in another part of the city. Nobody had. Finally, she called Phil.

"Phil's incredible," she said when she hung up. "Know what he said? Relax, go home, and have a good weekend. Said he'd contact the crew on the overnight van, to make sure they called him as soon as they found Tony, no matter what time it was. And he'll personally be in touch with the ER at Mass General."

There was nothing left to do but go home.

STREET LOGIC

Chapter 24

December 6, 2004

Monday morning, I arrived early to the office. Adrian was listening to the messages on our answering service from last night, still wearing her coat. She put the messages on hold to tell me that the van crew had looked for Tony, on foot even, but didn't find him over the weekend. I took my coat off while she listened to the rest of the messages. There was one from a doctor at Boston City Hospital. She was the chief medical examiner at the city morgue. She said she had an unidentified body that she believed was that of a homeless man. Maybe we could come down and try to identify the person.

"Could be anybody," I said. Adrian didn't reply. When Tina arrived and heard the message, she refused to go.

The doctor let Adrian and me in at the security door. I'd met her once before, when I'd been to identify someone. She led us down a cold hallway, and stopped before a set of swinging doors.

"His face was untouched," she told us. "The rest of him was crushed."

"Crushed? By what?" I asked.

"Car," she said, in a matter of fact voice. "He was pancaked, basically. The police report states that a car took the turn to the expressway ramp too fast and," she referred to a folder in her hand, "and flipped over the top of the concrete barriers where the unidentified male was sleeping." She looked up at us. Adrian had grabbed my arm. "Landed right on top of him. He probably died instantly. You look like you know him," she said to Adrian.

We followed the doctor into the cold, sterile room. There were several bodies on stretchers. She walked up to one and pulled the white sheet away from his face. Tony's beard had been trimmed down, his hair combed straight back. He looked ten years younger.

If there had been relatives in Tony Ruffo's stories, there were none at the funeral service in South Boston a few days later. I drove the whole team, five of us in the Lincoln. A priest who often visited Evergreen had offered to perform the service. Three nurses from Medical Care, the ones who had cleaned him up in the van on numerous occasions, showed up. A few outreach workers from other teams came. It was a short service. When it was over, we all filed past the simple, brown urn where his ashes were held.

We stood outside the church, telling Tony stories. The priest, a man in his sixties with experience in his lined face, came out of the church and walked up to us.

"I was wondering," he smiled, "since there's no family, maybe you folks would like to do something with Tony's ashes. Otherwise," he gave a shake of his head, "they'll just sit on a shelf somewhere, collecting dust." He paused, watching our faces. "Maybe he had a favorite place?"

We looked around at each other. Tina smiled at the priest and Ripley scratched his chin, like he was thinking. I glanced at Bette who had her mouth open and ready to say something, but she glanced first at Adrian. Nobody said anything for a minute. Adrian, I knew, was still upset. I turned to the priest. "That's a great idea. We'll take them. Him, I mean. His ashes." The priest nodded, and went back in the church.

"Gee, I think it's a swell idea," Bette said. "We'll think of a place."

Nobody said anything. The priest returned, carrying the urn in both hands, and handed it to me. "I'm sure all of you did whatever was in your power to do," he said. "Sometimes it doesn't seem like enough. I know it must be difficult work you do."

We stood around for a while longer. Everyone stared at the urn. It felt light in my hands. "You alright keeping those?" Adrian said to me. "Until we decide where to take them?"

"How about the harbor?" Bette said. "That was his place."

Adrian looked at me. "Why don't you stick them in your trunk for now."

"Sure," I said.

Before we piled back into the Lincoln, I placed the urn behind the spare tire, wrapped in an old beach blanket.

STREET LOGIC

Chapter 25

December 10, 2004

Despite the twenty-degree temperatures, there still wasn't any snow. I sat in the Lincoln and listened to the end of the radio banter about the Patriots' chances this weekend, then popped the trunk. The wind blew hard enough to disturb some loose newspapers from the trunk as I grabbed the beer and groceries. I noticed that my old football had rolled next to the blanketed urn, behind the spare tire. I set the bags down and opened the blanket. The small brown pot, probably clay, reminded me of a rock, a stone. The myth of Sisyphus came to mind. Rolling that stone up the hill, over and over, until finally being forced to decide that it's meaningful. Even though it's futile. Good old existentialism. I covered the urn up again and wedged the football next to it. I felt there was something better to do with his ashes than to spread them in Boston Harbor.

I let myself in to my warm studio, sat down on the couch and put my feet up on the glass table. My right ankle was sore. I thought about turning on some music, but didn't want to stand up. Halfway through my beer, there was a knock on the door. I opened it with the clicker.

"Hey." Holiday pushed past the door. "Am I bothering you?"

"Are you crazy? Never. Want a beer?"

"No, I have class tonight. Final exam. I just wanted to say hi." She walked over and sat next to me. "Hi. Did you hike all over the place today?"

"No, not really. I visited this guy Pete, the little old guy I told you about. He's been in the hospital. Checked himself into Mass General. The hospital notified us. He was having trouble breathing."

Holiday took my good foot in her hands and started massaging it. "Ouch, go easy there."

"No pain, no gain," she grinned. "So how was Pete?"

"Weak. But warm and sitting in bed watching cable television. Still thinks he can return to his old home in Milton once he gets some new legs. I think he liked having someone visit. I brought him a box of chocolate chip cookies."

"I'll bet he liked that." She dug her thumbs into my heel.

"He ate half the box while I was there," I said, feeling a jolt of pain in my lower leg. "Jesus, that hurts! I think you hit one of those pressure points."

She kept pressing into the tissue. "Relax into it," she said. "It's deep. Gotta work out the pain."

"I need something to bite on."

She gave me a seductive smile. "I'm sure you do. Drink your beer. What else happened today?"

I took a drink. "Well, you're not going to believe this one. I'm still blown away by it." She massaged a tender area, causing my foot to jerk.

"That's the spot," she said, going a little more softly. "What won't I believe?"

"This was incredible. I was on the elevator after seeing Pete, and the psychiatrist who was treating the Silent One, right, well he gets on. I'd met him at the commitment hearing. Anyway, he told me they'd finally managed to locate the kid's family. They got a Roger's order, which allowed them to medicate him. Apparently, it took effect, and once the Silent One started talking they couldn't get him to shut up. The kid gave them his family's names, his parents' phone number, all that info. Anyway, the incredible thing is that his mother happened to be in the hospital, at that very moment, visiting. The doc took me over to meet her."

She looked up. "Really?" She switched feet and started on my right ankle.

"That toe was broken once. And that's the ankle that hurts like..."

"I know," she said. "So what happened?"

"When we got to the psych unit, I saw them through the glass window of the nursing station. I didn't recognize him with his hair cut. Remember, I told you he had this great Afro? But now it was cut real short. And as I was looking at him, it hit me. I remembered where I'd seen him."

Her hands kept working. "What are you talking about?"

"Ever since I first saw him, I had a funny feeling that I'd seen him somewhere. Besides the street or the shelter. And now, with his hair short, I got it. It was just after I'd started, on the news. He'd gone missing from college. There was a picture of him, with his head shaved. They found him that time, but he went missing again, six months ago. It was him, wandering around Copley all that time."

"I'm surprised his family wasn't searching in Boston," she said.

"They figured he was in western Mass, like he usually was. But they did report it to the State missing children network. He just slipped through the net."

"He didn't bother anyone, that's why. Did you get to talk to the Silent One?"

"No, the doctor didn't think it was a good idea, and neither did I. Too weird for the kid. But I did talk to the mother."

"And how was she?"

"She was really cool. Thanked me for calling the ambulance and helping get her son into the hospital. And testifying at the commitment hearing. When she started to cry, I asked her if she wanted to get some coffee. We talked for an hour or so. This family's been through a lot. They have two other kids, and then a bright, schizophrenic twenty-year-old. She was angry that it took so long to find him."

"See, I told you. There needs to be a farm where they can take these kinds of people and hold on to them, and families would know where to go to find them. It's that simple."

"Plan F."

"Right. Did you find out why he'd never talk?"

"The doctor told me that Malcolm, that's his real name, had told him that the voices in his head had forbidden him to speak. That they told him not to take anything from anybody, and not to talk to anybody. Can you imagine that? Voices telling you what to do."

She murmured agreement as she let go of my foot, and began rubbing my lower leg. She stared at the glass table, seemingly lost in her own thoughts. "Voices," she said softly, after a few minutes.

We sat quietly for a while and she leaned against me, closing her eyes. I sipped my beer and considered what she had just said. When she opened her eyes, she reached across my lap and took my hand. "You know what my voices are telling me?" A tiny smile played at the corners of her mouth.

"Something good, I hope."

She jumped up from the couch suddenly, and pulled me up with her. Then she steered me toward the bed and pushed me backwards on to it, climbed on top of me, and brought her face up to mine. "They're good voices," she smiled. "And they're telling me that I have just enough time to drive you crazy before I have to go to class." She sat up and pulled her sweater over her head, then the long sleeve turtleneck. "Sound like a plan?"

"I'm all in."

Chapter 26

January 10, 2005

Christmas came and went. New Year's Day had lasted several days, up in a small bed and breakfast in Camden, Maine. Holiday and I had considered camping out on Mount Megunticook one night, but resisted it.

Peter Allen Hopkins, whose full name the hospital staff had discovered, had meanwhile walked out of Mass General wearing two layers of hospital johnnies under his overcoat, and a pair of loafers.

When Tina and I went to visit and didn't find him in his room, we paged Dr Patterson, who didn't know he was missing yet. "Must have left after I saw him this morning," he told us. He informed us that Pete had severe respiratory problems. The hospital social worker had already contacted the Department of Mental Health, who had old records on him dating twenty-five years ago. They were working on a plan to put him into supported housing with medical care. The hospital had agreed to keep him in the meantime. It was a good plan, but now he was gone.

Tina and I spent the entire day searching the Back Bay area, checking out all his usual haunts. The library, the Starbucks on Boylston, his camp in the back-yard alley. Nobody had seen him. His camp was totally abandoned now, the tarp blown down, snow covering the blankets and sleeping bag. At the end of the day, Tina and I walked back to the office from the Public Gardens. The sky was already dark at four-thirty.

"There's one more place to try," I told her. She gave me a surprised look when I told her about the Milner.

The receptionist remembered me. "He's here," she said.

Outside his door, Tina and I stopped. "You know, he's not going to want to come with us," I said. "And we don't have a legal section ready, although we could probably get one in a…"

"Forget about that." She knocked on the door.

There was no answer. Tina knocked again, hard, five times. Shortly, we heard the lock being turned, and then the door slowly cracked open. Pete stuck his face in the narrow opening above the security chain, his glasses hanging on the tip of his nose. His magnified eyes showed surprise.

"Oh, it's you two," he said, his voice soft and weak.

"Hi Pete," Tina said. "How are you?"

"Tired," he said. "How did you know I was here?"

"I'm sure you are tired," I said. "Hey, can we come in and talk to you for a couple minutes?"

He looked back and forth between Tina and me, slowly. I detected a little suspicion in his eyes. But mainly fatigue.

"Pete," Tina said. "I've always been honest with you. The hospital called us, and they're really worried about you. They asked us to see if we could find you. We looked all over the city today, and this is our last stop." Tina paused, seeing the confusion in his face. "We saw you come out of here once, a few months ago, when we were in the neighborhood." She glanced at me. I nodded to go on. "You know, Pete," she said, "we just want to talk with you about this, and you can decide whatever you want. We don't want to see anything bad happen to you. Your doctor told us that in your condition, until you're stabilized, you should be in a hospital under doctors' care..."

He closed the door abruptly. Tina looked at me in surprise, then raised her fist to bang on the door again when it opened. "Well, don't just stand there." Pete stepped back into the room. "Come on in. It's not much."

The room was small and neat, except for the newspaper spread out in sections on the bed. A box of crackers and a glass of water sat on the night stand. Wearing the hospital's pajamas and slippers, he moved across the room in small, slow steps, to turn off the television.

"Have a seat, Tina," he said. "Sorry Axel, there's only one chair." He gestured at the bed. "Sit there if you'd like."

"I'll take the desk," I said. "You can sit on the bed, Pete."

Tina pulled the chair out and sat down, and I leaned against the desk. Pete shuffled over to the bed and sat on one corner of it. He adjusted his glasses and then looked up at us.

"What are you going to do? Call the police?"

I shook my head. "No, Pete. We're not." The room was warm, but I left my coat on. Tina had taken hers off and draped it across her legs. I noticed Pete's overcoat on a hanger in the open corner closet. Tina sat forward on her chair, leaning toward him.

"In all seriousness, Pete, we know you value your independence and your privacy. But when people are sick, they need the best help they can get. At the hospital, they can treat what you have. It takes some time, and they really would like you to come back." Pete watched her closely as she spoke, paying attention, nodding his head now and then. "Of course," she said, "it has to be your decision."

He raised his bushy eyebrows and looked at me. "What do you think, Axel?"

"First of all," I said, "I think you did a heck of a job sneaking out of that hospital. Nobody saw you. You were like James Bond."

His face broke into a grin and he laughed his high-pitched laugh. Tina was smiling a little, but she kicked my foot and told me with her eyes to get serious.

"And second of all, 007," I went on, "Dr Pat, as you call your doctor, was concerned enough about the condition of your lungs that he called it severely dangerous for you to be out and about. They can treat it, but they need you there. And, on top of that, they're willing to help you make arrangements for a place of your own. I repeat, a place of your own."

Pete just smiled.

"Your doctor also told us," Tina said, "that even a strong-willed guy like you is taking too big a risk with your health, by not being in the hospital now. So," I could see she was getting impatient, "what do you think? You want to come with us back to the hospital, in a taxi?"

She sat back, folded her hands on top her coat, and smiled at him. It would've convinced me, but I wasn't so sure about Pete. I crossed my arms and waited.

"Well," his voice was just above a whisper, "I appreciate all the trouble you've gone to, and your concern. And you're probably right." He paused, looking around the room. "But for now, I think I want to stay here. A few more days."

Tina just looked at him, her face a mix of compassion and concern. "What then?"

Pete shook his head. "I'll have to cross that bridge when I get there," he said.

"Pete," I said. "Dr Pat said that every day you miss treatment puts you at even greater risk. You can't get that treatment here at the Milner. I don't know if you realize how serious your condition is."

He sat quietly and seemed to be thinking. At one point, he looked up and stared from me to Tina, as if he were wondering who we were. Finally, he stood up and walked carefully over to the night stand and took a drink of water. When he turned toward us, his face was set, but kind. "I'll think about it," he said.

We stayed another five minutes. Tina asked if we could visit him tomorrow. Pete said that would be fine. We had to settle for that.

Outside, we walked quickly against the cold wind back to the office. Tina was quiet. I called Dr Patterson at Mass General and told him we had found Pete. He said he'd call Emergency Services and request having a medical section issued.

"You know, those things sometimes take a while to arrange," Tina said as we neared the alley at Evergreen. "Maybe we have to get creative."

"That's what I was thinking, too."

Chapter 27

January 11, 2005

"Do you think this is going to work?" Tina asked.

"I hope so."

"What are you going to say?" Tina sat in the passenger seat, fidgeting with her hands.

"I haven't figured that out yet. It'll come to me."

We drove the short distance to the Milner and I pulled up outside the entrance, parking in a handicap spot. I had told Adrian that I needed the van to pick up Lamar Cleveland and take him out to Saint Elizabeth's Hospital. "How's it going with Pete?" she had asked us on our way out. "Any word yet from the doctor on that medical section?"

"He said it could take a while," I said.

As soon as Tina and I were in the van, I called the Mass General paging service and left a message for Pete's doctor to call me. "I hope he's not taking a day off today."

"No way. Good thing we have this," Tina pulled the handicap sticker from the glove box. "Wouldn't want to have our getaway car towed."

The woman behind the reception desk seemed to be expecting us.

"We're taking him out for breakfast," I said. She looked at us, then without a word picked up the phone and called his room.

"Mr Hopkins? There's…"

"Axel and Tina," I said.

"Axel and Tina here to see you." She listened for a minute and then hung up.

"He said to go on up."

"Thanks," Tina said.

We took the elevator. "Yesterday she let us go up. Today she calls," Tina said.

"That's the Milner tradition of excellence," I said.

Outside his door, Tina grabbed my arm and whispered something about whether this was such a good idea. "Tina, we've got nothing to lose." I knocked on the door.

Pete smiled when he saw us, and unlatched the chain to open the door and let us in. "Back again, huh?"

"I said we'd stop by," I said. "How are you feeling this morning?"

"Ah, so-so," he said, his voice sounding even weaker than yesterday.

I looked around the room. The cracker box was still on the night stand. "Well, Pete, today's your lucky day. We're taking you out to breakfast. And I'm not taking no for an answer. It's on me."

He looked a little surprised, and then shuffled over to the bed and sat down. "I appreciate it, Axel. But I don't think I have the energy."

"That means you must be hungry. A good truck driver's special, and you'll feel like a million bucks. You have a coat?"

I saw him glance towards the open closet. I took his overcoat off the hangar. "Stand up, sir. Your carriage is waiting."

"Well, I suppose I could." He was just tired enough not to resist. He stood, and let me help him on with the coat. Tina looked around the room to see if there was anything important he might need. Pete reached into the coat pocket and pulled out his wallet, looked at it, then put it back. "Well, maybe a little breakfast is a good idea. But I'll treat."

"If you insist," I said. "You have everything of value, Pete? You know how hotel maids can be."

He nodded his head. He seemed much weaker today. I escorted him on one side, Tina on the other. My phone rang as we were on the elevator, but I let the voicemail answer it. We led him slowly past the receptionist and out the entrance. The van was only a ten-foot walk. While Tina held on to his arm so he wouldn't fall, I opened the sliding rear door and jumped inside.

"Right this way, sir," I said, reaching out a hand.

He stuck one of his slippered feet on the sideboard, held the door of the van with one hand and gave me the other. Tina helped him take the first step, and I pulled him gently into the van. I maneuvered him into the seat behind the driver's side. Once he was settled, I buckled him in. Tina climbed in the passenger door. I started the van and let it warm up, and adjusted the rearview mirror so I could see Pete. "You comfortable, Pete?" Tina asked. His eyes searched around the van briefly, then he rubbed them. I saw them droop a little. When the engine was warm, I cranked the heat to high and directed it so it flowed to the back of the van. Then I pulled out of the handicap spot and drove.

Around the Commons and Public Gardens first, glancing in the rearview now and then. Tina kept her eyes on him. She looked at me a few times, indicating that he was almost asleep.

On the third lap around the Gardens, I could see Pete's eyes close. I aimed the van up Beacon, driving slow, and took a right on to Storrow Drive. The exit to Mass General came up almost immediately. By the time I pulled into the emergency room parking lot and shut the van off, Pete was sound asleep. I kept the engine running.

"Wait here," I said to Tina. "I'm getting a wheelchair." I eased the door open and closed it quietly. At the entrance to the ER, there were several wheelchairs lined up along the wall. I rolled one quickly back to the van. Tina opened her window. "Now what, Sherlock? You going to lift him out of here yourself?"

"I'm thinking, Watson. You're in pretty good shape. Between the two of us, we can get him under the arms..."

"Hi folks." The deep voice came from behind us. "Just to let you know, you can't leave the van here."

The security guard stared at us, his hands in his pockets while he looked at the side of the van. "Evergreen Shelter, huh?" He was a big, young guy who could probably help get Pete out of the van.

"We've got an emergency here," I said. "Heart condition, started convulsing on his way to an eye exam. He's unconscious. We have to get him inside."

He stepped quickly up and looked in Tina's window. She gave him one of her special smiles. Pete was slumped over in his seat, unmoving, eyes closed. The security guard's face grew serious, and he looked back at me.

"Want me to lift him out?" he said.

"That would be great."

I jumped in and unbelted Pete. When the guard stepped into the van, the undercarriage groaned from the extra weight. He picked Pete up like a bag of groceries and stepped out of the van with him. Tina pushed the wheelchair close, and he carefully set Pete down into it. Pete's eyes fluttered open and he stared around him.

"Are we there yet?"

"We're there, Pete. Just relax. We're going to wheel you in. First class."

His eyes looked around briefly at his surroundings, and then they closed. I heard Tina let out a deep breath.

"Thanks," I said to the guard. "Couldn't have done it without you."

"Need any more help?"

"Can I leave the van here for ten minutes?"

"Sure. But you gotta move it soon."

"Soon as I check him in," I said.

We wheeled Pete into the ER entrance and through the maze of long hallways until we reached the elevators for his floor. The wheelchair ride hadn't woken him up, and as we rode to the seventh floor, Tina started giggling. "Almost," she said.

The elevator opened. We wheeled him up to a desk. I asked a nurse if she could page Dr Patterson. A minute later, she handed me a phone.

"Axel Hazzard," I said.

"Dr Patterson here. I got your message."

"Can you meet me at the nurse's station?"

We waited about five minutes. When Dr Patterson rounded the corner of the hallway, he stopped in mid-step. He was a tall, older, distinguished looking doctor, and as his eyes went from mine to Pete, it seemed that he knew what we were doing. Pete was still asleep with his chin on his chest. Dr Pat set his clipboard on the nurse's desk and walked over to us. "Hi Axel, Tina. I tried to call you back." He bent down and looked closely at Pete's face. "Emergency Services has the paperwork ready." He listened to Pete's raspy, labored breathing, and then straightened up. His serious expression lightened for a moment, and he smiled. "But I see that's not necessary now. We'll keep it on file, just in case."

STREET LOGIC

Chapter 28

January 21, 2005

"Remember Ed Sullivan?"

"The code?"

"Exactly. So, if he's making you nervous at all, hit the eject button. Just say we have to meet with Ed. Don't bother with the Sullivan part."

"Instinct," Bette said. "Right."

It was the team code for "Let's get out of here!" If we were talking to someone, or a group, strangers especially, and anybody on the team began to feel nervous or threatened in any way, Ed Sullivan was the sign to move. No discussions.

"Wow, I always wanted to use the secret code," Bette laughed.

We walked up the hill and approached him from the front. It was cold, in the twenties. We were bundled up in full gear. So was he. A black wool cap covered his head and his hands were gloved in the yellow fleece mittens donated to the shelter. We had hundreds of them in the office. He heard us crunching across the frozen grass and lowered the binoculars, eyeing us briefly. Then he resumed his surveillance of the skyline, no doubt inspecting the communication towers and transmitters. We stopped five feet in front of where he was sitting.

"How's it going today, John?" I said.

He muttered something that sounded like 'focus' but continued peering through the lenses. The leather jacket ballooned out from the heavy hooded sweatshirt he wore underneath. I looked at Bette and raised my eyebrows in a question. She shook her head.

"Hi John," she said. "Beautiful day out, huh? I think I would just about freeze to death out here after a while, though." She laughed a little. "Doesn't it bother you at all?"

He grumbled some more, scanning the horizon. The only people I saw in the park were a woman and her son, walking toward the frog pond with ice-skates hung over their shoulders. "Damn things," John muttered a little more loudly. His head twitched several times, a tick I'd noticed developing over the last few weeks. Lowering the glasses, he glared, first at Bette, then me. "It's your fault these goddamn binoculars don't work the same! I can't see up close, not anymore!"

It was Ed Sullivan time, as far as I was concerned. I turned to Bette, who already had her backpack open and was pulling out socks and underwear, dropping a few on the ground. "Oh darn. I forgot them."

"Bette," I said, watching John stare at her while she bent down to retrieve the underwear. "I think…"

"I don't need any of that stuff." John suddenly sat straight up, talking under his breath.

"Ed," I said loudly.

"I didn't mean these." Bette straightened up, holding out the men's boxers. "I meant the pair of binoculars that we have in the office. Thought I had them with me. I'll have to bring them out tomorrow." She saw John's face and stopped talking. Under his beard, his mouth was working furiously, his mumbling intensifying. The words were coming out fast. "Never shoulda given 'em to you in the first place, my mistake, but then you had to go and throw them, I was only trying to tell you something." His face contorted in anger as he dropped the binoculars. I stepped back a foot and pulled Bette with me.

"Never should've given them to you in the first place," John repeated. He pulled one leg up like he was ready to stand. Bette zipped her pack shut and threw it on her back in one motion at the same time that John kicked his leg out and hooked my foot with his boot. I stumbled backwards but didn't fall. Bette screamed as John took another kick, this time grazing my calf.

"Get out of here!" he yelled at us.

"We're gone, John." I grabbed Bette by the arm and turned her quickly and began walking fast.

"Jesus, Axel, that was an assault!" Bette hissed loudly. "Are you alright?"

"I'm fine," I said, looking over my shoulder. "He's not coming, but let's get the hell out of here."

"I'm so sorry!" She clutched at my arm. "You said Ed, and I was dropping underwear! God, I'm an idiot!" When we were out of earshot, she pulled out her phone. "I'm calling 911," she said, breathing heavily. "Or Emergency Services! The 'danger to self or others' criteria. Others. It fits."

I kept her walking and glanced again over my shoulder. He was on his feet, searching the ground for something. "Keep going, Bette. But you're right. Absolutely right. When they start lashing out like that, physically aggressive, it's time. It's telling us something."

"And it's not about the binoculars," she said.

"You're the clinician."

We reached the street and crossed over to the Starbucks on the corner. I stayed near the window, watching John pace around the tree. Bette called the Emergency Services Team first, identified herself as a clinician with Evergreen, and exaggerated the level of the assault. "This is perfect," she said after hanging up. "We witnessed it first hand, you were the victim, and it's the most guaranteed way to have someone evaluated. Someone who badly needs it."

"I hope he stays in sight," I said. "Hate to have to tail him around."

"No shit. In this cold, in his state of mind. No thanks."

"Hey, nice work on the assault-with-high-intention-to-do-serious-bodily damage description."

"They're obligated to respond to that," she said. "Gee, sorry again about missing the secret code."

"No one will ever know," I grinned at her.

Five minutes later, they called to tell us the ambulance was on its way. They wanted to confirm his location. As Bette told them where he was, a couple of park rangers came riding down the hill on horseback. "Oh my God!" Bette gasped on the phone. "They're coming on horses!"

"They're federal rangers, Bette..."

"They're going to trample him!"

The ambulance arrived as the rangers rode up on him. John took off, running toward the frog pond, his black leather coat flapping behind him, before the ambulance could reach him. The rangers galloped after him, branching out one on either side.

"This is just crazy!" Bette said. "Look at him go! He's heading toward the rink!"

John raced full speed on to the ice of the frog pond skating rink and then slid, as if he'd done this before. The rangers stopped their horses at the edge of the ice, blowing their whistles. John kept running and sliding toward the other side, past the woman and boy. They stared at him, and then skated away. A police cruiser pulled up at the opposite side of the pond with its lights flashing. They had him surrounded.

"They're going to freak him out with all this firepower," Bette said.

We stood at a safe distance and watched. He fended them off at first, holding up a stick. The rangers went on to the ice, and were talking to him. The police waited on the edge of the ice near their car. Finally, they started walking toward John. He dropped the stick and put his hands in the air. I felt a stab of guilt as the two policemen walked him carefully across the ice to the ambulance. Once he was in and the rear doors had been closed, we walked over to talk with the paramedics.

"Bette," I said before we reached them. "You know and I know Leather Pants didn't exactly assault me with intent to kill. Are you OK with simple assault? We want psychiatric help for him, not jail."

Bette kept marching toward the ambulance. "Axel. Do I look like a fool?"

"I'm not going to answer that."

She gave me a little push and laughed. "Smarty pants. Don't worry," she said. "I'm on the same page. It's simple. He kicked you several times. In clinical parlance, he acted out aggressively, demonstrating an inability to be safe toward others. Something like that. And he's going to be a hell of a lot safer in a hospital."

"Why don't you do the talking, Bette. Use your credentials."

"You betcha," she said. "I can do that."

Chapter 29

January 25, 2005

"This is the truck driver's breakfast you promised me?"

Pete looked even thinner, and when he breathed, his pipes rattled. I held out today's copy of the *Boston Globe* and a bag of chocolate-chip cookies.

"You know what, Pete. I'm sorry about that. I had to do what I felt was in your best interest. I hope you can understand."

He opened the bag and peered inside. "Starbucks, huh? Well, I guess I can forgive you." His voice was still weak, but it had a touch of humor in it. I pulled a chair up next to his bed.

"They treating you alright here, pardner?"

"They seem to know what they're doing." He pulled out one of the cookies. "Want one?" He offered the bag.

"Sure." I took one. "Thanks."

He pushed the cookie into his mouth, crumbs falling on to his sheet. He didn't notice. I handed him a napkin from the table next to his bed. "They have a room at a place called Wilbur House for you," I said. "I saw it myself. Beats the Milner, hands down. It's an old governor's mansion in the Back Bay, top of the line. You have your own room, private bathroom, a great view of Clarendon Street, and it's a short walk to the library. When you're up and moving again. Plus, they have nurses on duty. Night and day. In case you need anything."

He looked at the newspaper for a while, without saying anything. I stared out the window at Beacon Hill and the Charles River in the distance, and thought about Tony Ruffo. One day short on luck, but then, what did I know. His time had come, that was certain. I thought about Plan F, and my mind momentarily drifted to Plan S. Another one of Holiday's plans. Pete coughed a few times, blew his nose and continued reading. I considered how much easier my job would be if we could just take a highly vulnerable person directly to some place, The Farm, or something like it, with its own medical clinic and treatment facilities. For six months minimum. Good food, good activities. Ruffo could have been one of the charter members, along with Pete Hopkins, John Leather Pants, and guys like Lamar Cleveland, whose legs weren't going to get him around Mass Ave much longer. A place where someone like the Silent One could be taken and families would know where to look. But until then, it was like this. Fitting the pieces together, in whatever way opened up.

"I think it's a good place for you, Pete."

He took another cookie and offered me the bag again. "Are the nurses pretty there?"

Chapter 30

February 2, 2005

"Bette told me this morning that Leather Pants was committed," Tina said, looking for the addresses on the brownstones. "Long-term."

"That's great," I said, watching for an empty parking spot.

"Oh yeah, and he had to be restrained for busting one of the orderlies in the nose. Broke it."

"Old Leather Pants can still pack a punch. Guess I was lucky to escape unscathed." We were driving the short distance to Mariah's Restaurant in the South End, even though we could have walked it in ten minutes. But we were both tired from the long day and I'd offered to give her a ride home afterwards.

"Bette also told me you danced out of harm's way like Fred Astaire."

I glanced at her. She was smiling at me in that way she had when she was really happy.

"I thought I was more like Muhammed Ali, actually."

She made a playful jab at me. "Dodge this, Cassius," she laughed, punching me lightly in shoulder.

"We got lucky with Leather Pants," I said. "He was going to lose it sooner or later. Get into it with someone on the street."

"Must be hell for him to be cooped up like that."

"Must've been hell to be cooped up behind that a-c unit."

"True."

Tina pointed out the restaurant. "Wow, looks like a good one," she said. I found a visitor's parking spot. We sat quietly for a minute, neither one of us making a move to get out of the car. "This should be interesting," Tina finally said.

"Looks a little chi-chi to me."

"Chi-chi? You mean gay?"

"No. Fancy."

"Come on. Let's enjoy it." She opened her door. "We deserve it."

The interior of the restaurant was what I thought it would be. South End upscale, newly renovated, cozy, with a mahogany bar in the back. White tablecloths and track lighting. A young guy who could have been a *GQ* model led us to a table where the Silent One's mother was sitting with another woman.

"Well, here we go," I said to Tina.

Ruth greeted us warmly, embracing both of us with affectionate hugs. "I'm so glad you could make it," she said. "I hope you don't mind, but I just had a meeting with Senator Woodson," she nodded toward the other woman, "and when I told her who I was meeting for dinner, she asked if she could come along."

"How nice to meet you." The senator stood, extending her hand first to Tina and then to me. She had a strong grip. "I'm Karen Woodson. Ruth's told me all about how you helped Malcolm get the care he needed."

Karen Woodson cut an impressive figure. Her dark skin and black suit gave her beautiful smile an extra whiteness. It was a charmer of a smile. But I detected genuineness in her voice. "Nice to meet you, Senator," I said.

"Please, call me Karen."

We sat. I recognized her now. She was a state senator from Roxbury with a reputation for being a fierce advocate for women and children. And the homeless.

The waiter came and took our drink orders. I let the ladies go first. When Karen and Ruth suggested we order a bottle of champagne, I glanced at Tina. I knew she didn't drink. She nodded her head anyway. "I'd like a Seven-Up also, on the side," she said. When the waiter returned and opened the bottle, he poured four tall thin glasses with the bubbly.

"Cheers," Ruth said. "To some exceptional people."

She held her glass up, and Karen and I raised ours. I glanced at Tina, who picked up her glass of Seven-Up. The two other women didn't notice, or if they did, they didn't show it.

I sipped the semi-sweet champagne and relaxed, and listened to the conversation between Tina, Ruth and Karen. The senator and Ruth laughed a lot, the kind of laugh that people who know each other well share. Ruth told us she was a political consultant to the senator on issues pertaining to inner-city poverty, especially single-parent mothers. She had graduated from Boston College with a PhD in sociology. Her husband Richard, Malcolm's father, had wanted to drive into the city to meet us for dinner, but apparently had a last minute emergency. He was an oral surgeon. Ruth emphasized how appreciative he was of our help with Malcolm.

The subject of homelessness didn't come up as we ate, but I felt it simmering under the surface. Our food arrived and most of the conversation centered on lighter subjects, such as work-out regiments – all three women at the table were runners – and the best beaches in Mexico. Ruth had been on several vacations in the Yucatan. Tina insisted the best beaches were on the Pacific coast, south of Acapulco.

Malcolm's progress was mentioned briefly. He had returned home after six weeks in the hospital. He was stable, and taking medication. "I don't like it, that he has to take those medications, but without them, he's lost." She expressed her hope that Malcolm could return to UMass eventually. We were almost finished eating when I caught the senator watching me, with a curious look on her face.

"So," she said. "I just wanted to know what it's like to do the kind of work you two do?" Her smile was encouraging. I took a last fork-full of lasagna and looked at Tina. She had her mouth full and nodded at me.

"Well," I started, "there's a lot to say about it. The street is different from anywhere else I've ever worked. It's their territory, and they don't necessarily welcome our help. It was a tough six months in the beginning."

Karen and Ruth sat quietly, ignoring the last of the food on their plates. Karen leaned forward and put her elbows on the table and rested her chin on her hands, her eyes bright and disarmingly attractive. I focused on the candle's flame in the center of the table.

"I believed at first that I could convince people, once they knew me, to accept some kinds of help. To take advantage of the options that were available. When I sent people into treatment, into detox, into the hospital, or to the clinics in the shelter, at first it felt like something was happening. But they kept coming back to the street. Once in a while, somebody sought further treatment. Not many, though."

I stopped and took a drink of water. Tina was still eating. Ruth had leaned back in her chair and had her hands in her lap. Karen urged me to continue with her eyes.

"When I came across people in desperate conditions, with open, bleeding injuries, and they refused to have them treated in a hospital, I had to rethink what I was doing. So I ended up talking to them about their situations, and found, on the whole, that there were plenty who could at least talk about needing help. They would cry about it. They would volunteer that they had to do something. But when it came to making a decision, well, there are a lot of tomorrow people out there, if you know what I mean."

"Anyway," I went on, "that's what I saw going on. Or not going on, as the case was. It became a matter of checking in with people, and letting them get desperate enough to maybe ask for help. Regular contact. A lot of networking with nurses and doctors, bringing them out to the street to treat people. Picking people up, literally, and taking them into the shelter. The ones who worried me the most were the older people, and the ones with psychiatric issues. Like Malcolm."

"And you can't force them to take help, I know," Karen said. "Except in cases like Malcolm's."

"Yes. And a few others."

"But those are rare?"

"It doesn't happen often. The majority of cases involve people who, even if they are aware that they need help, they just can't do anything about it. They're stuck. Although sometimes I think they're doing what they need to do."

"What do you mean?" Ruth said.

I wasn't sure how to put it. I took another drink of water and wished I had a cigarette. Karen and Ruth looked at me, patiently, waiting.

"This might sound off the wall, but it seems to me that their physical survival is sometimes secondary to their psychic survival.

They're on the street for a reason. Almost all of them are running from something that's always faster and bigger and stronger than they are. Their life, I suppose. It's hard to fit in. The street is the last little bit of freedom they can have. Freedom from having to face themselves, and make some changes. You know, when life is a constant state of chaos and all about survival issues, like it is on the street, then there's no time to look at yourself. Looking in the mirror isn't easy for anybody."

Karen sat back in her chair and let out a deep breath. She glanced at Ruth, who had a sincere, thoughtful expression on her face. "Because they can't," Karen said.

Tina nudged me under the table with her foot. She mouthed the F word at me. I frowned, and shook my head.

"What's that, Tina?" Karen said.

I returned Tina's foot kick. "Why don't you tell them?"

Tina put on her charming smile as she drilled me with another kick in the shin. "It was Axel's most famous speech," she said. "Tell them about your plan." Tina turned toward me, smiling innocently.

I put my boot on her foot and pressed down. She continued smiling, without a flinch. Karen and Ruth were waiting.

"Well, to tell you the truth, it's not really a plan," I said. "It's more like a healthy fantasy. The kind that doesn't really seem realistic, given the way reality is. Plus, I can't really take credit for it. A friend of mine voiced it, someone who'd lived outside one winter." I wanted to find a way to say it right, but plunged in before they could ask about that person. "This person thought that for the ones who clearly can't make it on the street, the extreme cases, there should be a place to go outside of the city. Not just the shelters. Somewhere in the country, a nice facility on a big piece of land, a farm, perhaps. A healthy, natural environment, where people can have time to recover their health. And missing people, maybe someone like Malcolm, even, could be treated out there instead of in a hospital. Families would know where to look if someone went missing. Outreach workers could identify the most vulnerable, and a judge, with a program in place, might be more likely to send them there for, say, six months. Save on ambulance and ER expenses, too. I know, it kind of sounds like it's taking away someone's personal liberty, to take them off the street against their will. But, when you're out there and see what it's like, well…" I looked at Tina.

"It seems," Tina said, "that it would make more sense to use all that money that goes into those ER visits, hospitalizations, revolving-door detox programs, to create a therapeutic environment, an alternative to what is happening now."

Karen nodded, her face thoughtful. "Which isn't enough," she said. "That's very interesting. On that note, I want to let you know that I'm chairing a conference on chronic homelessness next month. And believe it or not," she smiled, "the conference is titled, 'The Ten Year Plan to End Homelessness'. You two should attend. It's going to be an opportunity for people to share ideas, as part of a bigger scheme, for which we're seeking support in Washington."

Inside, I knew it was all good. But for me, those kind of meetings seemed like just a lot of talk. It reminded me of Saint Bernie's comment about a whole lot of people blowing smoke.

"That sounds interesting," Tina said. "I'd love to go."

Karen looked at me.

"Count me in," I said.

"That's great," Ruth said. "I'm sure your perspective will be appreciated."

The waiter came and brought coffee. Ruth insisted that we have dessert, and while we ate their special of the day, hot apple pie à la mode, the conversation shifted back to the best beaches in the world. When Tina and Ruth excused themselves and went to the restroom, Karen and I sat quietly, drinking our coffee.

"There was this guy who used to live on the waterfront," I said. "We all knew he was slowly dying in front of our eyes, and a lot of people spent a lot of time making efforts to help him. Nurses were cleaning the defecation off him, right there on the street. Finally, a doctor agreed to commit him. At least for a ten day evaluation. It took a few days to get the thing lined up. When it was all set, we went to his spot. But he was gone. The night before, a car had jumped across the barrier where he slept, and landed on him."

Karen stared at me over the top of her coffee cup. "That's awful. What was his name?"

"Tony Ruffo."

Tina returned and sat back down.

"That's where ideas like the farm, and Plan F, almost make sense. They might sound a little crazy, but when you're running out of solutions, you start thinking in different directions. You're forced to either give up and abandon ship, or keep going. For me, it's a challenge to find the good in these kinds of situations. But I still believe that good always comes with the bad. The only problem is figuring out what the good is, exactly, and what to do with it."

Ruth came back to the table and sat down, and waved to the waiter to bring the check.

"That almost sounds like you don't believe things can change," Karen said.

"No, I haven't lost total hope yet," I smiled. "But seeing is only seeing. Doing something about what you see is the hard part."

We walked outside together. Ruth embraced us both again, thanking us. We exchanged cards with Karen.

"I'll email you about the conference," she said. "I think it's important that you say these things to a bigger audience. And thanks so much for sharing what you know. Especially the story about Tony Ruffo."

"Speaking of Tony," Tina said to me. "Adrian wanted to know if you still have his ashes in your trunk?"

Karen and Ruth looked at us. I walked to the trunk of the Lincoln and opened it, and took the urn out from under the blanket. I held it up for their inspection.

"My goodness," Ruth said. "I must have missed that part of the conversation."

"We've been meaning to take his ashes down to the harbor, where he used to sleep."

Karen stared at the urn thoughtfully. Something passed across her face. "May I have a look at that?" She reached out and I handed it to her. "He had no family?"

"No," Tina said. "None that we were able to locate."

"Is that what he wanted?" she asked.

"You mean to be cremated?" I said.

"No. The harbor."

"We just thought he might like it, because he used to sleep down there. He talked about the sea a lot."

"You know what?" Karen said, quietly. "I know this sounds a little, well, strange. But would it be possible for me to keep these for a while? It occurred to me that with the conference coming up, and a lot of key people passing through my office during that time, I could set Tony's urn somewhere where they can't miss it. When people ask about it, I can tell the story you just told me. Unless," she paused, looking at us. "You think he would have rather..."

"I think that's a great idea," Tina interrupted. "I'm sure Tony would have liked to be a source of inspiration, in some way."

Karen looked at me.

"Sounds perfect," I said "Tony talked all the time about some of the great rides he used to have. I thought it was kind of appropriate that he's been riding around in the trunk of my Lincoln, but I'm sure he'd prefer a senator's car. What are you driving, Karen?"

Karen laughed. "I hope he liked Mercedes," she said.

"His favorite," Tina said.

Tina and I walked them to the senator's black Mercedes sedan. Ruth hugged both of us again as we stood in the street, then she stepped into the car. Karen opened her door and turned sideways, sliding into the seat with the urn cradled protectively in her arm. She rolled the window down and gave us a hopeful smile.

"I imagine," Karen said, "that his own, real ride through life could've been a whole lot smoother than it was."

I wasn't so sure, but I nodded my head. As she fastened her seat belt, I glanced down to where Karen had placed the urn between her legs. "I'm sure he'd appreciate this last ride."

"Well, I hope so," she said. "It was so nice to meet you both. I'm sure we'll talk soon."

As they drove up the street, Tina began to giggle.

"What?"

"I'm sorry, it's just that…" She paused, trying to control her laughter. "It's just seeing Tony there, in the arms of a beautiful senator, driving off in a Mercedes, into the sunset, no less…"

I looked up the street and watched Tony Ruffo's last good ride turn at the corner, and disappear. Tina wiped her eyes, back in control.

"So what do you think?" she asked.

I opened the passenger door and stepped back, facing her. "I think you bruised my shin in there, for one thing. And between the Ten Year Plan and Plan F, well," I shook my head and grinned at her, "I think we better plan on showing up for work tomorrow."